Bello:

hidden talent rediscovered

Bello is a digital-only imprint of Pan Macmillan,
established to breathe new life into previously published,
classic books.

At Bello we believe in the timeless power of the imagination,
of a good story, narrative and entertainment, and we want to
use digital technology to ensure that many more readers
can enjoy these books into the future.

We publish in ebook and print-on-demand formats
to bring these wonderful books to new audiences.

www.panmacmillan.co.uk/bello

B E L L O

Ann Cleeves

Ann Cleeves is the author behind ITV's VERA and BBC One's SHETLAND. She has written over twenty-five novels, and is the creator of detectives Vera Stanhope and Jimmy Perez – characters loved both on screen and in print. Her books have now sold over one million copies worldwide.

Ann worked as a probation officer, bird observatory cook and auxiliary coastguard before she started writing. She is a member of 'Murder Squad', working with other British northern writers to promote crime fiction. In 2006 Ann was awarded the Duncan Lawrie Dagger (CWA Gold Dagger) for Best Crime Novel, for *Raven Black*, the first book in her Shetland series. In 2012 she was inducted into the CWA Crime Thriller Awards Hall of Fame. Ann lives in North Tyneside.

Ann Cleeves

THE BABY
SNATCHER

BELL◎

First published in 1997 by Macmillan

This edition published 2014 by Bello
an imprint of Pan Macmillan, a division of Macmillan Publishers Limited
Pan Macmillan, 20 New Wharf Road, London N1 9RR
Basingstoke and Oxford
Associated companies throughout the world

www.panmacmillan.co.uk/bello

ISBN 978-1-4472-5024-1 EPUB
ISBN 978-1-4472-8901-2 POD

Visit www.panmacmillan.com to read more about all our books
and to buy them. You will also find features, author interviews and
news of any author events, and you can sign up for e-newsletters
so that you're always first to hear about our new releases.

Chapter One

The knock at the door surprised Ramsay. He received few callers at the cottage in Heppleburn and Jack Robson, who turned up occasionally to take him to the pub, knew better than to come this early. Ramsay seldom arrived home from work before eight and then he had to eat. If he arrived home at all. These days there was Prue, the woman in his life, and he was just as likely to stay at her home in Otterbridge.

He went to the door expecting to find someone collecting for good causes and on his way he looked through a pile of mail to see if there was a charity envelope he'd overlooked. It was just starting to get dark and he switched on the light in the storm porch.

He recognized the girl who waited on the step but for a moment he could not place her. Then he realized she was one of the walkers. That was how he thought of the couple who seemed to carry out most of their business on foot. There was this girl and an older woman. They walked miles. He had passed them on the roads out of Heppleburn and wondered about them. He was surprised that a teenage girl would choose to spend so much time with her mother. He assumed that the older woman *was* the mother. There was a family resemblance. They had the same large, unblinking eyes, and there was the walk, purposeful, long-strided, fast.

The girl was attractive. She had been bonny enough at least to catch his eye, to make him look again as he drove past them on the long, straight road from Otterbridge to Heppleburn. She was fifteen or sixteen, with very blond hair, white and frizzy, which might have been considered angelic in a toddler, but in the young woman seemed unnatural. Of the mother he had taken less notice.

Ramsay stood inside the porch and waited for the girl to speak. She was wearing the uniform of Otterbridge High School in a manner which was unusually chaste and tidy. Often the skirts came up to the girls' buttocks and the ties were loose, bulky knots. Her respectability made him think again that she was probably collecting. For the Guides perhaps or a church group. He looked over her shoulder expecting to see the mother. He'd never seen the girl on her own before. Then he realized she was nervous, shaking.

'Yes?' he said kindly, then, sensing that it wasn't shyness which roused the trembling, but fear, he asked, 'Is anything wrong?'

'You are a policeman?' Her voice was not what he had expected. It was educated. There was hardly a trace of accent. Before tonight if he'd had to place the women socially he'd have put them down as the deserving poor. A single mother and her daughter struggling to make ends meet in a council house. Walking everywhere to save the bus fare. Now the voice as much as the question confused him.

'Yes,' he replied. He did not ask how she knew. In a village like Heppleburn that sort of information was common knowledge.

'It's my mother.' She spoke in a rush. 'I'm worried about her. I didn't know what to do.'

'You'd better come in.'

As he opened the door wider he wondered if he was being entirely sensible. There were rules about this sort of thing. But he could hardly leave her on the doorstep when she was so distressed and she didn't seem the attention-seeking type. He couldn't imagine her running off and crying rape. All the same he sat her in the chair by the window so the table was between them and said, 'If it really is police business, you know, you should call the station. Or 999 if it's an emergency.'

'We haven't got a phone at home. Anyway, I thought she might be in the dene. Then it started to get dark and I saw the light in your window. I thought you'd know what to do. I'm sorry. I suppose I'm being silly. I expect she's all right.'

'Tell me what happened.'

'She wasn't home when I got in from school.'

He waited for a further explanation but that, it seemed, was it.

'Doesn't she work?' he asked.

'Oh no!' She seemed quite shocked by the notion. Ramsay wondered what Prue would make of that. She had taught her daughter to be independent.

'And she's usually there when you get in?'

'Always. I've got a key for emergencies but I've never had to use it before.'

'And *how* old are you?' He didn't quite manage to keep the surprise from his voice.

'Fifteen.' Then, in a pompous, rather preachy way, 'Mummy thinks family life is important. We all do.'

'So it's not just you and your mother?'

'Of course not. But my father's working tonight. I don't know exactly where so I can't get in touch with him. Then there's Claire. It didn't seem fair, to worry her too.'

'Claire's your sister?'

'My aunt. My mother's younger sister. She lives with us.'

They sat for a moment in silence. To his embarrassment she began to cry.

'Look,' she said. 'I know it's unusual. Other people's mothers go out all the time. But Mummy wouldn't. Not without leaving a note saying where she was going. Not when she was expecting me back from school. I know something's happened to her.'

'Where do you live?'

'The Headland.'

That too was unexpected. His perception of her shifted again. The Headland was an odd, isolated community on the coast, hardly considered part of Heppleburn at all. Young women who lived there did not usually speak of their mummies. The Headland had been formed when a Victorian pit owner had cut a channel in the rock and built a canal so he could ship out his coal, effectively splitting a small promontory from the surrounding land. Now the canal had been filled in and all the gully contained was a sewerage outflow. Ramsay supposed that the double row of terraced cottages had been put up to house the workers on the canal. There was no other reason for them to be there. The Headland was still separated from the main road, though now it was by a railway track which had superseded the canal and carried coal to a power station up the coast.

People had no reason to visit the Headland. There were no scenic attractions, no beach. All that remained were the two rows of redbrick houses, facing each other across the single road, and a redbrick social club, grotesquely large in proportion to the number of people who used it. There was also, Ramsay thought, some sort of coastguard building but he could not be sure of its purpose. It had been years since he'd crossed the railway line.

'What time did you get in?' he asked, then, before she had a chance to answer, 'I'm sorry, I don't even know, your name.'

'Marilyn Howe.'

He thought Marilyn was a very flighty name for such a respectable girl. Reading his thoughts she said, 'My father liked the pictures.'

'Ah.'

She muttered something under her breath.

'I'm sorry?'

She looked up at him and repeated it fiercely, angrily: 'At school they call me Billy No Mates.' She saw that he was confused. 'That's what they call people without any friends.'

'I'm sorry,' he said again, awkwardly. It seemed a desperate sort of confession.

'I get in at 4.40.' She answered his original question as if the outburst had not occurred.

'How did you get there?'

'School bus. It stops at the club.'

'And there was no sign of your mother then?'

'No. At first I wasn't worried. Not really. I mean I thought it was odd but in a way I was pleased. It meant she was letting go. I mean I suppose she is a bit clingy.'

'Where might she have gone? Into Newcastle? To a friend's for coffee?'

'Oh no.' Marilyn seemed slightly amused by the idea. So, Ramsay thought, the mother was a Billy No Mates too.

'What made you look in the dene?'

'She'd talked about going blackberrying.' It was the second week of September. The blackberries were past their best but there were still some for the taking. 'I waited until six, then I was really worried. I thought she'd walked through the dene, fallen, had an accident.'

'So you went to look?'

She nodded.

The dene was a wooded valley which ran from the base of the Headland right into Heppleburn Village. Ramsay's cottage looked over it.

'I walked along the main footpaths shouting,' Marilyn said. 'I met a couple of horse riders and a jogger but they hadn't seen her. Then I saw your light. I'm sorry. I suppose you're off duty. If you could just tell me who I should ring and let me use your phone.'

'Why don't you let me take you home first,' Ramsay said. 'Perhaps after all this time she'll have come back.'

'Oh God!' Marilyn clapped her hand to her mouth. Her eyes were round and shiny as marbles. 'If she's arrived home and I'm not there she'll be frantic.' There was a pause, a small, confiding smile. 'She'll probably have called the police.'

The road to the Headland ran parallel to the dene. There was a farm with a lot of empty out-buildings and a big sign which read: 'FOR SALE, BARN SUITABLE FOR CONVERSION'. The paint on the sign had faded. It had been there since Ramsay had moved into Heppleburn. As it approached the coast the dene flattened into scrubby grassland. The stream ran into the cut to the sea.

When they came to the railway line they had to wait at the level crossing. The train moved very slowly and Ramsay sensed that Marilyn's impatience was turning into hysteria. She tapped long fingers on the dashboard, muttered under her breath.

The last truck rattled past and the barrier lifted. The road became single track. It led first to the jetty where the coal boats had once been loaded, with the social club beside it, then to the houses. The Headland was a promontory which rose slightly at its tip. Beyond the houses and above them was the whitewashed building which Ramsay remembered as a Coastguard Station. It too apparently had been suitable for conversion because now it was a private house. The sky was quite dark but clear and there was a moon. There was something mythic about the view through the terraced houses to the white house on the hill beyond, with the full moon behind it.

'Our place is on the left,' Marilyn said. 'At the end.'

'Well, someone's in.' Ramsay was relieved. 'There's a light on. Or did you leave it like that when you came out?'

'I can't remember.'

When they got out of the car Ramsay could hear the sea on either side of them and a snatch of music from the club. Marilyn in her school uniform was shivering.

'Go on then,' he said. 'You've got a key.'

The front door opened into a narrow hall. The light Ramsay had seen had come from there and shone through the small glass panes in the door. Steep stairs led to the first floor. The door into the living room was open. Ramsay had expected the house to be tidy. A full-time housewife surely would care about that. But it was small and cluttered. In the centre of the floor stood a large wooden spinning wheel and a box of uncarded sheep's wool.

Ramsay expected Marilyn to call out for her mother but she walked quietly down the passage to a room at the back. It was as if she were afraid of disturbing someone. She opened the door and switched on the light. There was a dining table folded against one wall; a sofa with a crocheted rug thrown over; a standard lamp with a fringed shade; and a rocking chair. It reminded him very much of the back room of his parents' house when he was a child. Before his mother started reading women's magazines and bullying his dad into DIY. Nothing in it had been bought after 1960, though Marilyn's parents would have been children themselves then, perhaps not even born.

In the rocking chair sat Marilyn's mother. She was dressed as he had always seen her out walking, in a grey skirt and a faded pink anorak and little suede ankle boots lined with fur. Her skin was smooth, unlined as a girl's and the hair, dusty brown, unfashionably long for a woman of her age, fell loose over her shoulders. At first he thought she was asleep. Then he saw that she was so astonished to see them, so shocked by the sudden light, that she could not speak.

'Mummy!' Now Marilyn did shout. 'Where were you? I was worried.'

'Who's this?' Mrs Howe asked. She stood up.

'He's a policeman. Don't you realize? I was so worried I went to the police.'

The woman stood, blinking furiously. Ramsay wondered if she were ill. Depressed. Schizophrenic. She seemed lost in a world of her own. Then she seemed to regain awareness of her surroundings. She took a small, apologetic step towards her daughter.

'Darling,' she said. 'I'm sorry. I must have fallen asleep and you startled me.' She turned to Ramsay. 'You know how that can disorientate when one wakes up suddenly . . .'

'But where were you earlier?' Marilyn demanded. 'You never go out.'

'Don't exaggerate, darling. I went for a walk. I told you I might. For blackberries.'

'But I came to look for you.'

'Then we must have missed each other.' The voice was firm. She would tolerate no further argument. She turned to Ramsay. 'I'm so sorry to have troubled you, Constable.' He did not correct her about his rank. 'I'm afraid Marilyn panicked. Perhaps she's come to rely on me too heavily.'

'So long as everything's all right now.' He looked at them both. It was almost a question.

But it seemed to Ramsay that things in the little house were far from fine. He could see through a door to the back kitchen, to the formica-covered units and the white enamel sink. There was a door with a lift-up latch which would lead to the back yard and the outhouse where once the lavatory had been. Where perhaps it still was. On one unit, quite out of place, stood a microwave oven. But there were no blackberries.

Chapter Two

Emma saw her pregnancy as an act of rudeness. How inappropriate, how impolite to be blossoming at this time of grief! Brian had invited Mark Taverner to stay with them for a few days after the death of his wife and whenever she saw him she felt herself blushing. But then Mark had always possessed the knack of making her feel awkward.

Emma had come to motherhood relatively late and took to it with a passion and energy which surprised her colleagues. They'd expected her back in harness straight after maternity leave. Not for the money. Husband Brian more than provided. But because they couldn't imagine the Human Resources Department without her.

She didn't return to work. She had two boys in quick succession and now she was pregnant again. *Hoping* for a girl, of course, she confided to her new mumsy friends, but happy to take what came. And then Sheena Taverner had died sooner than they had expected, and the pregnancy seemed some sort of dreadful social gaff.

Emma had suggested to Brian that she might stay away from the funeral but he had insisted that she should be there. He said Mark would want it. Brian and Mark had been friends at university and had stayed close since, which was odd, Emma thought, because they had nothing in common. So she went. At least it was cold for September and she could wear a loose woollen coat which hid the eight-month bump. From a distance you wouldn't have been able to tell she was expecting. And Mark did seem pleased to see her. Outside the church he hugged her, held on to her with a desperation she had not expected. She pulled away from the embrace feeling quite shaky, with a surge of emotion which had little to do with missing Sheena. Hormones, she told herself. And wondered if the friend who was looking after the boys would remember about Owen's allergy to oranges.

After the funeral they went back to the house in Otterbridge where Mark and Sheena had lived for ten years. It wasn't a grand house a narrow three-storey terrace in one of the back streets behind the market, with only a couple of steps to separate the front door from the pavement. It was not at all the sort of house, Emma thought, where you could bring up children. But Sheena had never wanted that even before the illness. She had wanted a quiet place to work, her books and her pictures. Emma had always supposed that was what Mark had wanted too.

People expected the Taverners to live somewhere grand because Sheena had been a writer. But although her novels had been well reviewed they were hardly best-sellers. Certainly they weren't Emma's idea of a good read. She had ploughed through one or two but preferred something with a story. A thriller, even a historical romance. Secretly she thought Sheena should have gone out more, even found herself a job, mixed with people other than the arty friends who seemed very similar to her. Then she would have had something to write about. Towards the end, of course, that would have been impossible.

After the funeral there was quite a crowd in the little house. Teachers from the High School where Mark worked. Friends of Sheena, many of whom Emma thought were unsuitably dressed for the occasion. Mark introduced her perfunctorily to some of them: 'This is Margaret from the Flambard Press, this is Chaz, this is Prue.' He must have hired caterers because trays of rather unappetizing food stood on a table. If Emma had not been pregnant she would have taken charge of the proceedings – handed out plates, offered drinks. As it was she kept out of the way, not because she didn't feel up to it but because of the same embarrassment which made her uneasy in Mark's company. Eventually her legs began to ache so she settled herself in a chair by the window with a glass of orange juice and a cardboard vol-au-vent.

From her corner she watched Mark move restlessly from one chatting group to another. He was attractive in an intense, rather humourless way and the women turned towards him as he approached. His face was strained and it was obviously an effort to be polite. Brian must have realized that too because he went up to Mark and put an arm round his shoulder. There was nothing to say.

Emma thought that perhaps there had never been much to say, not even when Sheena was first diagnosed. Nothing that did any good, though Brian had railed at length about the mastectomy and the chemotherapy and the radiotherapy. He had been angry and uncomprehending on Mark's behalf. Mark himself had said little.

Brian peeled away from the group and stood beside her. He was big and dark, given to sentimentality and outbursts of temper, but only when he'd been drinking. At work he was cool and quite determined, willing to take risks if the odds had been properly weighed.

'A drink?' he asked.

'I could murder a cup of tea.' The house had been empty for nearly a week and it was not very warm. 'But I don't know if that's on offer.'

'Don't worry,' he said. 'I'll fix it.' And he went away into the kitchen glad to have something to do. She thought that was Brian all over. He was the fixer, the dealer, the person who made things happen. But not even Brian could fix it for Sheena to get better though he'd tried hard enough, yelling at consultants when appointments were cancelled, hunting out information about the best doctors, the best centres, pretending to be Mark over the phone so he'd be taken seriously. Now he had to admit defeat and it didn't come easy.

He brought her tea on a little tray painted with blue and white flowers. When she'd drunk it she asked if he minded her going home. Suddenly she felt very tired.

'I'll get a taxi if you like,' she said. 'You can bring the car back later.'

He said he would come too. She knew the decision to leave early had little to do with concern for her. He'd never liked sharing Mark with other people. Except Sheena, of course. He'd never seemed to object to her.

It was half past three. The children were coming out of the Infants School on the corner of Mark's street. Emma thought sadly that soon Owen would be starting school and that he had grown up too quickly.

It had been Brian's idea to buy the Coastguard Station on the Headland and knock it through into one magnificent house. She hadn't been very keen. Even then, five years ago, she'd been dreaming of babies and thought a modern house on a quiet estate would be nice. Somewhere with other middle-class mothers to invite in to coffee during the day, pavements for trikes and dolls' prams. She had kept her misgivings about the Coastguard House to herself. Brian was so generous to her in other things and he was so enthusiastic about the venture that she encouraged him. She had even pretended to share his excitement.

The house was wonderful now. She had to admit that. There was so much space that they wouldn't be cramped even if the latest baby turned out to be triplets. There were magnificent views out to sea on three sides. All the same if she were offered the chance to move she'd jump at it. She felt isolated on the Headland. She wouldn't call herself snobbish but felt she had little in common with the residents of Cotter's Row. She wouldn't be happy for her children to play down there. Physically, too, the place made her uneasy. Although there was a high whitewashed wall right round the garden and the cliffs weren't steep, more like rocky shelves down to the water and quite easy to scramble on, she worried that the children would fall. It was a secret nightmare and some nights she would wake up sweating to a picture of one of them limp and lifeless, battered by the waves at the foot of the cliff.

The car bumped across the level crossing, jolting her back to the present. She saw with relief that they were nearly home. Her friend had offered to give the boys their tea so she'd have time to put up her feet, perhaps watch the television news, before they arrived back.

'Shit!' They were driving between the rows of houses when Brian slammed on the brakes, hit the horn and shouted. A woman had run out into the street in front of them. He missed her by swerving on to the pavement. The woman stood for a moment like a rabbit caught in a headlamp's glare, then she ran off. Her pink anorak, unzipped, flapped behind her.

'Idiot!' Brian said. 'She could have been killed.' But his fury had passed. The BMW, his pride and joy, was unharmed. 'Do you know her?'

Emma shook her head and said nothing. She thought she recognized the woman but she had her own reasons for keeping quiet.

Brian got out to open the double gates into the yard, drove in, then went to shut them again. She struggled out of the car with difficulty. She enjoyed being pregnant but she would be glad when it was all over.

She was standing on the doorstep, rummaging in her bag for her keys, when her waters broke.

'Oh God!' Brian said with a trace of disgust, when she explained what had happened. Both thought with relief that at least it hadn't happened when she was getting out of the car. Think of the leather upholstery.

The daughter was born at midnight. Brian was there during labour though he disappeared regularly during the early stages. There was a television in the Visitors' Room and Newcastle United was playing in a Cup match. His howl of dismay when Arsenal scored rivalled the cries of the women giving birth. He was with Emma when she needed him, and afterwards he sat beside her on the bed and stroked the baby's cheek with his little finger. For an awful moment she was afraid he'd suggest they called the baby Sheena but he said: 'Helen, then? Like we decided?'

The hospital was on a hill and from the high bed where she sat, propped up with pillows, she had a view all over the town. Helen seemed dull and unadventurous all of a sudden, but it was his mother's name and better than Sheena. Perhaps she could come up with something glamorous too.

'Of course,' she said. 'Helen.'

She had planned coming out of hospital after twenty-four hours but Helen had a nasty bout of jaundice and she ended up having to stay in for a week. She quite enjoyed the rest. On the third day, unexpectedly, Mark came to visit. He was on his own and was carrying a huge bunch of flowers – flame-coloured chrysanths and those huge, round, tightly filled blooms which she'd only seen before at village produce shows.

'Brian said you wouldn't mind,' he said.

'Of course not.'

But she felt coarse, blowzy. Her breasts were spilling milk and her dressing gown was grubby. Helen was asleep in the plastic fish tank the hospital used as a cot.

'So this is Helen.' He set the flowers on the locker and peered in with a genuine interest, watched the balletic movement of the girl's hands. She could tell he wanted to pick the baby up.

'Helen Scarlet,' she corrected.

'Scarlet?' He seemed faintly amused. 'Brian didn't tell me that.'

'Brian doesn't know yet.'

Then they giggled together, quietly, so as not to disturb the baby, like school kids at the back of the class. Before he went he kissed her forehead and told her it was the first time he had laughed since Sheena had died.

Chapter Three

When baby Helen was born Emma and Brian took on a young woman to help with the boys. Emma had been thinking about it for some time. She had had her eye on just the right person but had been reluctant at first to discuss the idea with Brian. He made comments occasionally when he came home from work and his dinner wasn't ready or there were toys all over the floor.

'Good God, woman. You managed a department of fifty people. Can't you handle two toddlers? I don't know what you do all day.'

This was said in a good-natured way and was supposed to be a joke but she sensed real irritation behind it. If she asked for help in the house would he think she was quite incompetent?

When she broached the subject, however, on her arrival home from the hospital, he was all for it. Perhaps employing a nanny was like owning the BMW. It confirmed that he was successful at last.

'It'll give me more time to spend with Helen,' she had explained.

'Bugger that!' he had said. 'It'll give you more time to spend with me.'

Claire was nineteen and had completed an NNEB course at the local college. She lived on the Headland which made her ideal. References from the college were good but she had spent the whole summer without a nannying job. Emma, who had appointed many staff in her career, thought Claire would come over very badly in interviews. Even now, in February, when she had been with them for nearly five months she volunteered little information about herself. Her silences were intense and deadening. She was tall and stately and always dressed smartly in dark skirts and white blouses.

She looked like a waitress in a pretentious hotel. Emma thought it unlikely that this dress code had come from the college and imagined Claire's nannying friends in jeans and sweaters. Though perhaps she was not a person to have many friends.

Emma liked Claire because she was reliable and seemed to dote on the boys. She never lost her temper or raised her voice. She generated an air of implacable calm and was as obsessed as Emma about safety. Emma confided to the other mothers in the baby clinic that she thought she had discovered a treasure. The girl was mature beyond her years. Brian called Claire 'the dumpling' which was unkind but reassuring. Brian was at a dangerous age and Emma had heard enough stories about middle-aged men making fools of themselves with luscious au pairs to be cautious.

At the end of February David would be three. Emma wanted a big party, not only to celebrate David's birthday but the safe arrival of Helen. They had no plans to have Helen christened though Brian would have quite liked it. Mark's influence again. Emma had insisted that the party would have to do instead.

She discussed the party with Claire one morning over coffee. At least, Emma drank coffee. Claire still had a child's taste and always chose fizzy pop or milk. It was a grey, cold day and even in the kitchen with its big window facing east the light was on. Helen and David were having a nap and Owen was at playgroup. The house seemed unnaturally peaceful.

'I want something really special,' Emma said. She stretched her hands above her head, tightening her stomach muscles, and thought she had got her figure back well this time. She wasn't in bad shape for a woman who was nearly forty, more firm anyway than the young woman who sat opposite her.

Claire looked at her over a tumbler of milk and said nothing.

'There'll be adults, of course, besides the kids.' Emma stretched again, looked with satisfaction through the open door to the enormous living room which had been created when the Coastguard buildings had been knocked together, thought Brian had been right after all about this place. 'It's just as well we've got plenty of space.

I was thinking of laying something on to amuse the little ones. A children's entertainer. You know the sort of thing.'

'My brother-in-law's a magician,' Claire said and Emma nearly fell off her chair, in surprise, because Claire had never volunteered any information about her family before and it was such an odd thing to come out with. It was like saying 'My Granny's a witch.'

'Oh.' For once she was the one who couldn't find the words.

'He does kiddies' parties,' Claire said. 'He's very good.' There was a pause. 'I live with him and my sister.'

'Oh.' Emma was confused. 'Oh, I thought they were your parents. And doesn't he work for the DSS in Newcastle?'

'He's only a part-time magician,' Claire said, scornfully.

'Of course. Yes. I see that he would be.'

Emma's knowledge of the other residents of the Headland was sketchy. She had little reason to meet them. Her friends lived in the smarter parts of Otterbridge or in the rural, villages away from the old coal fields. Any information she had came from Kim, a single mother with a daughter the same age as Owen. The nearest playgroup was in the church hall in Heppleburn Village centre and Emma often gave Kim and her little girl a lift home. It was from Kim that she had heard about Claire, who had trained to be a nanny but who was having problems finding a job.

'Not worth going to college, is it?' Kim had said cheerfully. 'All that work then nothing at the end of it.'

Then, when they were coming home one evening after a playgroup trip to Edinburgh Zoo, Kim had pointed out the middle-aged man standing with his bike outside the house where Claire lived. He was bending to pull the bicycle clips from his trousers.

'They say that cycling makes you fit,' Kim had said with a giggle. 'He cycles all the way into the Ministry in Longbenton every day and look at the state of him!' And it seemed to Emma that the man did look remarkably unhealthy with his flabby stomach, his thin hair and pale greasy skin. She had assumed automatically that he was Claire's father.

Now, sitting in the Coastguard House kitchen, she did not know what to say.

'My parents died,' Claire said. 'Bernard and Kath took me in.'

'Oh I am sorry.' To Emma it seemed the worst sort of tragedy.

'Kath's seventeen years older than me. I suppose I was some sort of mistake. Mum died when I was a kid, and Dad was never very well. Not really fit for as long as I can remember. We lost him four years ago.' Without changing the tone of her voice she added, 'Shall I ask Bernard, then? About doing the show?'

Emma hesitated. She felt she was being rushed. She would have liked to consult the mothers at the very nice mother and toddler group in Otterbridge where she went with David and Helen before coming to a decision but she didn't want to offend Claire. Claire was a treasure. And how could she refuse after hearing what she'd suffered?

'Why don't you ask him to come and see me?' she suggested. 'We could discuss the sort of thing he does.'

'OK' Claire said, and lapsed into her customary silence, as if the exchange had quite exhausted her.

The next evening Bernard Howe turned up at the house. It was dark and rainy and if Emma had been on her own she might have been quite scared by the figure that stood in the security light. He wore a black PVC cape and his hair was dripping. But Emma was not on her own. Mark had called in after school. He had helped Claire to bath the boys and put them to bed, had jiggled Helen on his shoulder when she refused to settle. He had started coming to the Coastguard House after school quite often though he knew that Brian often worked late. Mark said he didn't enjoy being in the Otterbridge house on his own any more. It held too many ghosts. Besides, he loved playing with the children.

When the knock came at the door Emma was feeding Helen in front of the fire in the living room. The fireplace had been one of Brian's grand ideas. It was big enough to hold whole logs and spit-roast a pig. Mark was there too. Emma was being very discreet, holding Helen under one of the baggy sweaters she'd bought while she was pregnant and still wore, but all the same she felt quite brave. She had never been one of those women who could expose themselves in public.

So it was Mark who went to the door while Emma pulled the sleepy baby away from her breast and buttoned herself up.

'There's a magician to see you,' he said in a deadpan voice, as if it were the most natural thing in the world. He was standing in the living-room doorway leaning against the frame, more relaxed than he had been for months. She liked to think she was responsible for that.

The front door must have been open too because she could feel the damp wind against her face.

'Oh.' She felt suddenly flustered and again thought she was being rushed into something which had not been properly planned. 'You'd better show him in.'

And when she looked up again from straightening her clothes there Bernard Howe stood, dripping on the parquet floor. He must have come directly from work because his trousers were bunched around bicycle clips. He was large and clumsy and the baggy trousers made her think more of a clown than a magician. He smiled nervously.

'Claire said . . .' He took off the black cape and looked for somewhere to hang it. Mark took it from him. 'But perhaps I'd best come back another time.'

'No, no.' Emma had regained her composure. 'Please. Do come in.'

He took a chair opposite her, still close to the fire. His socks were thick, hand-knitted and they began to steam. There was a hole in one toe.

'I thought you'd want to see . . .' He seemed incapable of finishing a sentence.

She sat back with the sleeping child on her knee, waiting for him to continue. Instead he launched into his magic act and all of a sudden silk scarves were being pulled from his sleeves and sweets from his ears and balloons from his nostrils. Although she sat near to him she could not see how it was done, and despite her irritation at his just turning up on the doorstep, she was swept away by the magic. She gasped at each new trick. He beamed. When he finished she turned and saw Mark clapping behind her. It was an amused, self-conscious clap which made her enthusiasm seem foolish, as if he were an adult and she were a little girl.

'That's the sort of thing . . .' Bernard Howe muttered. His clumsiness had returned when the act was over. 'And I end with a cake. All the ingredients put into a bowl. Sugar, flour, eggs. And then there's a finished cake with icing and the candles all lit. The kiddies love that.'

'Oh yes,' Emma said. 'I can see that they would. You must come if you're available. Would you like a deposit? What do you charge?'

'I don't know about charging. You've been so good to Claire.'

'Of course you must charge. And Claire's been very good to us.'

So it was arranged that Bernard Howe, otherwise known as Uncle Bernie, would perform at David Coulthard's birthday party. As he prepared to go out again into the rain he turned back to them.

'Thank you, Mrs Coulthard. Mr Coulthard.'

'Oh no,' Emma said awkwardly. 'Oh no. This isn't my husband.'

The magician gave a strange stare before walking out into the night.

Chapter Four

They woke on the morning of the birthday party to an unexpected snow fall. The boys wanted to be out in it immediately. Usually Emma would have shared their excitement but today she was edgy and irritable. She'd had a bad night. The boys came chasing in from the cold and she moaned at them for the footprints on the kitchen floor, the sodden pile of outdoor clothes. Then, when Brian said he might go to work for a couple of hours, she turned on him.

'But it's a Saturday,' she said.

'It's a good time to catch up. When no one's there.'

'I could really do with your help here, you know.'

'Na. I'd just get in the way.'

She thought he was like a big spoilt kid standing there, grinning. His nose was still slightly twisted from a crunch during a school rugby match. He'd been a single child and he'd been able to get away with murder in his parents' house.

'Oh, go on then!' she said and he smiled more widely, thinking she'd fallen for his charm again, not realizing that at that moment she couldn't bear the sight of him.

She stood in the kitchen with her hands flat on the bench, breathing deeply, until she heard the BMW start and the garage door close automatically behind it. She was still standing there when Claire stamped past the window, flat footed in elephantine wellingtons.

During her wakeful night, while the baby snuffled in her cot, Emma had been thinking about Claire. She had reason to wonder how loyal to the family she really was. Now, seeing her march through the yard those suspicions seemed ridiculous and Emma thought if she needed someone to talk to, Claire might be the person she would choose. She was so solid and practical, more sensible surely than her friends from the Childbirth Trust, or old colleagues from work.

'It'll not last long.' Claire nodded through the window to the churned-up snow, the remains of the boys' snowman. 'The wind's gone westerly. Just as well. You'd not want twenty-five kids walking that much snow through your house.'

'No,' Emma said, quite calmly, thinking, If I can just get today over I can work out what we're going to do.

At one o'clock Brian came back, anxious to make amends by shifting tables and blowing up balloons. The snow had gone but there was freezing fog and occasional squalls of sleety rain.

'Mark phoned,' Brian said.

'Oh?' She kept her voice flat. She did not ask how Mark had known Brian would be in the office. Or why they seemed to need to communicate with each other every day.

'I told him to come round this afternoon. It might be a laugh for him.'

Christ, she thought. That's all I need.

'You don't mind?' His voice was slightly anxious. Surely you *can't* mind, he was saying. This man lost his wife less than six months ago. You're not going to make a fuss about this.

'Of course not.'

'I told him to come about two and I'd buy him a sandwich and a couple of pints in the club.'

So that's the strategy, she thought. Make me feel guilty, then I can't complain about the two of you sneaking off to the club for the afternoon. She said nothing and he added defensively, 'Well, the party's not supposed to start until four, is it?'

'That's right,' she said. 'Four o'clock.'

'And there's nothing more you want me to do?'

'Not at the moment.'

'We'll make sure we're back for four, then. On the dot.'

'I should bloody well hope so!'

He shot her an amused glance, thinking she was teasing.

'I mean it!' she shouted, suddenly furious.

'OK.' He held up his hands as if she had threatened to shoot him. 'I told Mark to leave his car at the club so there'd be more room up here for parking.'

What do you want, she thought, a medal for consideration?

'I'll go, then,' Brian said. 'Meet him there.'

'Fine.' She made an effort to keep the sarcasm from her voice. She didn't want to spoil David's birthday. 'Fine.'

He stood by the back door, pulling on his Berghaus jacket. It was raining again.

She turned to see Claire standing just inside the kitchen. The nanny gave no indication that she'd been listening but it gave Emma a start.

'I thought I'd nip home for a bit of lunch,' Claire said. 'I've put on a video for the boys. They'll be quiet for a while.'

'Oh.' Emma was disappointed. 'I thought we could have some lunch together.'

'I'd best go back.' She gave no reason.

'Oh,' Emma said. 'All right.'

'I'll be back in an hour.'

'Fine,' Emma said again. Brian was still hovering in the doorway. He opened the door and a blast of cold air came into the kitchen, before he went out and slammed it behind him. Claire put on her wellingtons and followed.

The boys' playroom was at the top of the house. It was long and narrow and looked down the Headland towards the level crossing. Emma heard the music of the video as she climbed the stairs. It was an old one – *Ivor the Engine* – and the boys must have been tired because they watched in silence. David was curled up on a bean bag with his thumb in his mouth. They looked up when she walked into the room but turned their attention immediately back to the screen.

She stood by the small window. It was streaked with salt but she could see Claire and her husband walking together to the double gates. Beyond that the rain closed in, and as they moved down the track she lost sight of them. Emma wondered what the girl, usually so unwilling to speak, could have had to say to her husband.

The Headland Club had the faded grandeur of an old theatre, and it *had* been grand once, on the northern circuit attracting big stars and big audiences. Now it was a miracle it stayed in business.

When Brian closed the heavy door behind him the temperature only rose by a couple of degrees. The drinkers standing by the big bar were still wearing overcoats and scarves.

He had joined the club when they moved to the Coastguard House. Emma thought it was an affectation. Occasionally he liked to make a show of his working-class roots. She never thought he would actually go. He was more at home in the wine bars, and smart restaurants of Jesmond, the Newcastle suburb where he had his office. But he had taken to going there regularly on Friday nights and staggering home in the early hours of the morning. One of the lads. He was even nominated for the committee and was tempted to accept. Committee meetings were an excuse for drinking late. In the end he decided, reluctantly, to turn it down. There were other demands on his time.

The manager of the club had his pint on the bar before he reached it. Les was a small, weaselly man with a mouth uncomfortably full of crowded teeth.

'By man!' Brian said. 'Can't you turn the heating up? It's like a morgue in here.'

'You're getting soft in your old age.' Les turned away, sensing that someone on the other side of the room needed a drink.

'I'm expecting Mark. You've not seen him?'

'Not yet.'

They all recognized Mark. He'd shocked them when Brian first brought him into the club by asking for a Perrier. He'd never lived that down.

The faded posters on the noticeboard flapped in a sudden draught and Mark came in. Brian looked at him with affection and concern. He'd lost weight in the last year, but Brian had thought he was starting to come to terms with his grief. Today, though, he looked pale and drawn and there were dark rings under his eyes. At university they'd nicknamed him the Monk. It wasn't only the shaved head, the skeletal features. He was the only one of their group who ever went near a church and he'd never, drunk much, even then. Never swore. You'd have thought he'd be the butt of their jokes but he wasn't. If anything they'd fought for his friendship. Today he looked more like a monk than ever.

Brian thought he needed a woman. Not an intellectual like Sheena. Someone easy and comfortable who'd feed him up on the wrong sort of food and enjoy plenty of sex.

Mark leant against the bar and Brian saw that he was shaking.

'When was the last time you had a decent meal?' he asked, following that recent line of thought. 'You need something to keep out the cold.'

Mark said nothing. He shook his head as if the question wasn't worth considering.

'What's the matter?' Brian demanded. 'Has something happened?' He had seemed so much happier lately.

Mark paused then shook his head again. Brian didn't want to push it.

'Mavis'll rustle us up something.' Brian shouted to the manager. 'Won't she, Les? Mavis'll stick something in the microwave?'

'Whisky,' Mark said. 'That'll warm me up.'

'Of course.' Brian kept the surprise out of his voice. 'A double Teachers when you're ready, Les. Medicinal.'

He led his friend to the table by a radiator. It gurgled and churned like the inside of someone's gut, but it gave out a little heat. Another couple of drinks and Mark might talk, Brian thought. Really talk. Like those long nights in the crappy students' bedsits in Durham. What he really wanted was to put his arm round Mark's shoulder and hold him tight. Just for comfort. But that wasn't the sort of thing you did in a working men's club. Unless your football team had just won the Cup.

He bought another round of drinks but Mark didn't seem inclined to confide in him. They sat for a while making desultory conversation. About a new contract Brian was bidding for – some insurance company based in Belfast. And about one of the kids in Mark's school who was making his life hell. Then they left and walked up the hill together to the Coastguard House, well in time for the four o'clock deadline.

The children loved Uncle Bernie from the moment he tripped over his feet on his way to the front of the room. Emma had been afraid that he wouldn't hold their attention but though he spoke so quietly that they had to strain to hear him, he held his audience spellbound. He performed in the big living room. The chairs were cleared to the walls and the children sat on the floor. The curtains were shut because outside the weather was so chill and grey.

Most of the adults stayed in the kitchen with their glasses of wine and their pints of beer, glad of the peace, but Emma, Mark and some of the other mums stood at the back to watch. The local news had been full of stories of a child who'd been abducted from a birthday party in a burger bar in North Shields. This wasn't the same but they knew better than to leave a stranger in charge of their little ones.

Uncle Bernie had a costume: wide check trousers and a loose jacket with a silk flower in the button hole. He asked for assistants and seemed to make a serious decision, considering the forest of hands that shot up with a frown. He chose David because it was his birthday, and Owen, because David was really too young and would need some help, and a pretty little girl with braided hair and a flowery frock.

The show was coming to an end.

'Now,' Uncle Bernie asked. 'What is it that makes a birthday special?'

'Presents,' they shouted.

'Yes,' he agreed. 'But what else? To make it really special?'

'Friends,' pronounced a precocious boy with glasses.

'That's a very good answer but it's not what I was thinking of.'

'A cake,' called the pretty little girl.

'Yes,' said Uncle Bernie with something approaching relief. 'A cake. Now, here are all the ingredients I need for my cake. If you shout them out I'll tip them into the bowl.'

Eggs were cracked. Flour was sieved. Margarine was scraped out of a tub. The children giggled appreciatively. They liked nothing better than a mess. David was allowed to stir and told to make a wish. When he didn't answer Bernie put it down to shyness and continued, 'Now, what do you need to cook a cake?'

'An oven!'

'That's right. An oven. But we couldn't have an oven here. Not close to so many children. That would be dangerous, wouldn't it? So we'll need some magic. What's the magic word?'

'Abracadabra.'

'Not loud enough!'

'ABRACADABRA!'

As he pulled away the white cloth to reveal a cake, with icing and three candles already flickering and running with melted wax, the adults' attention was distracted. Someone was hammering on the front door and shouting. Emma waited for a moment, thinking that Brian would answer it. But he was in the kitchen swapping blue jokes with some lads from the rugby club and he pretended not to notice.

The audience turned back to Uncle Bernie to give him his due applause and Emma went to the door. She opened it to a teenage girl with wild white hair. Traces of moisture hung to her hair, like frost on a spider's web, and her breath came in clouds.

'Please,' the girl said. 'I need to talk to my father.' Then she saw him through two open doors. Owen was holding the cake, and Bernie was already packing away his equipment in a cheap suitcase.

'It's Mum,' she shouted towards him. He looked up and saw her for the first time. 'She's gone again. Disappeared.'

As if, Emma thought, the woman had been part of his magic act. As if he had covered her with a cloth and she had vanished, like the mixing bowl full of ingredients.

Chapter Five

Ramsay had the weekend off but on Sunday morning he went into the police station anyway. He would have been more reluctant to volunteer for extra duty if Prue had been around. Prue was his lover. Not live-in, though he spent much of his free time in her house in Otterbridge. According to his mother he might as well be staying there. Mrs Ramsay was a chapel-goer and expected him to make an honest woman of Prue.

'If you think that wife of yours will come back to you, you're fooling yourself,' she'd said. She'd always had the knack of putting him down. And perhaps she was right and he *was* hoping Diana would turn up one day on his doorstep, laden with expensive shopping, her adventures over.

Now Prue was away. She worked as director of a small arts centre and was touring the Highlands and Islands with her youth theatre group, playing in schools and community centres. It was as much about giving her unemployed Tyneside teenagers a good time as developing acting and directing skills, she said. They would end up at the Youth Drama Festival in Kirkwall.

She was obviously enjoying every minute of the trip. When she remembered, she phoned up to rave about the scenery, the history, the whisky. He missed her more than he had expected, became quite sentimental when he thought about her.

'Why don't you come?' she'd suggested during the last phone call. She'd sounded tired, exhilarated and a little bit drunk. 'Take a couple of days' leave and fly up for the weekend.'

He'd been grateful for the invitation but he'd turned her down. It would be like taking *her* out to view the scene of a crime. As one of Prue's arty friends would have said, they both needed their own space. He knew Prue would prefer to work without distraction.

So on Sunday morning he went into the office. Sally Wedderburn was working too, clicking furiously at the computer keyboard, determined to make her mark on a high-profile case. There had been a number of child abductions in the area and the most recent had hit the headlines. The press hadn't made a connection with the previous incidents. Perhaps the police themselves had been slow in considering a link, had been reluctant even to take the cases seriously. At the beginning the children had turned up safe and well close to home. They were very young – all under five – and their stories were confused. There was no evidence of assault. Perhaps they had just wandered away. Perhaps the stranger with the sweets had been a friend of the family – someone at least, with no malicious intent – or a figment of the child's imagination, an excuse to cover naughtiness.

'How's it going?' He sat on the edge of her desk, so close, that he could smell her perfume. Prue teased him sometimes about his 'worklings', the eager young women who turned to him for support and advice, but the thought of any social entanglement embarrassed him.

'Slowly. The place was packed. You'd have thought someone would have seen what happened.'

In the most recent incident a three-year-old boy had been taken from a burger bar in a retail complex on the outskirts of Otterbridge. He was a guest at a birthday party which was being held there. His mother had taken him inside and waited until he'd handed over the present, then she'd gone shopping. She'd bought wallpaper from a DIY store and wandered round a car showroom, eyeing up the family saloons. When she returned to the burger bar an hour later the boy was gone.

'I spoke to the people who held the party myself. Of course they were devastated, but you can understand how it happened. It was Saturday afternoon, and they had a long table in the main restaurant. There were twenty kids, all riotous. None of them would sit still.

They ran back and forwards to the toilet. It must have been hard to keep track of them all.'

'Any witnesses where he was found?'

'Not yet. He seems to have materialized out of thin air.'

The boy had been found four hours later wandering along the seafront at Whitley Bay, clutching a bag of chips, crying. It seemed that nothing had happened during his adventure to distress him. The tears had begun after he'd been abandoned.

'The social worker's talked to him again but she hasn't come up with anything new. She can't even be sure of the reliability of what we've got.'

'What have we got?'

'A ride in a car and a fun fair.'

'The fun fair at the Spanish City?'

'Presumably, but most of the rides are shut at this time of the year and no one remembers a single bloke with a kid. I've left a pile of witness statements on your desk.'

'Thanks!'

She smiled up at him then returned to her computer screen. He moved on to his own office.

His desk was stacked with piles of paper which had appeared during the weekend – expense-claim forms for his signature, Home Office circulars, Sally's witness statements. He ignored them all and began by flicking through a file of incidents which had been reported over night.

At first he skipped over the missing person report without really taking it in. He was concerned about children and this was an adult. Then he went back to it. Kathleen Howe. The walker. He had seen her and the girl on the roads round Heppleburn several times since Marilyn had turned up, panic-stricken, on his doorstep in the autumn. Once the girl was carrying a violin in one hand and a music case in the other. Another time she recognized him and raised her hand in greeting as he drove past. It was an apologetic gesture. She didn't stop or break her stride. The mother never acknowledged him.

What had happened now? Had the girl overreacted to her mother's absence again? Perhaps this time she had taken his advice by phoning the station instead of knocking on the door of a stranger. He unclipped the form from the file and looked at it in more detail.

It had been the husband, not the daughter, who had phoned the station.

Ramsay considered the piles of paper on his desk, then swivelled his chair so his back was turned to them. He was curious and he wouldn't concentrate on other work until he had checked this out. He picked up the phone.

'This missing person from the Headland?' he asked. 'She turned up yet?'

'If she has no one's told us. But, they don't always, do they?'

'I'll deal with it if you like. Talk to the family anyway.'

'Why?' The voice was suspicious. Routine missing persons shouldn't have interested Ramsay. 'Something going on there that we should know about?'

'Nothing like that.'

How could he explain his feeling that something was wrong? He could hardly say, 'I went there once. The lassie was more worried than someone her age has a right to be. And there were no blackberries.' He'd be a laughing stock. So he said nothing.

'Well, if you're short of work you're welcome to it.' The voice at the end of the phone had turned sulky. The receiver was replaced with a thud.

Ramsay drove back down the road along which he'd just travelled. There was a straight avenue of dripping trees before he came to the familiar grey terraces of Heppleburn and the road to the coast. As he drove he half expected to see the ramrod-straight figure of Kathleen Howe marching towards her home, carrying her canvas shopping bag and another excuse for her unexplained absence.

As on the previous occasion he had to wait at the level crossing. A coal train was rattling slowly on its way to the power station. On the other side of the line, beyond the barrier, a pedestrian was waiting to cross. He was a large man in a black PVC cape and Ramsay imagined the moisture trickling from the greasy collar into his neck. As the barrier lifted and Ramsay drove slowly across, the man peered into the car, sticking his head right up to the passenger window, so close that for a moment Ramsay was afraid he intended to jump in front of the vehicle. It occurred to Ramsay as he drove on towards the club that he should have stopped, and at least asked the man for his name and address. Already he was thinking of Kathleen Howe's disappearance in terms of a police investigation.

The Headland was covered with a fine drizzling mist which hid the Coastguard House from view. Ramsay drove slowly past the club and towards the houses of Cotter's Row. A red minibus loomed out of the fog ahead of him. He had seen it before parked in the street close to his cottage. It collected people who had no transport and took them to the ten o'clock service at the Methodist church in Heppleburn. He pulled in to let it pass and had a glimpse, through windows spotted with rain, of elderly faces.

He parked outside the Howes' and waited for a moment, suddenly daunted by the prospect of an encounter with Marilyn Howe. He thought he should have brought Sally Wedderburn with him, then told himself he was overreacting. When he knocked on the door Kathleen Howe would probably open it herself.

Chapter Six

The door opened while he was still sitting in the car so he felt awkward, irrationally guilty, as if he'd been spying. Marilyn stood on the step. She was dressed in clothes which her mother might have worn: a shapeless knee-length skirt, a roll-neck sweater, fluffy pink slippers. Her hair was pulled away from her face. The effect was of middle-aged dowdiness and exhaustion.

'Oh,' she said. 'It's you. I heard the car and I thought. . . Is there any news?'

He shook his head. 'Your mother's not back yet? You've not heard from her?'

'Nothing.'

'Perhaps I could come in. I'd like a word with you all.'

'I'm the only one here. Dad's out looking. He went as soon as it got light. I don't think any of us slept.'

'Is your father a big man? Wearing a black cycle cape?'

She nodded.

'I think I saw him on the road.' So the strange figure at the level crossing had been an anxious husband, not a suspect. Not yet at least. Marilyn continued. 'Claire's at work. She offered to stay but there didn't seem much point.'

'Claire's your aunt?'

'That's right.'

She moved away from the step to let him in and took him straight to the back living room. There was a fire banked up in the grate and the sulphurous smell of smokeless fuel which reminded him again of his mother's house. In one corner a clothes horse was draped with towels and the windows ran with condensation. The dining table was spread with textbooks.

'I was trying to do some homework,' Marilyn said. 'I thought it would take my mind off Mummy but I couldn't really concentrate.'

He sat in the rocking chair where Kathleen Howe had been when he had surprised her on his previous visit to the house. In the hot, steamy room it would have been easy to doze off.

'Why don't you tell me what happened?'

'We don't *know* what happened!' the girl cried. 'She just disappeared.'

'Well, when did you last see her?'

'At breakfast yesterday. Then I went out.'

'Where did you go?'

'To school.'

'On a Saturday?'

'There was a special choir rehearsal. We're taking part in a music festival at the Cathedral.'

'What time did you get home?'

'Two o'clock.' She paused then continued like an ordinary schoolgirl, chatty, enthusiastic. 'We'd taken packed lunches because Miss Winter thought the practice would drag on into the afternoon but it went really well and we finished early.'

'Your mother wasn't expecting you back then?'

'Not until later. That's why I didn't worry at first.'

'How did you get home from school?'

'I got a lift.' There had been a slight hesitation. A flush of embarrassment. Or was it pleasure?

'Who from? A parent? One of the sixth-formers?' He had seen them, the kids coming out of the High School. They all seemed to have cars these days, and not just old bangers either.

'No.' She hesitated again. 'One of the teachers sings with us. Mr Taverner. He was coming this way.'

An adolescent crush, Ramsay thought.

'Was anyone in when you got home?'

'My father. He went out at about four. He works as a children's entertainer. He had a booking at a kids' party.'

'Didn't he tell you where your mother had gone?'

'He thought she might have walked into Heppleburn, to the Co-op.'

'Wasn't he sure?'

'Not really.' She had been standing with her back to the table. Now she leant forward. 'When you meet my Dad properly you'll understand. It's not that he's stupid. He's absent-minded. When you talk to him he doesn't always listen. Especially to Mummy, who tends to nag. I think it's because his head's full of tricks and illusions.' Again she saw the need to explain. 'He's a magician. Brilliant. Anyone round here will tell you. He's only part-time, of course. His real job's with the DSS at Longbenton. The insolvency section.'

'I see.'

Ramsay was glad he had visited Marilyn Howe in his own time and alone. He wondered what his sergeant, Hunter, would have made of the family. Hunter's prejudices were widespread and various. He distrusted anything outside his own experience. A household without a car or a television would have struck him as sufficiently odd to raise his suspicions. But a part-time magician ...

'When did you start to worry about your mother?'

'Soon after Dad left to go to the party. Even if she'd left just before I'd got home she should have been back from Heppleburn by then. She's a fast walker.'

Ramsay gave a brief smile. 'I know.'

'I didn't want to panic or make a fool of myself like last time. I told myself she'd soon be home. I looked to see what she'd taken with her, to try to work out where she might be. Then I knew something was wrong. Her coat was still here and her shopping bag and her purse. She wouldn't have gone to Heppleburn without them.'

Her face crumpled and Ramsay was afraid she would cry. He felt a stab of anger because she was being put through this anxiety. Parents should be the ones to worry. It was part of the job description. But she hadn't asked to be responsible for two middle-aged eccentrics whose thoughtlessness had caused this panic.

He gave her a moment to compose herself then asked, 'Has your mother ever been ill?'

'What do you mean?'

'Has she ever had any nervous trouble, suffered from stress or depression, anything like that?'

'No,' she said uncertainly. 'I don't think so.'

'Who's your GP?'

'Dr Lattimer in Heppleburn.' She looked up at him and he saw that despite her sheltered life she could be mature and perceptive. 'You think she's had a sort of breakdown?'

'It's one possibility.'

'She wouldn't have committed suicide,' Marilyn said, and again he was surprised at her ability to follow his train of thought. 'Absolutely not. She wouldn't want to leave me alone.'

'No.' He saw what she meant. 'But the breakdown? She did seem rather tense when I came here last September. Did she ever really explain what happened that afternoon?'

'Not to me.' It was said too quickly but he didn't feel it was the time to push her.

They waited for a moment in silence.

'I'm not doing much good here,' Ramsay said, 'but I don't want to leave you alone. Can we get your aunt to stay with you? I could talk to her employer. Explain. Where does she work?'

'She's a nanny to the kids in the Coastguard House. Don't go up there. They think I'm daft enough already. That's where Dad was working yesterday and I burst in and made a scene. Claire will be home soon. She's only gone in for a couple of hours to help clear up after the party. Anyway, I don't mind being on my own.'

'Well,' Ramsay said. 'If you're sure . . .' She had, after all, been on her own when he found her. 'Perhaps I'll have a walk around the Headland. See if your dad's come back.'

Outside it seemed very cold and the mist was thicker than ever. Ramsay carried on up the track until he arrived at the high, whitewashed wall which surrounded the Coastguard House. To the south a fog-horn belched, marking the mouth of the Tyne.

36

He called tentatively, 'Mr Howe,' then decided that only a maniac would be wandering along the cliff tops in fog. Besides, if Kath Howe's husband had returned to the Headland he would surely have called home. Ramsay supposed he was still searching the footpaths in the dene.

He walked back between the double row of houses towards the club and the jetty. It was only eleven o'clock but there were lights on in the front rooms. In one a pretty little girl was playing at dressing up. She wore a frilly white garment which might once have been her mother's night-dress, and twirled round and round so the skirt spun away from her body.

The club was still shut. The door was covered by a grille, the windows by steel shutters. The tide was well on its way in and the gully which had been cut through the rock to let out the coal boats was nearly full.

Four children were playing on the jetty. They were rowdy, foul-mouthed, cocksure. Future customers, he thought. The oldest had probably already been up before the Juvenile Bench and he'd guess they were all on some register or another. They were throwing rocks at a target floating in the water, swearing indiscriminately whether they hit or missed.

Ramsay approached them and shouted. They stopped briefly and looked at him, then continued their game, deciding he was nothing to be scared of.

'Hey!' he called again. 'Come here.'

'Sod off!' one of the boys shouted, not taking his eyes off the target. 'We're allowed. It's not private.'

'I was looking for someone. Mrs Howe. Do you know her?'

They didn't answer immediately but they did stop throwing stones. They turned and gave him their attention.

'Why?'

'I'm a policeman,' Ramsay said.

'Na!' The boy was probably too young for school. 'We know the copper round here. PC Whelan. He's not on duty today though. Weekend off.'

Ramsay thought that crime prevention couldn't be best served if a gang of bad boys knew the rota of the only local policeman. Then the target the lads had been aiming at drifted into his field of view. A dead animal, he thought at first. Not a dog. Something with long, grey hair floating on the surface like fine seaweed. The position of the animal shifted as it was buffeted by a wave and he saw that it was wearing clothes.

'Do you know where PC Whelan lives?' he asked.

'Heppleburn Village.' The answer was grudging but they were bored and curious.

'I suppose that's too far for you to go on your own.'

'Don't be dumb!' They were scornful.

'Would you be able to go and fetch him? Tell him that Inspector Ramsay is on the Headland and needs him urgently. If you can remember that.'

It was enough of a dare to send them running across the railway line and up the short cut through the dene. That was all Ramsay wanted. To be rid of them before they realized what was floating in the cut. He used his mobile phone to call Otterbridge Station. He talked to Sally Wedderburn.

'You'll set it all up then. I'll wait here.'

'Sure.'

'And get here as soon as you can, Sal. I'm going to need you.'

She was ambitious and he heard her resistance.

'For an accidental death?' The child abductions were far more glamorous.

'For a suspicious death.' He didn't want to be on his own when he told Marilyn Howe that her mother was dead.

Chapter Seven

'She was dead before she reached the water.'

It was Monday morning. Hunter was so excited that he was almost drooling. He stood at the entrance to Ramsay's office. In the room beyond a phone was ringing. Members of the public were still calling to report the sighting of a single man with a young boy.

'How did she die?' Ramsay hadn't waited on the jetty to see the body lifted out of the water. He couldn't bear the idea of the gang of kids or an excited neighbour telling Marilyn that a woman had been found in the cut. Especially if Marilyn were still alone. Later the doctor had refused to commit himself over the phone.

'She was stabbed. A violent attack, the pathologist said.'

Ramsay wondered briefly how stabbing could be anything other than violent.

In fact when he and Sally had arrived at the house at Cotter's Row, Bernard Howe was already there. He was sitting at the table in the back room, his hair still wet, his face red and blotchy through coming into the heat from the cold. In front of him was a foil container on a plate and he forked an unappetizing ready-cooked shepherd's pie into his mouth. There was a recent gravy stain on his sweater. Marilyn opened the door to them and it seemed to Ramsay that she had already prepared herself for bad news. It was Bernard who was shocked. He was the one who couldn't take it in. He sat with his fork halfway to his mouth while the food dripped on to the oilskin tablecloth.

'We'll need you to identify the body,' Ramsay had said. 'Until then there's no certainty.' Although he had seen the long hair as the waves jolted the body towards the rocks and was quite certain.

But still Bernard Howe had seemed unable to move.

In his office Ramsay looked up at Hunter who blocked the doorway.

'A full-scale murder inquiry, then,' he said. 'As if we haven't got enough on our plates. You know the ropes.'

Hunter nodded but remained where he was.

'You knew her, didn't you?' he asked. 'The victim?' He could be as nebby as an old woman, started most of the canteen gossip.

'Not really. I met her once and I've seen her around.'

'They're a funny bunch out on the Headland,' Hunter said. 'I went out with a lass from there once. Her dad took me to the club. You'd have thought I was a Martian. No kidding. The place suddenly went quiet and they all stared.'

'They don't like outsiders?'

'Oh, they're friendly enough when they get to know you but if there's not a member of your family who can remember the Cotter's Row street party at the end of the war, you're a newcomer.'

Well, Ramsay thought, there were still plenty of communities in Northumberland like that. He wondered how long the Howes had been living on the Headland. He could not imagine that they belonged.

'Sal Wedderburn stayed the night with the family,' he said. 'She was there when I told the girl about her mother.'

'Aye.' Hunter was disapproving. 'I'd heard you'd called her in to play social worker.'

Ramsay wondered if it was time for a warning about the petty rivalry which flared between the two officers occasionally but decided against it. Gordon Hunter was given to sulks and flounces and he could do without that now.

'They seemed to take to her.' But as soon as the words were spoken he wondered if that were true. There had been no hostility but the family had hardly seemed to acknowledge Sally's presence. When he'd said that he'd like her to stay – for support, to fend off the press if that proved necessary – Bernard, had emerged briefly from his stupor to say, 'But where will she sleep? Claire uses the spare room.'

Ramsay had explained that the sofa would be fine and there had been no more comment. He had hoped that Marilyn would form a relationship with Sally, would confide in her, but realized now that this was unlikely to happen.

'You think one of the family's involved, then?' Hunter asked.

'I don't know anything at this stage.' The words were sharper than he'd intended and he added, 'No. That's not why I asked Sally to stay. The girl was very close to her mother. They went everywhere together. She'll know better than anyone if Kath Howe was anxious, frightened. I'd hoped she'd see Sal as a friend.'

'Ah.' Hunter was relieved. 'Like I said. Playing the social worker.'

'I'd like you to come over to Heppleburn with me,' Ramsay said. 'I want every single person on the Headland talked to. I don't mean a plod asking a couple of questions on the doorstep. I mean a pot of tea on the table and someone listening for as long as the chat goes on. Gossip. Not just about the Howes but about anyone living in the place.'

'You think we're looking for a local, then?'

Ramsay shrugged, tried not to show his frustration at Hunter's demand for easy answers. 'It's not the sort of place a stranger would wander across to by chance. Especially in the weather we've had this weekend. I don't suppose we've got a time of death yet?'

'Nothing specific. Some time Saturday.'

'Ah.'

'Problem?'

'The Coastguard House has been converted to private use. On Saturday afternoon there was a kiddies' party. I presume that means carloads of strangers visiting the place. Not exactly a problem. More of complication. We'll need a list of visitors, car registration numbers. It certainly doesn't make life easier. Anyone unfamiliar on the Headland that day would have been put down as a guest of the Coastguard House.'

'Do you want me to talk to the owners?'

'No,' Ramsay said. 'I'll do that.'

'Leave me to deal with the peasants? Is that it?' Hunter grinned to show there were no hard feelings, exposing teeth which seemed very white in an even brown face. He'd been on a package holiday to Turkey in the autumn and he'd topped up his tan regularly since then on the sun beds.

'Charm the old ladies more like,' Ramsay said. Hunter liked that and grinned again.

The jetty was still roped off with blue and white plastic tape. Despite the drizzle a small group of onlookers stood in the car park of the Headland Social Club. Mostly old men with pitmen's coughs. One of them was blind and had his arm linked with that of his companions who provided a running commentary on the proceedings. Not that there was much now to comment on.

A blue transit van with a noisy exhaust rattled to a stop beside the group. On the side ERIC WILSON MOBILE SHOP was painted in uneven white letters. This was the excuse for the gathering, though Ramsay thought that on normal Mondays it would be the women who'd be waiting. Perhaps the men had persuaded them it wouldn't be safe to be out.

Eric Wilson jumped out and opened the back doors of the van. Apparently from nowhere a group of children came running down the road. They pushed to the front of the queue and began pointing at the trays of improbably coloured sweets and chews which the shopkeeper stored sensibly out of their reach. The men muttered disapproval but did not try to stop them. It was as if they were scared to. These were the children who had been throwing stones at Kath Howe's body.

Ramsay waited until they had been served then made his way towards them. They munched silently, surrounded by a scattering of dropped sweet wrappers. In other circumstances he would have ordered them to collect the litter, but he resisted the temptation and said mildly, 'Shouldn't you be at school?'

They grinned as if they had caught him out.

'Na. Half term, isn't it?'

It was only later that he realized he'd seen the school-crossing lady in Heppleburn Village. A sudden death on the Headland had been too much for them to resist.

'Were you playing round here on Saturday?'

'We might have been here.' As if playing wasn't a concept they recognized.

'I need your help.' He began walking away from the men buying bags of potatoes and tins of beans. The children followed. When they could not be overheard he said, 'It's a murder inquiry.'

That had them hooked. They wanted to know if Mrs Howe had been shot, stabbed or had her head cut off. They acted out scenes from particularly nasty videos and pretended to be carrying automatic machine guns. Every other word was an obscenity. Ramsay felt out of his depth. He'd been imagining the Gorbals Diehards not these manic addicts of celluloid pornography.

'Was it a serial killer?' one of them asked. 'Was it?'

'No!' he said, more sharply than he'd intended. 'And if you're going to be stupid I'll ask someone else to help.'

Then they calmed down because above everything else they were bored.

'What time were you here on Saturday?' he asked.

They looked confused. They didn't own a watch between them.

'Before tea or after tea?'

Again that had little meaning. They seemed to eat continually when they weren't at school, scrounging crisps and biscuits from whichever mother they could con into providing them.

'What was on the television before you went out?'

'*Live and Kicking*. When that was finished there was only the sport.'

'And what was on when you went back in?'

'*Baywatch*'. It was the oldest boy. He gave a lecherous smirk. 'My dad always watches that.'

'So you were out all afternoon?'

They nodded.

'Where did you go? Were you down by the jetty?'

'Earlier on.'

'Did you see anything?'

43

'The murder, you mean? Na.' He shook his head, disappointed, then gave a blood-curdling scream, an imitation presumably of a woman being stabbed. 'Later we hung around the Coastguard House. There was something going on. Loads of big cars.'

'It was a birthday party,' one of the younger boys said almost wistfully, then added, 'Not that we'd have wanted to go.'

'Na!' they all joined in.

'Did you see Mrs Howe that afternoon? You would all recognize Mrs Howe if you saw her?'

'Course we would. She was an ugly bitch. And a stuck-up cow.' A pause. 'That's what my mam says.'

'Did you see her on Saturday afternoon? At the jetty?'

They shook their heads, quite certain.

'What about later? You'd have had a good view down the Headland from the Coastguard House.'

They looked at each other. Ramsay thought they were taking the question seriously, trying to reach a consensus.

'We didn't see her. But we mightn't have. It was drizzly and misty. Like today only worse. And it was sodding cold. You couldn't see much. Especially when it started to get dark.'

Ramsay imagined them, banned from their homes by the men who wanted to watch *Grandstand* in peace, hovering round the gate of the Coastguard House, attracted by the noise and the flash cars. Being a nuisance. Getting in the way. If they were noticed at all.

'So you didn't see anything unusual?'

But by then they'd lost interest and they were already swaggering away, back to the jetty, to swing on the blue and white tape and shout insults at the constable on duty.

Ramsay walked up the hill to the Coastguard House.

Chapter Eight

Claire didn't turn up for work at the Coastguard House on Monday morning. Emma hadn't really been expecting her to. She'd heard about Kathleen Howe's death from Brian who'd gone down to the club for a pint after his Sunday lunch and found the jetty cordoned off, the place crawling with coastguards and police.

'What a terrible accident!' Emma had said, meaning it at first and only thinking of the implication later. Then there was a feeling which was not so much relief as gratitude.

'Not an accident.' Brian's words were slightly slurred. The club might have been shut but he'd had a few cans at home and most of a bottle of Rioja with his roast beef. 'That's what the talk is. The lass spoke to the blokes who fished her out.'

She hadn't replied. Couldn't. She would have expected Brian to go on about the tragedy all afternoon, making sick jokes, even phoning his friends to tell them. Luckily he never mentioned it again.

When the doorbell rang late on Monday morning Emma hoped that it would be Claire, deciding that she would be happier at work after all. Claire would know what was going on.

But Claire would have gone round to the back and let herself in. Instead there was a man who waited patiently while Emma unlocked the door and tugged at it. It always warped in the damp.

'Yes?' she said briskly. She tended to become officious when she was nervous.

'Mrs Coulthard?'

'Yes.'

'My name's Ramsay. I'm a detective inspector with Northumbria Police.' He paused. 'It's about Mrs Howe.'

Ramsay was a man who wouldn't be easily fooled. Emma saw that at once. Before the babies she'd headed up the Human Resources Department of an electronics firm which had moved to Wallsend and she'd worked with men of authority. She'd admired them. Not the bullies, the pushy, lippy little men – they almost always *were* men – who blustered and posed and did sod all work if they could help it. But the one or two decent managers who meant what they said. Always.

He was not particularly impressive to look at. About her age. Possibly a bit older. Tall, bony and angular with long limbs like a marionette. Dark hair which could do with a cut. She was too nervous to focus on his face but she saw dark eyebrows almost meeting in the middle which left the impression of a continual frown. He was wearing a raincoat. It was too big for him and hung over the shoulders, dragged out of shape by the weight of the material so it looked like a cavalry officer's cape.

'Claire's not here today,' Emma said quickly. 'I don't expect she could face it.'

'She hasn't been in touch?'

'They haven't got a phone. She'd know I'd understand.'

'Of course.' Ramsay paused so long that Emma wondered if that was it, if now he would turn away and walk down the hill to Cotter's Row.

'It was really you I wanted to talk to,' he said at last. 'You or your husband. Perhaps I could come in. If it's convenient.'

'The children are here.'

'Oh, I won't need to disturb them.'

'But they might disturb us. That's what I'm saying.'

He smiled. 'We won't mind that, will we?'

So she had no alternative then but to stand aside and let him into the house. He thought it was a place where he could have lived. There was a lot of polished wood and white paint. It was not so tidy that it was intimidating. They sat in the kitchen with the door open so Emma could keep an eye on the boys playing in the other room. The floor was covered with toys. He knew nothing about children but it seemed to him that so many could only confuse. It was very different from the houses where his work usually took him.

'It was David's birthday at the weekend,' Emma said. 'He had loads of new things. It should keep them quiet for a bit.'

But almost as she finished speaking there was a scream of rage from the other room. The smaller boy had been fixing together pieces of wood to form a railway track. The blocks making a bridge had fallen apart. He picked up the painted train and hurled it away from him, then lay on his back, pounding his feet on the floor. Emma went in to him. When she tried to comfort him he pushed her away, punching at her with his fists. At last the sobs subsided and he fell limp in her arms. She set him gently on the floor and returned to the kitchen.

'Just a temper tantrum,' she said. 'Now he's past the terrible twos perhaps they'll stop.' Then, as if she felt some explanation was necessary, 'David's speech is very poor for his age. They say there's nothing really wrong. Boys are often slow developers. But he gets frustrated when he can't communicate.' She caught her bottom lip with her teeth and he had the impression of a real anxiety.

'I'm sure he'll be fine,' he said. He felt she needed reassurance.

'I hope so. My husband says I'm making a fuss about nothing, but he doesn't speak at all.'

Through the open door they watched the boy return to his game.

'You have two children?'

'Three. The baby's asleep. Coffee?'

'Please.'

She ground beans, fiddled with a percolator. There was a jar of instant on the work top and he wondered why she didn't use that. Was she trying to impress or did she need time to collect her thoughts? She poured coffee into pottery mugs.

'This is a murder investigation,' he said. 'Mrs Howe didn't die by accident.' He waited for some response. 'You're not surprised?'

'There's been talk. The men that helped pull her out of the water thought . . . You know what the gossip's like in a place like this.'

'I shouldn't have thought you'd get involved in that. Not living up here.'

'Brian – my husband – goes to the club.'

'Ah.' They'd used the club as a base the day before. It was somewhere the pathologist could get out of the rain. Of course there'd be talk.

'We believe Mrs Howe was killed on Saturday,' Ramsay said. 'We need to eliminate anyone who was on the Headland then. I understand you held a party. We'll need a list of all the guests and an address or a phone number for each one.'

'Of course.' She looked up from her coffee. 'But no one who came here knew Mrs Howe. What reason would they have to kill her?'

'As I said, it's a question of elimination. And of finding witnesses.'

'Yes.' She seemed reassured. 'I see.'

'Besides,' he went on gently, 'it's not exactly true, is it, that none of the visitors to the Coastguard House knew Mrs Howe? Both her daughter and her husband were here on Saturday afternoon. And her sister is your nanny.'

'I didn't mean. . .' She blushed. 'I wasn't trying to hide anything. I meant the guests. They wouldn't have known the Howes.'

'They didn't mix in the same social circles?'

'No, well, I suppose not.'

'But you will be able to give me a guest list?'

'Of course. I put a list of names and addresses on the computer before I sent out the invitations. I'll print you a copy.'

She returned with a sheet of paper and a baby. The baby was round faced with downy hair and curls damp and flattened where she'd been lying in the cot. She was still sleepy. It was the closest Ramsay had ever been to a child so young. He wondered if some comment was expected about her prettiness, a question about her age, but he just took the list of names and scanned it quickly. There was no one he recognized.

'And this is it?' he asked. 'There was no one else?'

She paused for a moment and shifted the baby into a more comfortable position against her shoulder. 'There was one extra. Mark Taverner. He's a friend of my husband.'

'Taverner?' The name was familiar then he remembered where he had heard it in connection with the case. 'Is he a teacher at Otterbridge High School?'

'That's right. RE and music. Why?'

Ramsay shook his head, smiled. 'Nothing sinister. It ties in with information from another witness.'

Marilyn Howe had said she'd been given a lift back from the choir rehearsal by Mr Taverner. He'd told her he was coming to the Headland anyway.

'I'll give you his address,' Emma said. 'I don't know why Brian invited him. It wasn't really his thing. We try to include him in family events because he lost his wife recently. He must get lonely.'

I lost my wife, Ramsay thought, but to a BBC news reporter with a blond moustache and a red sports car. And no doubt he's lost her now, too.

'Tell me about Mrs Howe,' he said. 'Did you have any dealings with her?'

'What do you mean, dealings?' The reply was sharp. It was as if he had suggested something improper. And he thought, for the first time, that he heard anxiety in her tone, perhaps panic.

'I employed her *once*,' Emma said reluctantly. He had the very strong impression that she would have preferred to keep this to herself but realized it was impossible. 'It was just after Christmas. The house was a tip and I was expecting Brian's family to stay for New Year. He was rushed off his feet at work. Never here.' She smiled. 'Not that he'd do much if he was. Claire has her hands full with the kids. I can't expect her to do much cleaning.'

'So you employed Kath Howe as a cleaner?'

She nodded. 'For a two-day blitz. To do the house from top to bottom. I asked Claire if she knew anyone who'd want the work and she suggested Kath.'

'Was she satisfactory?'

'Not really.'

'What was the problem?'

Emma gave a brief smile. 'I don't think her heart was in the job.'

He waited.

'She considered cleaning was beneath her. And she definitely didn't like being told what to do.'

'Why did she take the job then?'

'I suppose she needed the money. Teenagers don't come cheap, do they?'

'Probably not.' But he didn't see Marilyn as the demanding sort. He couldn't imagine her wheedling for smart clothes or nights out with her friends. There were violin lessons, though. They didn't come free these days even if they were arranged through school. Exam fees. The instrument itself.

'You weren't tempted to employ her again then? Not even before this recent party?'

'No, even if she'd been any good. Brian wouldn't have approved. He thinks I sit around all day drinking coffee.' She paused. 'He never knew I took her on that first time.'

'What was she *like*?' he asked. 'As a woman, I mean, not just as a worker.'

The question surprised her, but he could tell she was interested by it.

'I don't know,' she said slowly. 'She wasn't very chatty. That's one thing at least she and Claire have in common. I mean, even then I thought she was Claire's mother. I didn't realize they were sisters.'

'But you must have formed some impression?' It seemed she was just giving herself time to collect her thoughts. She would reply in the end.

'I used to work as a personnel officer,' she said. 'I'd assess candidates' suitability for employment every day.'

'So, what did you make of Kath Howe?'

'Let's say I wouldn't have given her a permanent job.'

'Why?'

'She'd never have made a team player. Too sure of herself. Arrogant almost. She was bright enough and in areas of dispute she'd probably be right but she'd offend all her colleagues by telling them so. A loner.' She looked up at him. 'Look, this probably isn't fair. A first impression. I hardly knew the woman. . .'

'I know,' he said. 'But it's useful all the same. You say she was bright. Wasn't she frustrated staying at home, not working?'

'I can hardly comment on that, can I? It's what I've chosen to do.' Her words were reassured, calm. '*I* don't regret it.'

'Your situation isn't quite the same. Your children are younger.'

She chose her words carefully. 'I think Mrs Howe would have found it difficult to adjust to employment, for all the reasons I've explained. Perhaps she was glad of an excuse to stay at home. She could potter round the house. She had interests. And she could tell herself she was making a sacrifice for her daughter's sake. I had the impression she was an ambitious woman, but for her daughter, not herself.'

It was probably an accurate impression, but Ramsay thought it of some significance that despite her previous career Emma Coulthard could come up with such a considered judgement of a woman she hardly knew.

He set down his coffee mug, stood up.

'Was Claire happy living with Mr and Mrs Howe?'

'I suppose so, I don't expect she'd have told me if she were miserable. Claire's a very private person.'

'You never suggested that she live here?'

'No. That never arose. We chose Claire as nanny because she lived locally.'

'When did you last see Mrs Howe?'

'I don't know. Weeks ago probably. And then not to speak to. She was with Marilyn on the Heppleburn Road. Walking.'

Chapter Nine

Hunter, would have been happy to stay at number six Cotter's Row all day. All night if it came to that. And he didn't think Kim Houghton would object. She seemed a sociable sort of girl.

He'd knocked on the door of number six expecting another old granny with time on her hands but nothing useful to say. Instead there was Kim, wearing a little lacy top stretched to ripping point by a Wonderbra and jeans so tight it would take an hour to pull them off. If the situation ever arose, which it already had in Hunter's imagination. She turned to let him in and he saw she was wearing a silver chain round her ankle. He'd tried to persuade successive girlfriends to wear an anklet but they'd all refused. They'd said it would make them feel dirty.

The ground floor had been knocked through to make one room and Hunter thought that someone had made a good job of it. The kitchen units were oak and there was nothing cheap or tacky about the furniture. So she was probably married, he decided with only a little regret, to someone who brought in a decent wage. There'd be a steady boyfriend at least.

'Do you live on your own?' he asked, speaking loudly because she'd offered him coffee and she was in the kitchen at the other end of the long narrow room. The kettle was humming. 'Or is your old man at work?'

'Na!' she cried. 'I'm not married. Not any more.'

She walked back to him across the shag pile carpet, carefully carrying a mug in each hand, her bum swaying. She'd kicked off her shoes in the kitchen. She sat on a deep easy chair with her feet tucked under her. She hadn't asked what he was doing there. He'd introduced himself and she'd invited him in. Sociable.

He looked pointedly around the room. His eyes took in the television and the videos, and lingered over the marble fire surround which he'd been pricing out himself at the Northern Gas showroom over the weekend.

'You work, then,' he said. You didn't live in this sort of style on the Social.

She looked at him over her coffee mug, teasing, 'Oh, you know. Bits and pieces where I can. Nothing regular. I can't, can I? Not with a little girl to take care of.'

'You've got a daughter?' That surprised him. There was nothing to show there was a child in the house. No toys or picture books. No mess. Then he saw a silver-framed photo on the mantelshelf. A blond-haired little girl in a pink sweater, with silver rings in her ears and a silver chain round her neck.

'Kirsty.' Kim explained. 'She's at playgroup.'

Hunter thought perhaps the child explained the way she lived. The Child Support Agency had got its claws into a wealthy father. He wondered briefly what bits and pieces of work Kim Houghton had had a go at, but decided it was probably best not to dwell on it. He needed to concentrate.

Kim set her coffee mug on the glass-topped table. 'I suppose you're here about Kathleen. Mrs Howe.'

'You knew her?'

She shrugged. 'Saw her about. We never spoke. She thought she was too good for me.'

'What's the story, then?'

'What do you mean?'

'Tell me about the Howes. What do people say about them?'

'That they keep themselves to themselves. That's what the charitable ones say.'

'And the others?'

'That they're stuck-up gits.'

'And you?' He leant forward confidentially. 'What do you think?'

'They're not normal, are they?' The answer was flip. She didn't really care one way or the other. This was a bit of drama, a bit of fun. There'd been reporters knocking on the door and now this detective. Very tasty. She'd always kept her distance from the law but if anyone could make her change the practice of a lifetime. . .

'In what way not normal?' His tone was more serious and she struggled to explain.

'They don't drive, don't drink, don't have a telly. They never go out except to walk. That's not normal, is it?' For the first, time she was on the defensive.

'Are they religious?'

She looked blank.

'Do they belong to one of those sects? Jehovah's Witness or something?' It was the only explanation he could come up with for the aberrant lifestyle.

'I don't think so.' She rushed a little giggle. 'They haven't tried to convert me.'

'How long have they lived on the Headland?'

'Just over five years. They moved in about the same time as Ray and me.'

'Any family connections on the Headland?'

She shook her head.

'So why move here?'

'Same reason as me and Ray I expect. Because the houses were dirt cheap. Ray's a builder and he knew he could do the place up. The Howes speak posh but I don't think there's much money there. Bernard works on the computers at the Ministry but it's all agency staff now and they pay peanuts.'

'How do you know?'

She shrugged again. 'People talk. You know how it is.'

'I wonder what they say about you?'

She answered immediately, but without rancour. 'They say I'm a dirty slut because I threw out Ray and I'm bringing up the bairn on my own. And because I like a night out with my friends once in a while. A few drinks and a laugh and a bit of a dance down Whitley on a Friday night.'

'How do you manage that with a kid to look after? Does your mam live close by?'

'Na, and she wouldn't be keen if she did. She still likes a night out herself. She thinks she's too young to be a gran.'

'So who minds the bairn?'

'Claire. She'll always sit if she's free. Glad to get out of that house, I expect.'

'Claire?'

She looked at him as if he was stupid. 'Claire Irvine. Kath Howe's sister. They took her in when her parents died. She works as a nanny up at the Coastguard House, but they don't need her much in the evenings. Like I say, I think she's glad to get out – can you imagine being shut up with those weirdos and no *telly*? But she owes me a favour anyway. It was me that got her the job.'

'How was that?' Hunter thought this was probably irrelevant but the boss had ordered gossip and he was following instructions. Besides, it was more pleasant here than in some of the houses he'd visited, with their smells of old age, talcum powder and cat pee. He thought again he'd be happy to stay here all day.

'I take Kirsty to the playgroup in. Heppleburn. There's no nursery round here. Mrs Coulthard from the Coastguard House sends her oldest boy there too. Sometimes she gives me a lift home. She was talking about getting a nanny and I mentioned that Claire had done the course and was looking for a job.'

'Very convenient.'

'Yeah, though you wouldn't think she'd need a nanny, would you? It's not as if she works. Some people have got more money than sense.' There was a silence. She twisted a bangle on her wrist. 'Is it true what they're saying?'

'Depends what they're saying.'

'That Kath Howe was murdered. It wasn't an accident.'

'She was stabbed.' Hunter said. He drained the last of his coffee noisily. He wouldn't have minded another cup, wouldn't have minded anyway another glimpse of her bum as she bent over the sink to fill the kettle.

'Jesus!' She seemed honestly shocked. 'I thought it was just talk.'

There was a pause. 'Was she mucked about first? You know what I mean.'

'There was no indication of sexual assault.'

'Oh.'

'When did you last see her?' Hunter asked. She was still so dazed that he had to repeat the question.

'I'm not sure.'

'Did you see her on Saturday?'

'Saturday? No, I don't think so.'

'Where were you that day?'

'Here for most of the time.'

'Didn't you go out at all?'

'Not in the morning. Unless you call standing on the doorstep going out. I'd been down Whitley on Friday night and a friend stayed over. I went out to wave him off. I didn't see anyone then. Except the bitch across the road who had her nose pressed to the bedroom window.'

'I'll need the name and address of your friend.'

There was a moment of uncertainty then she said, with an attempt at the old flippancy, 'You'll be lucky.'

'What do you mean?'

'I mean we weren't on those sort of terms.'

'You only met him that night?'

'Na, I'd bumped into him a couple of times. He'd been back here once before.'

'You must have a name for him then.'

'He called himself Paul.'

'You don't think that was his real name?'

She shrugged. 'Could have been. But he's married, and he wasn't giving much away.'

'And where did "Paul" live?' Hunter recognized no contradiction in his previous fantasies about Kim Houghton and the disapproval of her behaviour which expressed itself in sarcasm.

She seemed not to notice. 'Newcastle.'

'You can't be more specific?'

She shook her head.

'What about a phone number?'

It wasn't that sort of thing. Just a bit of fun. At least it was supposed to be.

'What do you mean?'

She had been smoking a cigarette and stabbed it out fiercely in a glass ashtray.

'Went all weepy on me, didn't he? About how his wife didn't understand him. About how screwed up she is. Just what I needed. Not.'

'How did you get here on Friday night? Taxi or his car?'

'His car.'

'Which was?'

'A red Mazda. Very fancy. Very fast.'

'Number plate?'

'New. N reg. That's all I noticed.'

'And it was parked in the street all night?'

'That's right.'

Hunter sat back in his chair and looked at her. 'Didn't it bother you? Folks knowing you had a bloke to stay. Going out in the morning to see him off?'

He imagined her standing there in her dressing gown. With nothing on underneath.

'Stuff them,' she said. She picked up the packet of cigarettes from the table, knocked one out, lit it. Her hands shook slightly but her voice was steady. 'Stuff them. They could do with some excitement in their tired lives.'

'What time was that?'

'I don't know. Too early.'

'You didn't see Mrs Howe's daughter? She walked down to wait for the bus into town.'

'I didn't notice.'

'What about later?'

'I didn't see anyone. I put on a video for Kirsty and went back to bed.' She caught his eye and held it. 'I was knackered, wasn't I?'

'Did Claire Irvine babysit for you on Friday night?'

'Yes.'

'So she will have met your friend Paul. When you got back.'

'No. He waited in the car until she'd gone home.'

'Tactful.' Again the sarcasm was intended.

'Yeah!' she blazed back at him. 'Tactful. If you must know he was really nice. We had breakfast together, him, me and Kirsty. He made a real fuss of her. He didn't have to do that.'

'Did you talk to Claire before you went out?'

'A bit. While I was getting my things together, waiting for the taxi.'

'How did she seem?'

'Same as she always seems. About a hundred and fifty. And it's not surprising, is it? Wiping kids' bums all day and staring at the walls in that house all night. I've offered to take her out clubbing with me but she'll not go.'

'Did she mention Mrs Howe at all?'

Kim shook her head. 'All she could talk about was the kiddies' party and how good it would be.'

'Did your daughter go to that?' Hunter was surprised.

'Oh yes! Kirsty and me had a royal invitation. Very honoured too. No one else on the Headland was asked.'

'What was it like?' He was intrigued.

'It was all right. I mean, I only went because I thought Kirsty would like it and she's friends with Owen at playgroup. But it was OK. Plenty of booze. Decent food. A proper buffet, not just stuff for the kids. And that Bernie Howe was good. I was surprised. You'd never think it to look at him. I mean, he could make it really big. He's better than blokes I've seen on the telly. And though most of the mothers were stuck-up cows, the fellas were friendly enough once they'd had a few drinks. Yeah, it was a good party. Until mad Marilyn came knocking on the door, shouting that her mam was missing.'

Chapter Ten

On his way down the hill from the Coastguard House Ramsay saw Hunter leave Kim Houghton's house. The sergeant paused for a moment outside number eight, leaning his notepad on the window sill to scribble a few notes, then he knocked at the door. It was opened immediately by a large elderly woman brandishing a mop like an offensive weapon. She seemed nervous about letting him in, stood, blocking the doorway, feet apart, but Hunter must have talked her around because when Ramsay looked again the door was shut and Cotter's Row was quiet.

The whole Headland was quiet. There were no dog-walkers or pram-pushers. Even the washing lines along the backyards were empty. The only activity was in an area around the jetty. There a group of overalled officers were stooped, searching, but they were too far off for Ramsay to hear voices. The cloud had lifted and there was pale sunshine, a view down the coast as far as St Mary's Island.

He was tempted for a moment to walk on down to the jetty to ask what had been found. He would have welcomed evidence that Kath Howe had been killed *there*, her body tipped immediately into the cut to be carried away and brought back on the next tide. It would have been something to work on. But it seemed a dreadful discourtesy to walk down Cotter's Row without calling on the Howes and at number two he stopped. He stood on the pavement, preparing what he might say, especially to the girl.

In the house across the road a curtain was lifted then fell back into place. He tapped gently on the door. Sally Wedderburn answered it and let him in.

Sally was a redhead with a pale, freckled skin and brown eyes. Hunter thought Ramsay was grooming her for stardom, and perhaps he was. Perhaps he wanted to prove to Prue that he could take positive action to push a woman up the ladder, that he was doing what he could to support her cause. Recently he had recognized the danger of trying to please Prue and made an effort to be more clear-sighted. Sally was a good officer but she needed to learn patience. Which she would be doing sitting in this tiny house with nothing to do but listen.

'How's it going?' he asked in a whisper. They were standing very close together in the narrow hall.

'The women are in the living room. Mr Howe's upstairs. He said he wanted to be on his own.'

'Distressed?'

'Not outwardly. He was all set to go to work this morning until I persuaded him it probably wouldn't be a good idea. More puzzled. As if he can't get his head around the idea that his wife's dead.'

'And the women?'

'Shocked I suppose. No tears. Not while I'm there at least. They don't talk. Not to each other or to me.' She was disappointed. She had hoped to have something for him and felt she had failed.

'Time enough for that.' But he was disappointed, too.

'Do you want to come through?'

'I'll see Mr Howe first. Don't announce me. I'll go on up.'

He found Bernard Howe in a room at the front of the house. Although it was clearly the biggest bedroom most of the space was taken by a high double bed, spread with a blue candlewick quilt. There was a wardrobe but no chest of drawers and clothes were piled untidily on shelves which covered one wall. The shelves also held books and the equipment for Uncle Bernie's magic act. There were strings of brightly coloured ribbons, chiffon scarves, wooden boxes. A cup hook had been fixed to the highest shelf and hanging from it, by its neck, was a ventriloquist's dummy. The latex head was egg shaped, bald at the top with long wispy strands of hair at the back and the sides. It looked remarkably like Mr Howe, a mirror image of the man who sat on the bed, playing with a pack of cards, shuffling and twisting them with supple fat fingers.

'Practising?' Ramsay asked.

Bernard Howe looked up, startled. He had not heard the footsteps on the stairs.

'I find it very relaxing,' he said. 'The doctor wanted to give me tranquillizers, but Kath wouldn't have approved of that.'

'Wouldn't she?'

'No. She was a strong woman. She didn't like props of any sort.' He set down the cards and gave both hands a little flick so the cuffs of the shirt and the cardigan he was wearing settled back over his wrists.

'Who are you?' he asked. It was a direct, childlike question which Ramsay found unnerving.

'Stephen Ramsay. I'm a detective inspector. In charge of the case.'

'There is a case then? She didn't just fall? No one's said. Not really. I mean perhaps Miss Wedderburn explained but I didn't take it in.'

'We weren't sure until this morning. But she didn't just fall. She was stabbed.'

'Ah.' All his reactions seemed very slow. Ramsay thought they would have made an odd couple: Kathleen with her principles, her tense and purposeful marching, and Bernard. He groped for a word to describe Bernard and came up with simple. Not in the sense of unintelligent because it was clear he held down a reasonable job, but uncomplicated, easily satisfied.

'How long have you been married?' Ramsay asked. He took a seat beside Bernard on the bed.

'Nearly seventeen years.' He had not had to think about it. 'We both worked in the same office. Clerical officers with the Civil Service. And then we got married.' He still seemed mildly surprised at that as if he had woken one morning to discover he had a wife. He turned to face Ramsay. 'She took me on,' he said.

'And you're still doing the same job?'

'More or less. It's not the *same*. It was all paper then. Now it's computers. I quite liked computers once I got into them.' And

Ramsay could see that he would. He would enjoy the clear instructions, the simple rules. He would get lost in the patterns.

'I haven't progressed much in the organization.' Bernard smiled sadly. 'Not management material I see that. Kath would have been better at it than me – much more assertive – but she gave up work when Marilyn was born. Most people did in those days.' He paused, considered. 'I think she might have been happier if she'd carried on working. Not so restless.'

'Did you suggest that?'

'Oh no!' He was shocked by the idea. 'It was her decision, wasn't it? Mother offered to look after Marilyn but Kath said that would only cause trouble and I could see she was right.'

'Was it Mrs Howe's decision to move to the Headland?'

'Yes.' Of course, Ramsay thought, it would be. 'Before that,' Bernard continued, 'we lived with my mother in her house in Newcastle. There was plenty of room even when Marilyn came along and it was handy for work.' His voice was wistful. 'And the pictures.'

'But your wife decided she wanted a home of her own?'

'Perhaps she did.' It seemed a new idea. 'Though it wasn't just that. Marilyn was coming up to secondary school age. Kath wanted her to go to Otterbridge High. She'd looked at all the schools in the area and thought it was best. Especially for music. She took the decision very seriously after proper research. The children from the Headland go to Otterbridge and there's a school bus. We couldn't have afforded to live anywhere else in the catchment area.'

So the lives of the family had been disrupted to satisfy Kathleen Howe's ambition to send Marilyn to a good school.

'Didn't your mother mind being deserted?' Ramsay asked lightly.

Bernard's head jerked up. The dummy's head pulled by its string. 'There was a row,' he said. 'It was horrible.' He paused. 'She said some, very unkind things about Kathleen. Mother and I quite fell out for a while.'

'But you patched it up?'

'Oh yes. Mother couldn't stay cross for long. Not with me. I go to see her every Thursday night after work. She's very good for her age, still living in the same house.' He smiled confidentially. 'She cooks my supper. Always the same thing, cauliflower cheese. My favourite.' He hesitated. 'She wouldn't speak to Kath, though. She wouldn't have *her* in the house again.'

'Has she ever come here?'

'Oh no! I don't think Mother would feel at home in Cotter's Row. It's not at all what she's used to.'

'And Marilyn? Does your mother see her?'

'Occasionally, though Kath didn't encourage it.' He looked up with a sudden bright thought. 'I suppose we'll be able to visit Mother together now. That'll be nice.' The absence of grief in the statement shocked Ramsay. It also occurred to him that someone who could come out with something like that to a detective was either very innocent or very clever.

'Tell me about Saturday,' Ramsay said. 'The day Mrs Howe disappeared.'

Bernard did not reply. He was smiling to himself and Ramsay saw he was still planning the reunion between Marilyn and her grandmother.

'Was it an ordinary Saturday?' he persisted. 'Had anything unusual happened?'

Bernard shook his head.

'The four of you had breakfast together?'

'That's right. And then Claire went to work at the Coastguard House. Marilyn was going to school. As I said, she's very musical. Kath's always encouraged that. She started the violin when she was four and she's passed all the exams. But this time it was the choir. I'm sure that's right. An extra rehearsal before the music festival.' He screwed up his face in concentration, became again the latex mask hanging on the wall.

'Kath walked with her to the bus stop. She said she needed some fresh air. The school bus comes right on to the Headland to pick up the children but because it was Saturday Marilyn had to get the service bus and the stop for that's on the other side of the crossing. They had a bit of an argument about it. Marilyn said it would look stupid, her mother seeing her on to the bus at her age.

Kath insisted. She said, "You shouldn't care what people think". She was always saying that. She's right, of course, but it does matter, doesn't it, when you're sixteen?' He paused for breath. Ramsay was surprised by the insight. He hadn't given Bernard credit for sufficient imagination to put himself in the place of a sixteen-year-old. 'Anyway,' Bernard went on, 'in the end they must have gone off together.'

'And then a little later your wife came back?'

'Yes. I think so.'

'You don't sound entirely certain.'

'No.'

Ramsay felt a sudden urge to shake him.

'Why aren't you sure? Can't you remember?'

Bernard Howe pleated the candlewick quilt with his fingers.

'I was up here, preparing for the afternoon's performance. It takes a lot of concentration.' As seriously as an actor about to play Lear. 'I'm sure I heard the door open and shut and I called down, "Is that you, Kath?" Something like that. I hoped she might make some tea. She usually did in the mornings. I thought she'd bring it up.'

'But she didn't?'

'No.' He was at least certain about that. It still rankled.

'And you didn't see her again?'

'No. When I came down to get some lunch she wasn't there. I thought she'd probably gone out to the shop in Heppleburn.'

'Did she tell you at breakfast that was what she intended to do?'

'No,' he said uncertainly. Then, with sudden inspiration, 'She said something about dyeing wool. I'd forgotten. It's something she'd taken to lately, spinning. She had these fads. She hoped to make money out of it but I didn't think anything would come of it. I suppose it gave her something to do. Now Marilyn didn't need her so much.'

'And she was going out to dye the wool?' Ramsay didn't know much about the process but he'd supposed it was something you did inside, boiling water in a big pan, stirring with a long stick.

'She was going out to collect lichens to make the dye,' Bernard said. 'At least I think that was it.'

'But she didn't shout up that she was going?'

'No.'

'Did you hear the door slam shut again?'

'I'm sorry,' he said. 'I really can't remember.' He stared out of the window as if he expected the interview to be over.

'Mr Howe.' Ramsay spoke quietly. 'We need to find out *why* your wife was attacked. There was no sexual assault and so far as we know she didn't disturb some other crime. Motive is important. You do see that, Mr Howe?'

'Yes.' He seemed to find the idea interesting.

'Mr Howe, can you think of *anyone* who might have wanted your wife dead?'

He gave the matter proper consideration. He didn't dismiss it out of hand.

'No,' he said at last. 'I can't think of anyone who would have killed her.'

Ramsay was halfway down the narrow stairs before he realized that Bernard Howe had not actually answered the question.

Chapter Eleven

Ramsay took the three women out to lunch. He'd only been in the house for half an hour and he couldn't stand it any longer. He thought *they* must be going mad.

'What about Bernie?' Claire had said, but when they asked Mr Howe he said a sandwich would do for him and continued to practise his magic tricks. So Ramsay called in an eager young constable to stay in the house and they drove away from the Headland, Sal Wedderburn in the driving seat and Marilyn and Claire silently in the back. He was surprised there were no reporters waiting for them in the street. Only the slight movement of upstairs net curtains marked their going.

Ramsay took them to an Italian restaurant in Otterbridge. The food was good and if Claire and Marilyn had unadventurous tastes there was pasta and pizza. All young people ate pizza these days. He felt, unconsciously, that he wanted to give the girl a treat, a small comfort.

He and Prue used the restaurant often and the owner was a friend. It was late and the place was nearly empty. The last customers were preparing to go. Ramsay said gravely that he hoped the restaurant wasn't about to close. They had been hoping for a place to talk. Marco would understand. And Marco did understand. He flapped a white napkin over a table by the window and said they could stay, all afternoon if they liked. He was there anyway. And with a wink, in an aside to Ramsay, he said that it was always a good idea to keep on the right side of the police.

The restaurant had long windows which looked out on a courtyard, one side of which was formed by the ruins of the town wall. The small trees in the courtyard still looked lifeless but underneath had been planted a bed of crocuses, bright orange, and purple and lit by the pale afternoon sun.

Ramsay watched Marilyn read the menu, hesitantly, always turning back to the cheaper items on the front. At Cotter's Row money would have been tight and if the family had eaten out at all choice would have been restricted.

'Have whatever you like,' he said. 'It's on expenses.' Which it probably wouldn't be but she always seemed so anxious that he wanted her, at least, not to have to worry about this. He ordered pasta with a spicy spinach sauce and, on impulse, a carafe of house red. Across the table he could sense that Sal Wedderburn was perplexed, wondering what he was up to, what he was hoping to get out of this. What the bosses would say.

What Claire made of it he could not tell. Meeting her for the first time in the cramped and claustrophobic living room at Cotter's Row she had seemed entirely out of place. She was a statuesque young woman, large boned, dark haired, dark eyed. Here in the restaurant, with the other guests having left for their offices and only the Italian staff waiting quietly by the bar she seemed more at home. She could have been one of them. She ate with pleasure, drank the first glass of wine quickly and accepted the second when it was offered. You would have said she was there for a family celebration, yet, Ramsay thought, Kath Howe was the nearest thing she had to a mother.

They did not talk of the murder until they had finished eating. By then the sun had left the courtyard. Marco brought coffee in a thermos jug and said he would leave them to it. Throughout the meal Sal Wedderburn had attempted to catch Ramsay's eye in an unspoken attempt to start the ball rolling. Each time he had ignored her. Now, quite openly, she looked at her watch. He saw it was a torture for her to sit and wait.

'I expect,' he said, 'there are questions you'd both like to ask.'

'We don't know anything,' Claire said flatly. 'It's not right, being kept in the dark like this.'

'That certainly wasn't deliberate. We didn't want to give you false information. The details in a case like this take longer to check than anyone realizes.'

'But now you do know? About how Kath died?' He tried to place Claire's accent, and decided north of the county. Berwick. Wooler. Had Kath Howe spoken like that? He couldn't remember.

'We know enough to be certain she was murdered. She didn't slip on the rocks and fall. She was dead when she entered the water.'

As he spoke he was watching Marilyn. The colour drained from her face though there were no tears.

'I'm sorry,' he said.

'When did she die?' Claire demanded. Her bluntness surprised him. She leant forward across the table waiting for an answer.

'Some time on Saturday. It might be possible to pinpoint the time more accurately once we know when she last ate but at the moment that's all we know.'

'How was she killed?'

'She was stabbed, possibly with an ordinary kitchen knife. We haven't found the weapon yet but we've begun to search.' He paused. 'We might need to look at your house too.'

She looked up, challenging. 'Why?'

He chose his words carefully. 'There's a possibility that Mrs Howe knew her killer. We don't think there was a struggle.'

He expected a denial, outrage that he could suggest that one of the family might be involved but perhaps she lacked the imagination to realize the implication of what he was saying. He continued. 'There's a possibility that Mrs Howe let someone into the house that morning.'

'Might she have done that?' Sally Wedderburn asked. 'Might she have let a stranger into the house? She wouldn't have been afraid?'

Claire shook her head. 'Not for herself. She wouldn't let Marilyn out of her sight but she thought nothing of walking the country roads at night. Besides, Bernie was upstairs all morning, wasn't he?'

'Yes,' Sally Wedderburn said. 'Of course.' She seemed thrown by Claire's confidence, her aggression, and fell silent.

'Obviously we're trying to form an idea of Mrs Howe's movements on Saturday,' Ramsay said. 'We need your help for that.' He turned to Marilyn. 'I understand from your father that she walked with you to the bus stop in the morning. Did she wait with you until the bus came?'

Marilyn looked at him blankly as if she had not heard the question and he had to repeat it.

'She waited until we could see the bus coming down the road then I sent her back. The crossing was clear for once and you can stand there for hours if one train follows another.' She paused. 'To be honest I thought there might be someone I knew on the bus. I didn't want any of my friends to see Mummy waiting with me.'

'When I spoke to you on Sunday you said the last time you saw your mother was at breakfast.'

'I was embarrassed,' Marilyn said. 'I didn't want to tell you that she wouldn't let me walk to the bus stop on my own.' She began to cry. Large, silent tears rolled down her cheeks. 'She was only worried about me. I never worried about her. None of us did.'

'Except the time when she was missing and you called at my house,' Ramsay reminded her gently. 'You were worried about her then.'

'I was, wasn't I?' She seemed consoled by the memory.

Ramsay waited until she had composed herself.

'Did anyone get off the bus when you got on? Someone who might have followed your mother up the Headland, perhaps caught her up?'

'No. No one.'

'Mr Taverner gave you a lift back from school that afternoon?'

'Yes.'

'Did he tell you why he was coming to the Headland?'

'He's a friend of the Coulthards who live at the Coastguard House.'

Ramsay turned to Claire.

'You'll know him then?'

'I've met him.'

'Is he a regular visitor to the Coastguard House?'

'He has been recently.' She gave a sudden smug little smile which vanished so quickly that he wondered if he'd imagined it.

'Oh?'

He was hoping for gossip, even scandal, but she said gravely, 'I expect he's lonely. His wife died a few months ago. She was Sheena Taverner, the writer.'

Then he realized why the name had been familiar. He had seen Sheena Taverner's books in Prue's house; had even met her once at some party to which Prue had dragged him. There had been so many thin, soulful women that he found it hard to place her, but he thought he remembered her. Had Mark Taverner been present too? He could not remember, and turned his attention back to Marilyn.

'Would your mother have known Mr Taverner?'

'She'd met him at parents' evenings. He was my tutor in Year Seven and now he takes me for music. She'd have recognized him.'

'Where did he drop you?'

'At the club. He was meeting Mr Coulthard there.'

'And you walked up the hill by yourself?'

'Yes.'

'Weren't you worried that your mother might be waiting for you at the bus stop?'

'No. I told you yesterday. She wasn't expecting me back until later.'

There was a silence. The restaurant was, by now, very gloomy and a little cold. Ramsay poured more coffee.

'Did you meet anyone as you walked up the hill?'

'I don't think so.'

'Perhaps you could concentrate. It's important that you're absolutely sure.'

'I didn't meet anyone,' Marilyn explained, 'but I saw Claire come out of the house and walk on up towards the Coulthards'. I don't think she noticed me. The weather was dreadful. She wore her hood up and her head was bent down against the sleet. I shouted but she didn't hear me.'

Claire did not speak. She continued to stare into the courtyard.

'I thought you spent all day in the Coastguard House,' Sally Wedderburn said.

Throughout the conversation Ramsay had been aware of a controlled hostility between the women, and wondered what lay at the root of it. Perhaps they had just got on each other's nerves cooped up in that house. Now Claire was unapologetic, even defiant.

'So I went home for something to eat? Why shouldn't I? Everyone else has a dinner break.'

'Was Mrs Howe there?'

'Of course not! I would have said, wouldn't I?'

'But Mr Howe was?'

'I suppose so. Upstairs. He spends hours up there practising.'

Claire lapsed into silence. The carafe of wine was empty but a little remained in her glass. She held it up so the fading light from the window caught it, then she drank it all.

Ramsay was thinking that this might be an explanation for Mr Howe's belief that his wife had returned to the house. A door had slammed shut and he had assumed it was Kath. But the timing was wrong. Claire's lunch break would have occurred much later than Mrs Howe's expected return from the bus stop. Was it possible that so much time could have passed without Bernard's noticing? Ramsay thought that perhaps it was. Bernard had been concentrating on his rehearsal, his mind, as Marilyn had once said, was full of magic and illusion. Ramsay decided they should work on the premise that Kath Howe had last been seen by her daughter, waved away across the level crossing before she could cause embarrassment.

'But what would she have done then?' He realized he had spoken aloud and continued in explanation. 'You were all busy. I was wondering how Mrs Howe would usually have spent her time on Saturday mornings.'

The similarity of the terraced house in Cotter's Row to the Coal Board cottage where he had lived as a child made him think of his own mother. When he reached school age she'd taken a part-time job in a draper's shop and Saturday had become her cleaning day. He'd been sent out to play in the street while she dusted and hoovered. He remembered her squatting on the stairs, a small, hard brush in one hand, furiously beating the fluff and the dust down into the hall, shouting at him through the open front door to clear out until she'd finished. He couldn't imagine that Mrs Howe would ever set aside a day for housework.

Her relatives seemed surprised by the question. They looked at each other. Neither answered.

'I understand she was interested in craft. Dyeing. Spinning.'

'Aye,' Claire said. 'That was the latest fad.'

'What were the others?'

'Botany, watercolours.' She looked at Marilyn. 'Is there anything I've missed?'

Marilyn shook her head. It was a gesture of distaste, not an answer to the question.

'Is it possible that she was following one of these hobbies on Saturday morning?'

'It's possible. Bernard would be able to tell you. That spinning wheel of hers makes a real racket and the living room's right under the bedroom.'

'What else might she have done?'

'I don't know,' Marilyn said. 'She walked a lot. Read. There was no regular routine.'

Claire leant forward. 'The trouble with Kath', she said, 'was that she'd never really grown up. She played at things. It was all too easy for her.' And with that she shut her mouth and became her old taciturn self.

Chapter Twelve

Brian Coulthard was running late. Emma was in the kitchen with the kids squawking around her and when he shouted down the stairs she didn't hear him. In the end he had to go himself. He stood in the doorway, bare chested, and said in as restrained a voice as he could manage, 'I don't suppose there's a clean shirt in this house.'

She was heating milk for the baby's cereal and hardly turned round.

'There are some in the tumble dryer. If you hang on a minute I'll iron one.'

'I need it now. I'm late already.'

She was still in her dressing gown and he felt like screaming, 'What the hell do you *do* all day?' But that would have provoked a row which would only have delayed him further.

'All *right.*' she said. The martyr. 'I'll do it now.'

She slammed open the dryer door and yanked the ironing board into an upright position.

When he left the house he tried to kiss her but she turned her cheek away. There were roadworks on the A19, and traffic was tailing back from the Tyne Tunnel to the Coast Road roundabout. He liked to be first in the office. Today his secretary was already there and the phones were ringing. A backlog of work to be cleared before he started.

Brian Coulthard had set up his computer software business in 1985. It had been a gamble going it alone, and it hadn't all been plain sailing, however it seemed from the outside. There had been times at the beginning when the banks had threatened to call in the debt and it was only Emma's wage which had kept the company afloat. He had seemed then to spend all his time on the road touting for business, giving presentations to an audience so obviously uninterested that he had known they had already decided to place their contract elsewhere. Now there was more work than he could handle. He employed a dozen programmers and they were all rushed off their feet. That was stressful too, though Emma didn't seem to realize.

Whenever he was asked he said his office was in Jesmond. People knew that was Newcastle's smartest suburb. In fact it was in Sandyford, close to the bus depot and the cemetery, near enough to the new Cradlewell bypass for him to hear the rumble of heavy traffic if he left his window open. It was in a gentrified terrace with a firm of accountants on one side of him and solicitors on the other. He was very proud of the office. He was buying, not renting it. Beside the door there was a brass plaque with COULTHARD COMPUTING engraved upon it. He parked the BMW in the space reserved for him and let himself in.

'Anything urgent?'

His secretary was a smooth-faced young graduate who'd given him the shock of his life when he'd turned up at Coulthards for interview. Brian had assumed the agency would send a woman though he hadn't been displeased. He preferred to work with men. The secretary was called Noel, a name of ambiguous gender which suited him.

'Mr Taverner rang.' Noel knew that Brian would consider that urgent.

'When?'

'About ten minutes ago, but he said not to phone him back because he's teaching all morning. Can you give him a ring at school at lunchtime? He was hoping you might meet for a drink this evening.'

'Right.' Brian wondered why Mark had not phoned him at home before he left for school. That was the usual practice.

'And Inspector Ramsay phoned again. He's been trying to get in touch for a few days, he said. He really would prefer to meet you during the day but he could come to your home this evening if that's impossible. He says you've got his number.'

'Yes, of course.' Brian had made a few desultory attempts to get back to Ramsay but they hadn't connected. Brian knew he could have organized a meeting if he'd made the effort. So did Noel. The last thing he wanted was office gossip about him obstructing the police.

'Give him a ring, will you, Noel? Tell him I can fit him in during my lunch break. Say about one o'clock.'

Ramsay arrived at exactly one. Brian went out to reception to meet him. He knew Noel was listening to every word.

'Have you eaten, Inspector? I'm afraid I'm rather hungry. It was chaos at home this morning and I didn't even manage a slice of toast.'

Ramsay shook his head. He wondered for a moment if he would be wined and dined.

'I usually buy some sandwiches from the deli in Cradlewell. In weather like this I like to eat them outside. It's a break from the office. Would you mind talking at the same time?'

So they walked together down the street. Ramsay noticed that for a man of such heavy build Coulthard had very small feet and a walk that was dainty, almost dancing.

'I usually sit in the cemetery,' Brian said. 'You won't find that macabre? Of course you won't mind. Not with a job like yours.'

It was a large Victorian cemetery, too big to keep tidy. The graves were covered in mounds of dead leaves and overgrown with bramble. Where the grass had been cut close to the paths there were snowdrops and in the tangle of undergrowth an overblown, greenish-white Christmas rose.

The weather was fine, unusually mild, and other office workers strolled down the wide paths. They found a wooden bench in the sun.

'I didn't know the woman,' Brian Coulthard said. 'I mean, you'll have gathered what it's like. I'm rushed off my feet. I'm hardly ever at home.'

'But you would have recognized her.' Ramsay was sure about that.

'No. I don't think so. Why should I?'

'She walked everywhere. You must have seen her on the roads round the village, striding out. Usually she has a girl with her.'

'Oh was *that* her? I have seen them. She always struck me as rather odd.' He paused. 'And it was the girl, wasn't it, who turned up at the party?'

'That's right.'

'Poor child.'

'Did you ever speak to Mrs Howe?'

'No. Never. Though I nearly ran over her once. I'd have spoken to her then if I'd had the chance.' He bit into a tuna roll, wiped mayonnaise from the corner of his mouth with a handkerchief.

'What happened?'

'She ran off the pavement like a lunatic, straight into the path of the car. I remember it because it was the day my daughter was born.'

'When was this?'

'Last September.'

It was in September, Ramsay thought, that Mrs Howe last disappeared.

'But I suppose you want to know what I was doing that day.' Coulthard seemed eager to move the interview on. 'When she died.'

'Last Saturday. Yes.'

'In the morning I came into work.'

'What time did you leave the Headland?'

'Nine. Nine thirty.'

'Did you see Mrs Howe or her daughter on your way out?'

He could have done. Marilyn had timed the bus's arrival at nine forty-five.

'No.'

'You seem very definite.'

'As soon as I heard the woman had been murdered I went over things in my mind. I knew you'd be asking.'

'But you didn't know then who Mrs Howe was.'

'I didn't see her on my way out. I know because I didn't see anyone adult. It had snowed and there were a few kids mucking around on the pavement using a black bin bag as a sledge. That was all.'

'Any strange cars?'

'A very flash Mazda parked outside Kim Houghton's house. I'd not have left a car like that in Cotter's Row. But I don't suppose he had car security on his mind.'

'You know Kim Houghton?'

'Only by reputation. They talk about her in the club.'

'Did anyone phone you at work?'

'At weekends all the phones are switched on to the answering machine. Except my personal line. I had one call on that. Mark Taverner – a friend. He paused. 'I put in a few hours then came home for about one. To a madhouse. Emma so wound up you'd have thought Princess Di was coming for afternoon tea, the kids as high as kites.' He turned to Ramsay. 'Have you got children?'

Ramsay shook his head.

'You won't understand what it's like, then. When they get excited they fizz.' He shook his head and smiled. 'Like an Alka-Seltzer. It starts off bubbling gently then gets wilder and wilder until it overflows.'

Ramsay said nothing – he could not imagine Marilyn Howe fizzing, even as a five-year-old – and Coulthard continued. 'I was glad to get out of the house again.'

'Where did you go? Back to work?'

'To the club. I'd arranged to meet a friend there.'

'Mr Taverner?'

'That's right.'

'Did you drive?'

'Walked. I knew I'd have a few drinks. I'm not sure of the time. Claire Irvine, the nanny, walked down with me. She'd probably know. I think she'd had enough of the madhouse, too. She usually stays for lunch with Emma, but that day she'd obviously decided she needed a break.'

'She walked with you to the club?' Ramsay was deliberately obtuse.

'No. Just as far as Cotter's Row, then I walked on down by myself.'

'Did she let herself into the house or knock on the door?'

'I think she had a key.'

'Was Mr Taverner in the club when you arrived?'

'No. I had to wait for him. He said he'd probably be late.'

And that would fit, Ramsay thought, because Marilyn had seen Claire when she was on her way back to the Coastguard House, her hood up, head bent against the sleet.

'Tell me about Mr. Taverner. Is he an old friend of yours?'

It was a polite question, not emotionally loaded, yet Brian found himself talking, rambling even, as he might in the rugby club after far too much beer to someone who wasn't really listening.

'We met at university. Durham. He was doing theology and I was doing applied maths. In the first year we had rooms on the same corridor, and we've been friends since then. Surprisingly, because we're quite different characters. Mark comes from the south. Worcester. He was the first southerner I'd really known. His father was a clergyman, something high up in the Cathedral. Mine was shop steward in a bakery. . .' He stopped abruptly, seeming to expect another question. Ramsay said nothing and he continued.

'Mark's the only one of the Durham gang I've kept in touch with. I was always into computers. I got a job with an electronics company straight out of university and stayed with them until I set up on my own. That's where I met Emma. She worked for personnel.' He paused again, remembering. 'We all thought Mark would be a priest, follow in his father's footsteps and I think that's what he intended until he met Sheena. His poet. That's what he called her. But Sheena wouldn't have made a vicar's wife. You couldn't see her running the Brownie pack or organizing the flower rota. That wouldn't be nearly poetic enough for her. Even if she was a Christian, which I don't believe she was. So he went into teaching.'

'You didn't like her?' Ramsay's voice was uncritical but surprised.

'It didn't matter what I thought of her. Mark loved her. That was enough for me. That's why I got involved when she was ill. Not because I fancied her, which is what some people thought.' He must have decided then to answer Ramsay's question because he added, 'No, I didn't like her. She was too wrapped up in herself. She treated Mark like shit.'

'What do you mean – you got involved when she was ill?'

'I suppose I hustled on their behalf. I tried to persuade them not to give in. When she was diagnosed as having breast cancer they both seemed to regard it as a death sentence. It was ridiculous. It can be a treatable disease. But neither of them would fight it. They wouldn't ask questions, press for different therapies. They just let it happen. I know I was interfering but I wanted to keep her alive for him.' He shrugged. 'I failed, didn't I? Made a fool of myself for nothing.' Suddenly he seemed embarrassed by the conversation. 'Look,' he said. 'I should go back. They'll be sending out search parties.'

Ramsay nodded and watched him hurry away, his little feet skipping across the damp grass.

In the office Brian phoned Mark but could not speak to him. He had forgotten how early a teacher takes his lunch hour. Mark was already in the classroom for the afternoon session. Brian left a message saying he'd be in the office until six and spent the afternoon distracted by work.

Chapter Thirteen

Mark Taverner waited in the staffroom for Brian's call. Usually he preferred to go out at lunchtime. When Sheena was alive he'd gone home. Even before she became ill he'd liked to check that she was happy. The colleagues in the staffroom had commented snidely on these absences. Once Mark had heard an ageing maths teacher say to another with the weary envy of a tabloid hack, 'There goes Taverner. Off for his midday bonk.'

In fact sex was never considered at these lunchtime meetings. Sex played little part in the relationship at all despite Sheena's obsession with it in her books. Or perhaps because of it. She wrote about sex as a symbol of violence or betrayal. Mark had read her stories before they married and made an effort in the beginning to be sensitive. He thought there must have been a previous relationship in which she had been abused or humiliated and he wanted to prove to her that he was different from the other men she had known.

It seemed that he had failed. Perhaps he was too careful. She had allowed the advances in a disinterested way but had taken little pleasure from the contact. Inexperienced as he was he had realized that. Only once, when he became angry, had she responded at all. They had both been shocked by the encounter and he had taken care not to repeat his outburst. Her illness had provided an excellent excuse for abstinence. He could understand that she was always very tired.

He had gone home at lunchtime to *see* her. He would let himself in at the front door and before even taking off his coat he would climb the narrow stairs and there she would be, in the little room she had turned into an office. The little room, where in the other houses in the street a baby slept. She would be leaning over the A4 sheets of plain paper on which she wrote, a fountain pen in her hand. She had refused to learn about computers.

She must have heard him come through the door but she pretended not to. It was an affectation. She liked him to think she was concentrating so deeply on her work that she had not noticed. Then she would turn and exclaim. 'Mark! Is it that time already?'

He would kiss her cheek and go down to the kitchen to make tea and a sandwich while she finished her sentence and collected her thoughts.

They would sit together at the kitchen table and she would talk about her work. She never asked how his day had been. Often she would need reassurance. Not about the quality of her writing – she believed implicitly in that – but because of some setback. Her agent had not been sufficiently enthusiastic about her latest novel. Attempts to break into the American market had come to nothing. He would tell her that of course it was a struggle but that recognition would come one day. Then he would wash the dishes and hurry back to school.

Sometimes he could not make it home at lunchtime. Perhaps there was a meeting or a parent demanding to see him. Then he would arrive, late in the afternoon, to find her looking out for him, distraught. He hated to see her unhappy, but those moments, when she clung to him as soon as he came through the door, made everything worthwhile. It showed how much she needed him.

After her death he never went to the house in the middle of the day. He preferred to walk into the centre of the town and sit in one of the cafés, watching the shop assistants in short skirts and clacking high heels, who hurried in to buy sticky buns to take away. And the harassed young mums with their babies.

Today he bought his sandwiches at the school canteen and took them back to the staffroom to wait for Brian's call, ignoring the conversation around him.

'Have you heard the latest? The head wants a policy document on pastoral care. Pastoral care! Who has time for that any more?'

'If the bloody Ofsted inspector can do any better with my Year Nine group he's welcome to try.'

Mark hated the staffroom. Too many people smoked. When the bell rang he collected his piles of exercise books with relief. He was disappointed that Brian had not phoned but thought they could probably meet up later. Brian would make the effort. He was a friend.

Otterbridge High was a comprehensive school but had once been the grammar and still made much of its academic reputation. It offered Latin, for example, and insisted on blazers. There were glass and concrete blocks – a Sports Hall, a Science Lab, which had been built in the early seventies when there was still money for that sort of thing – but the heart of the school was an impressive nineteenth-century building. Mark was pleased that he usually taught from a classroom in the old school. The ceiling was high and the acoustics were good, and there was less chance that the roof would leak. Teaching came hard to him. He would never have survived a soulless inner-city institution.

Only as he walked down the corridor past the jostling children did he realize that his next lesson was Year Eleven music, and that Marilyn Howe would be in the class. He knew she was back in school because he had seen her distinctive white hair from the stage where he sat during assembly. He was not sure how he would feel about meeting her. He was not quite sure what he would say.

In fact it was Marilyn who spoke to him first. They met at the classroom door. No other pupils had yet turned up.

'Hello, sir,' she said, and gave him that smile, flattering and insinuating. Then a group of children turned up. He could not mention her mother's death in front of them so he only nodded and held open the door for her to go in ahead of him. Even if they had been alone he would have found it hard to speak to her. He had found the smile profoundly shocking. Of course he had understood that the girl was infatuated. The devoted gazes, the questions once the lesson was over, all these had been a nuisance, but he had supposed that the death of her mother would put an end to them. Now, it seemed, the irritation would continue.

At four o'clock he phoned Brian's office again. Noel put him through immediately.

'Sorry about lunchtime,' Brian said. 'I had a visit from the cops. One particular cop. Inspector Ramsay. Has he had a go at you?'

'No. I gave a statement to a constable. A woman.'

There was a silence which was starting to become awkward when Mark said, 'I wondered if we might meet. There's something I need your advice about.'

'Great. Why don't you come to supper? Em could do with the company and we'll get a takeaway if she doesn't fancy cooking.'

'No. Just the two of us if you don't mind.'

There was a pause. 'Sure. Where should we meet?'

'I don't know. I hadn't thought. . .' Mark realized suddenly that this was probably a mistake. It wasn't the right time. 'Look, it doesn't matter. Em will be expecting you. You'll miss the children's bedtime.'

'Sod the children's bedtime. But not the club, then. She might see the car from the house and I'll have to tell her I'm working late or there'll be a row.'

'You shouldn't lie to her, you know.'

'None of us could live, could we, without lies?' Even then that seemed a peculiar thing for Brian to say. 'Look, I'll come over to Otterbridge. To the Tap and Spile in the market square. Early. Six thirtyish. Then I can earn a few brownie points by being home for supper.'

'All right.' Mark was still hesitant. He was trying to put together an excuse.

Brian said cheerily, 'Look, I've got to go. There's a call on the other line. I'll see you tonight.'

Mark sat in his classroom marking books until five, then he was driven away by the distant thud of pop music from the sixth-formers' aerobics class. It started as a mild irritation but after twenty minutes he was completely distracted, so he packed up and left. The corridors were empty. Outside it was nearly dark.

The front entrance of the school opened directly on to a suburban street. It was all steps and pillars like a municipal town hall, and would have been more in keeping facing a busy road in a town centre. Mark stood on the pavement wondering what to do next. There was hardly time to go home and still be in the pub for Brian. He felt ridiculously conspicuous and undecided. He looked at his watch to suggest that he had an appointment, a real purpose in lurking on this street corner, then he set off.

Almost immediately he thought he was being followed. There were footsteps which he was certain were not an echo of his own. When he turned round no one was there, but he imagined the pursuer flattened into the shadow of the high wall which marked the boundary of the school grounds. He felt his hands sweat and his heart pound. Occasionally Sheena had been the victim of panic attacks. Objectively, he recognized the symptoms, but still he was convinced that he was on the verge of a heart attack, that he was about to die. He stood still and forced himself to breathe deeply. There were no scuttling footsteps. When he turned round again the street, better lit now, was empty.

He told himself he had been imagining things. It was his guilty conscience. He deserved, after all, to have nightmares.

Brian Coulthard arrived at the Tap and Spile five minutes late, expecting to find Mark already there. Mark's punctuality was legend. He checked both bars then settled down with a pint at a table by the fire. He had a view from there of the door. At seven, another pint later, he was beginning to become concerned. He was debating whether he should drive to the Taverner house in case there had been some sort of accident when Mark came in. He stood inside the door, dazed and blinking, like someone just woken from sleep and did not see Brian until he called out, 'Hey. Over here.' Then he stumbled to the table, his hands stretched ahead of him in apology.

'I'm really sorry. I left school early so I called into St Mary's Church for a few minutes. Just to sit, you know, and think. I lost track of the time.'

'No sweat,' Brian said. He did not ask what Mark had to think about. 'You've waited for me often enough. Drink? I've only got half an hour left, though. I promised Em I'd be in at eight.'

'It won't take long.' But now he was here it seemed even more difficult than he'd feared, his dreadful betrayal was impossible to put into words. And Brian didn't make it any easier with his bustling approach to the bar, his demand to be served. It was as if he were trying to avoid any serious discussion. By now the pub was filling up with men in suits needing a quick drink before facing their families, and there was a queue.

'I'm sure that cop will get in touch with you,' Brian said, as soon as he sat down with Mark's orange juice and his half-pint. 'Ramsay. He was asking all about you.'

'I hope he doesn't come to the school.' Mark had a picture of flashing lights, a uniformed policeman standing at the classroom door, children sniggering.

'He's not daft,' Brain said. 'He'll be discreet.'

'Look,' Mark leant forward across the table, felt spilled beer seep into his jersey at the elbows. 'There's something I have to tell you.'

But the noise of voices around them was now so loud that Brian had not heard. Or so it seemed because he jumped up suddenly and pushed his way through the crowd to the gents. When he returned he did not sit down.

'I'd better go.' He was holding his Burberry mac by the hook over his shoulder and his car keys were already in his hand. 'Em'll have my supper in the cut if I'm late again.'

'Yes,' Mark said. 'Of course.'

'Can I give you a lift?'

'No. I'd rather walk.'

They left the pub together, and standing briefly on the pavement Mark made one more attempt to say his piece. Brian cut him off with an excuse that he was already late, but Mark was certain now that he did not want to hear.

'Give Em my love, then,' he said.

'Sure,' Brian answered. 'Sure.'

When Mark walked home he stopped several times to listen, but there were no following footsteps.

Chapter Fourteen

The Shining Stars Day Nursery stood at the end of the street. Its corner position meant that there were gardens on three sides of the house. Marcia Frost, the proprietor, was a great believer in sending the little ones outside to let off steam. Now, however, it was dusk and too late for outside play. From her office on the first floor Miss Frost watched a group of high school students cross the road and make their way towards the town centre. They were late. Miss Frost realized that she had lost track of time. The lighter evenings had confused her. Already there was an adult standing by the high wooden gate. A father, presumably, waiting to collect a child, though he stood in the shadow and she did not recognize him.

Miss Frost hurried downstairs. She liked to be on hand when the parents arrived, to reassure. Fees for the Shining Stars Nursery were substantial. Clients were entitled to a personal service.

The nursery took children from newborn infants to four-year-olds ready to start school. Invariably the parents were professional. They liked Miss Frost because she was flexible and accommodating. Offspring could be dropped off at any time after seven thirty in the morning and collected as late as eight o'clock at night. She drew the line at weekends, though this service had been requested on a number of occasions.

Miss Frost, who had never suffered any maternal stirrings, wondered occasionally why some of these mothers chose to put themselves through the process. They saw their babies so infrequently. Hardly ever awake. She was very fond of cats. Her cat recognized her whenever she arrived home from work. Did these children recognize the parents who collected them, sleeping, from the baby room? What pleasure could there be in that?

At five thirty a rush of parents arrived. They stood in the hall, chatting to Miss Frost while the nursery nurses went to collect the children. Later Miss Frost identified this as the time when Tom Bingham must have escaped. One of the parents must have failed to shut the door properly. The staff had all been very carefully trained. She was emphatic that none of them could be responsible.

Tom's mother was fat and cheerful. She worked as a reporter on the local newspaper. There was no father, at least no one she would admit to. Miss Frost thought she was feckless and a little slovenly. It had been known for Tom to arrive wearing odd socks and without his packed lunch.

'How's he been today, then?' Jan Bingham asked, when she arrived at six o'clock. 'A terror as usual?'

'No,' Miss Frost said. 'He's been much more settled.' Though when she considered it she realized that she just hadn't been bothered by Tom. Usually he was running backwards and forwards into the hall at this time to look for his mother, getting under the feet of other waiting parents. She was looking forward to losing Tom to the infants school.

She called to the nursery nurse in charge of the three-year-olds, 'Tom Bingham, please, Hayley. His mother's here.'

Hayley returned a few minutes later, anxious and blushing. This was her first position after completing her training and she still found her boss daunting.

'I'm sorry, Miss Frost. I can't find him.'

A search ensued. They looked in the toilets, in the baby room and the garden. Eventually, at Ms Bingham's insistence, the police were called.

By chance two policemen in a patrol car found the boy on their way to answer the call. He was standing in the middle of the road, shivering because he had left the Shining Stars without a coat. He was lucky that a car had not hit him.

He would not tell the policeman what had happened to him or

how he had left the nursery, though he enjoyed the ride in the police car, especially when they made the siren sound for him.

Miss Frost refused to accept that any of her staff had been careless.

'Tom is a very wilful boy,' she said, making it clear where she felt the responsibility for the whole incident lay.

Ramsay heard of the missing boy while he was drinking coffee in the staff canteen. His shift was over but Prue was on her way back from Scotland and he'd promised to collect her from the arts centre. It wasn't worth his going home. He'd probably still be there anyway.

Hunter passed on the information. He too was working late. He was still trying to trace the man in the red Mazda who had stayed with Kim Houghton the night before the murder. The local press had been very helpful about publicity but he was no nearer a result. He was glad of a distraction.

'You hear there's been another one, then?' He carried a plate with a fried-egg sandwich. He sat at Ramsay's table without waiting to be asked.

'Another murder?' Please, Ramsay thought. Let it not be the girl.

'Na. Another kid's been snatched.'

'Oh.' The child abductions were no longer his problem.

'From a private day nursery near the high school.'

'From *inside* the nursery?' Despite himself, Ramsay was interested.

'The woman in charge claims not. She says that would be impossible and the boy must have got out somehow.' Hunter paused, grinned. 'But then she would say that, wouldn't she? She'd have her reputation to think of. I knew a lass once who was a nursery nurse. She told me there was a fortune to be made in private nurseries.'

Ramsay thought Hunter knew so many lasses that between them they could provide a comprehensive careers service.

'Is the boy all right?'

'Apparently. Two of our lads found him wandering in the middle of the road a couple of miles away from where he went missing.'

'We are sure that he was abducted, then? He didn't just go walkabout?'

'Well that's what everyone thought at first. He's a bit wild apparently and he's tried to run away before. But the timing's all wrong. The kids have tea at five o'clock and he was definitely there for that. And for the story afterwards. They reckon he must have gone at about a quarter to six. Lots of parents arrived at about that time and they think he could have slipped out in the scrum. Our lads found him just before six thirty. An adult could walk two miles in three quarters of an hour. But a three-year-old? In the dark? And it's a nice respectable neighbourhood. Nosy. A busy time of the evening with folks coming home from work. If anyone had seen a kid that small on his own they'd have taken him in, phoned us.'

'So there was a car, then? Like the others?'

'Either that or he was carried piggy back. And that's hardly likely.' Hunter grinned. 'Still, it's for some other bugger to sort out now. We've got enough on our plates.'

'He was all right, the boy? Unharmed?'

'So it seems.' Hunter paused. 'The woman in charge saw a bloke hanging round outside at about quarter past five. She thought he must be one of the dads. They're trying to trace all the parents who were there. So far no one's identified him.'

'Did the woman give a description?'

'Nothing worth having.'

'Did she see a car?'

'Na.'

'It'll all come down to the boy, then?'

'Aye. And the strange thing is, he's not talking. Not a word. He doesn't seem frightened or upset, and he's not known for keeping his mouth shut, but he'll not tell them a thing.'

Chapter Fifteen

The next day Mark escaped school at lunchtime. He didn't go into town because it was market day and he couldn't face the crowd. He bought an apple and a Mars Bar from a corner shop near the school. The place was packed with kids. They weren't supposed to leave the grounds at midday and it was a shock for them to see him there. He had a reputation for being strict. One of them muttered, 'Here we go. Detentions all round.'

But he didn't say anything. He just bought his apple and his Mars Bar and pretended he hadn't seen them.

He took his lunch to Prior's Park and sat on a bench near the children's playground. On the way he had the same sense of being followed as he had the night before, but he put it down to nerves. And to a guilty conscience. If he'd managed to talk to Brian perhaps he'd find it easier to relax.

In summer he hated the park, the regimented rows of bedding plants, the semi-naked teenagers lounging in the sun with their transistor radios and their cans of lager. At this time of year it was windswept and neglected. Tolerable. Banks of dead leaves still lay under the trees. The river was full.

There were no children playing on the swings, but a woman pushing a pram walked past him and sat on a bench next to his. He would have liked to get up to look at the baby. He could tell that it was very tiny, tightly wrapped in a white blanket and covered with a quilt. The quilt was blue so he supposed the child was a boy. One hand had escaped. It was covered in a cotton mitten to stop the nails scratching the face. A middle-aged woman could have gone up to the pram and asked for a peep and the mother would have been delighted to show her baby off but Mark knew this was out of the question for him. It was not considered normal for men to like babies.

He had spoken to Sheena about children. Hypothetically. Not wanting to put any pressure on her. Afraid, as always, of boring her. From the very beginning her reaction had been one of revulsion.

'Oh, God no. Don't worry, Mark. I'll spare you that at least. Really, darling, I'm not the broody sort. Never have been. Can you *imagine* the process of giving birth? I'd die!'

And, of course, she had died, though not through childbirth.

Occasionally he had heard friends talking without realizing he could hear them.

'At least,' they said, 'there were no children.'

Only Emma had seemed to understand the pleasure he took in baby Helen Scarlet and to her it was perfectly natural. She was potty about the baby, entranced by the way she stretched her hands, unseeing, groping for food. Why shouldn't Mark be? It was Brian's lack of interest which had astounded her.

'Tell me, Mark,' she demanded. 'How can he bear to spend so much time in the office? He's missing everything. Her first smile. She'll be crawling soon and then she won't be a baby any more.'

She had been delighted when Mark held Helen against his shoulder to wind her after she had been fed, when he jumped her up and down on his knee to make her laugh.

On his recent exile from the Coastguard House he had missed the baby as much as he had his contact with Emma.

The woman stood up from the park bench. She leant into the pram and put her hand on the baby's forehead to check presumably that he was not too cold. The baby woke and began to grizzle. The woman walked on briskly.

It was then that Mark noticed the tall man in the heavy raincoat. He had been standing by the wire mesh fence surrounding the playground for some time, though Mark had been too taken up with the baby to realize.

'Mr Taverner?'

He walked across the grass and sat beside Mark who had the

sudden thought that they were like spies in a Le Carré novel. He almost expected a password.

'Yes.'

'I hope you don't mind. One of your colleagues pointed you out. I thought it would be more discreet to talk here than at school. I'm the detective in charge of the Kathleen Howe case.'

So, Mark thought, he had been followed. Ramsay had watched him leave the shop and walk to the park. Then he had waited for the woman to leave so they would not be overheard. A patient man. Mark admired that.

'Do you have time to talk now?' Ramsay was asking. 'If you prefer I could make an appointment to see you at home this evening.'

'No,' Mark said. 'I've a free period first thing this afternoon. There's no rush to get back.'

'I know you gave a statement to one of my officers but there are a few points I'd like to clear up.'

'Of course.' Now that the moment had come, Mark felt quite calm, clear-headed. There was none of that ridiculous panic he'd felt last night on his way to meet Brian.

'Did you know Mrs Howe well?'

'Not well. I'd met her at parents' evenings. She came to school concerts.'

'You would have recognized her?'

'I suppose so.'

'But you didn't see her on the day she disappeared?'

'No. I said so in my statement.'

There was a brief silence.

'What was your opinion of Mrs Howe?' Ramsay asked. 'I mean as a parent.'

'She was supportive. Involved. I wish all our parents were as well motivated.'

'But?'

'But on occasions her interference could be irritating. And it didn't do Marilyn any good.'

'Perhaps you could explain.'

'Marilyn's a competent violinist. She works hard, passes all her exams, but there are other, more talented musicians in the school. Last term Mrs Howe barged into a rehearsal and demanded that Marilyn should be moved from second to first violins. It was perfectly true that Marilyn could have coped quite adequately with the music, but so could many of the others in her group.'

'How did you deal with the situation?'

Mark smiled, briefly. 'I left it to Mr Scott, our head of music, to sort out. That's what he's paid for.'

'What did Marilyn make of the fuss?'

He shrugged. 'Naturally she would have liked to play first violin. She's a competitive child. But she was profoundly embarrassed by the incident. I tried to make light of it, to make the others see that Marilyn could hardly be held responsible for her mother's . . . over-enthusiasm. All the same it can't have been easy.'

But Ramsay thought that his sympathy would have made it easier. No wonder the girl had a crush on him.

'Did you ever meet Mr Howe?'

'He was dragged along, rather reluctantly I suspect, to some events.'

'Is Marilyn popular at school?'

The question seemed to throw him.

'She's conscientious, well behaved. I'm sure most of the staff would welcome her in their class.'

'That's not really what I asked. Did she have friends? Close friends of her own age?' Or was she, as she had described herself, a Billy No Mates?

Mark Taverner considered. 'No. Not in the way that you mean. You mustn't assume, though, that she is unhappy at school. That there's bullying, for example. I don't believe there is anything of that sort. Some children are naturally solitary. Or they find it easier to form relationships with adults. I was like that myself. I didn't develop any close friendships until I left home and went to university.'

'When you met Mr Coulthard?'

'Brian. Yes.'

'And Mrs Coulthard? Would you consider her to be a close friend?'

'Very.' The answer came easily.

'Brian's marriage didn't affect your friendship?'

'Why should it?' Mark asked.

'Oh,' Ramsay said lamely. 'There can be an awkwardness sometimes in a threesome, can't there?'

Certainly he had felt awkward with some of Prue's friends. She had been single for years and had become very close to the women who had supported her. One or two resented the time she spent with him. Their jealousy had perplexed her.

'Why can't they just be pleased for me?' she had demanded, almost in tears, after one particularly hurtful remark.

Because they can't get a man of their own, he had wanted to reply. Only half flippantly. Knowing that was what Hunter would have said and not caring. But he hadn't been entirely sure that Prue would have found it amusing so he had kept his mouth shut.

'Not in this case,' Mark said firmly. 'Emma has always understood that Brian's friends were important to him. Besides, we weren't a threesome. I was already married when Brian and Emma met.'

'I see.'

'My wife died five months ago. She had cancer. Brian and Emma have been wonderful. I really don't know how I could have carried on without them ... That's how I came to the Headland the afternoon Mrs Howe was killed. Since Sheena's death they've been very good about including me in family events.'

'You drove there, straight from school?'

'Yes. That's how I came to give Marilyn a lift.'

'What car do you drive?'

'A blue Volvo estate. I told the other policeman.'

He was beginning to lose his patience. Ramsay ignored his irritation.

'How did Marilyn seem to you? She wasn't anxious? She didn't express concern for her mother's safety? I thought she might have confided in you.'

'Look, Inspector. Marilyn Howe's not the sort of girl to confide in anyone. She might possibly have talked to her mother. She certainly didn't talk to me.'

That night Stephen Ramsay took Prue to Marco's to celebrate her return. They were given the table near the window where he had sat with Marilyn and Claire. The town wall was floodlit from below and long shadows were thrown across the courtyard.

'I suppose,' he said, 'it's an anti-climax. Coming back here. After all the admiration and the glory.' Her group had taken a prize at the festival. There had been rave reviews in the Scottish press.

'At least I can catch up on some sleep.'

But not, Ramsay thought, tonight, I hope.

'And you've been kept busy? Gordon Hunter hasn't had you out clubbing in town, picking up unsuitable women?'

'Unfortunately not. He thinks I'm past it. It would be an embarrassment to be seen with me.'

She laughed. Marco himself came up with the wine, made a great fuss of Prue, then melted away.

'I have been busy though. This murder inquiry.'

'So you haven't missed me?'

'Hardly at all.' After a few drinks he might have answered more honestly but she hated it when he got heavy.

'How's the inquiry going?'

'Not very well. We can't trace an important witness – a man who stayed in the Headland the night before the murder. The victim was a middle-aged housewife. The family seem very respectable, quite ordinary I suppose. We can't dig up a motive. Why would anyone have wanted to kill her?'

'A meaningless act of violence, then?'

'No. I don't think it was that.'

Why not? he wondered. Because she disappeared so absolutely. Because the Headland wasn't like Newcastle on a Friday night. Because he had the sense, for some reason, that the murder had been planned.

'I think you know one of the witnesses,' he said. 'Mark Taverner. Didn't you work with his wife? You both sat on a Northern Arts committee?'

'That's right. She was a writer. She died last September. I went to her funeral.'

'Were you friends?'

'I don't think Sheena had friends. Not really. She didn't have time for them. She had admirers, though. Plenty of them. She was quite stunning in a dark anorexic way. She was desperately skinny even before she was ill.'

'You didn't like her?' He realised it was the same question he had asked Brian Coulthard.

'I think I might have done if she'd given me a chance. She was very driven, absolutely convinced that she could be a great writer. Nothing was allowed to stand in her way. Certainly not a night in the pub with a mate.'

'And was she a great writer?'

'I didn't think so. I found her too self-conscious.' Prue paused, considered. 'Perhaps she might have been if she hadn't taken herself so seriously. She came once to run a workshop for the kids in the arts centre and she was brilliant with them, very witty, very funny. They all ended up writing nonsense verse and laughing out loud. I asked why she didn't do more of that kind of thing. Why didn't she produce a book for children, for example? She said she'd love to but it would only be a distraction. As if something enjoyable couldn't possibly be worthwhile.'

'But her books *were* published. They sold.'

'Oh yes, she was published and she was well reviewed. I'm not sure what sort of living she made from them. I know she taught some adult education classes for the university though they wouldn't have paid a fortune. I don't think she could have survived without Mark's income.'

'She and Mark were happy?'

'He doted on her. More than was good for her I thought. Apparently she was an only child. Spoilt rotten. He took over from her parents. I didn't think it would last. You can't be a doormat for ever. Then we found out she had breast cancer and she died very quickly.' Prue looked up from her wine. 'She was only thirty-six. Younger than me.'

Chapter Sixteen

Emma Coulthard had become obsessed with her inability to sleep. She thought of little else even during the day. She could have understood it if the baby had been keeping her awake but Helen had slept right through from the age of six weeks and was no trouble at all. The boys had been terrors as babies. They'd hardly seemed to know the difference between night and day but Emma had staggered cheerfully out of bed to feed and change them, then returned to fall immediately and deeply asleep.

This was different. She could not rest. Even if she put up her feet during the afternoon while Claire had the children she could not relax. At night she lay tense and still listening to Brian's breathing. The bedroom curtains were thin and sometimes moonlight shone through so she could see him. His skin was very white and the layer of fat just beneath it reminded her of the goose he had once persuaded her to cook at Christmas. As the night wore on she became more startlingly awake. She watched the red flashing numbers on her bedside alarm clock mark the hours. Sometimes at four or five in the morning she would fall into a troubled doze. Sometimes she stayed awake to see the sky lighten over the sea.

Eventually Brian noticed her drawn face, the rings round her eyes, her short temper.

'What the hell's the matter with you?' he demanded. Then, in a panic when she didn't reply, 'You're not ill, are you?' She knew he was thinking of Sheena. His concern did not stretch, however, to ironing his own shirts.

At his insistence she had gone to the doctor, a fatherly Scot, who knew Brian from the rugby club.

'I'm not sure what you can do,' she said. 'I shouldn't have come.'

'How long's this been going on for?'

'Oh,' she replied. 'A couple of weeks.' Though she could time it exactly back to David's birthday. She had not slept on the night before that.

'Anything troubling you?'

Well, she thought, you could say that.

'No, no,' she said. 'Everything's fine.'

'You were a close friend of Sheena Taverner, weren't you? Perhaps that's it. Bereavement can take a long time to have an effect.' Then, a sort of joke: 'You're not worried, are you, that the police still haven't caught this murderer?'

'No!' she said, smiling to show that she would not be so foolish. And that, at least, was true.

'I'll prescribe you some sleeping pills. They're very mild. Don't use them every night or they won't work. But don't worry. You're not the sort to get hooked!'

He had known her during her time as a career woman, seen her through the trouble-free pregnancies and thought she was entirely sensible.

So now she had the pills; which were a secret from Brian. She took them when she was desperate. They did knock her out but they left her feeling doped up and befuddled the next day, so she still could not think clearly about what she should do.

Brian phoned at a quarter past four to say he would be late again.

'You said you'd be back before the boys went to bed.'

'I'm sorry, pet. Really. There's a chap I've got to meet. He can't make it earlier. I'll definitely be home for supper at eight. Look. I'll bring a bottle of wine. Something decent. We'll have a quiet night together like the old times.'

She said that would be very nice though there was scarcely an evening when he didn't open a bottle of wine and drink most of it himself before the end of the *News at Ten*. She felt a sudden urge to be out of the house.

Claire finished work at five thirty and she had become much

more punctilious about leaving on time since Kath Howe's death. Emma thought it sweet that she was taking her role as surrogate mother so seriously but sometimes, as now, it was inconvenient. Emma had suggested that Marilyn could come to the Coastguard House straight from school if she wanted the company. That would save Claire having to hurry away. Claire had thanked her but refused. She said Marilyn was going through a difficult time and needed her family.

Emma shouted up to the playroom where Claire was sitting with the children, watching cartoons.

'I'm going out for a walk. I just need some fresh air. I'll be back before you have to leave.'

She waited for a reply. None came, and she read in the silence criticism.

She put on a thick coat but outside it was surprisingly warm. The wind was south-westerly and later it would probably rain. At the jetty she sat in the last of the sun watching the tide ebb from the cut.

Stephen Ramsay, too, had felt the need for fresh air. Apart from his discussion with Mark Taverner in the park he had spent the day in his office. The drive to the Headland in the late afternoon sunshine made him feel like a boy sagging off school. He left his car at the club and walked up the peninsula, avoiding Cotter's Row, following the coast to the highest point where the cliffs fell in rocky steps to the sea. From there he had an uninterrupted view to the railway line and beyond. He saw Kim Houghton's little girl playing with her doll's pram in the street and Emma Coulthard leave the Coastguard House for her walk to the jetty. And they could have seen him if they'd turned to look.

So how, in such a small area, had Kathleen Howe disappeared without trace? The visibility had been bad on the day of the murder but surely not so dreadful that an attacker would have taken the risk of stabbing her in daylight. From his vantage point at the top of the Headland he saw clearly for the first time that there was nowhere to hide.

What did that mean? That she had been killed after dark? The pathologist's evidence was still inconclusive on time of death – it was possible perhaps, as Bernard had said, that she had been collecting lichens for dyeing. Then where had she spent the day? He knew she had taken off without warning once before, when Marilyn had arrived at his house asking for help. Perhaps Kathleen Howe had met her killer as she walked back to the Headland in the evening. She would have passed the jetty. Had she been killed there, close to where her body had been found?

It would depend on the tide. If the cut had been nearly empty as it was now there would hardly have been sufficient water to cover the body, certainly not enough to carry it away and sweep it back in on the following day's high water. The scene of crimes officer had commented at the time. He had been a fool not to give her report more attention.

When Emma returned to the Coastguard House Claire was waiting sulkily in the kitchen, already dressed in her coat and her outdoor shoes. Emma looked pointedly at the kitchen clock which said five twenty.

'I don't think it's *quite* time for you to go,' she said in the snooty, stuck-up voice which Claire hadn't heard for a while. Recently Emma had been much more apologetic and obliging. 'But as you're ready, I suppose you might as well.'

'Right,' Claire said. 'Thank you.' Inside she was fuming but it was all she could think of to say on the spur of the moment.

Out of the house her resentment grew. She let it simmer. It was just what she needed.

The cow, she thought. What right did Emma Coulthard have to speak to her like that? Any decent employer would have made sure she got home safely. It was dark, wasn't it? Nearly dark, anyway. And as far as Emma bloody Coulthard knew there was a murderer on the Headland waiting to strike again. She spoke out loud to herself. 'It's about time you told someone.' She'd only kept quiet out of loyalty and loyalty should work both ways, shouldn't it?

At Cotter's Row she paused for a moment outside number two.

The house was dark, the curtains undrawn. Marilyn must be home from school by now but she'd be in the back bedroom doing her homework. Bernie would still be on his way from work. Kath had always fretted about Bernie on his bike when it was windy, and she felt a moment of sympathetic concern. Then she walked on down the street and knocked on the door of number six.

She knew that Kim was in because she could hear the television. When Kim opened the door she kept her eyes on the screen. *Neighbours.* Kim knew it was for kids really but she'd become addicted. She couldn't bear to miss an episode. She always arranged to give Kirsty her tea when *Neighbours* was on. She loved her food and it was the only time you could be sure she wouldn't make a noise. Through the half-open door Claire could see the little girl sitting on a stool up to the breakfast bar, eating fish fingers and chips.

'Claire!' Kim sounded very friendly. 'How are you? Hey, I've missed having you around.'

What she meant, Claire thought, was that she missed having a regular babysitter. It was hard to ask favours of someone who'd just lost her sister.

'I'm all right,' Claire said in a wan, little girl's voice. Grief-stricken but trying to be brave.

'Is there anything I can do?' From the corner of her eye Kim watched a handsome Australian hunk take a bronzed teenage girl into his arms.

'Well, I wondered if you fancied going out tonight. If you'd like me to sit. I haven't wanted to leave Bernie and Marilyn before but I could really do with a change of scene. It's not much fun in that house. Well, you'll understand.'

'Of *course*.' Kim was all sympathy but she could hardly contain a smile. For the first time Claire had her full attention. 'What time?'

'Give me an hour to give Bernie and Marilyn their tea and clear up. Say seven. That all right?'

'Sure,' Kim said. 'That would be fine.' She was already planning what she would wear.

'Look, would you mind if I used your phone? Only a local call.

I don't like to ask but I don't fancy walking down to the phone box with this maniac about.'

Kim could hardly refuse after that.

'I'll do it upstairs then, shall I? So So I'll not disturb your programme.'

Before Kim could answer she was in the house and up the stairs. She knew where to find Kim's bedroom, had heard the Cotter's Row gossip about what went on there. And they didn't know the half of it! It had flouncy curtains and a frilly valance, much more to Claire's taste than the stuff in the Coastguard House. The carpet was deep pink. The phone was by the bed and she sat there, leaning back against the pillows and the padded head-board, sticking her feet out to the side so the mud on her shoes wouldn't stain the quilt.

First she dialled directory enquiries to get the number of Otterbridge Police Station: 999 seemed a bit over the top. When she was connected she asked for the murder incident room. Ramsay wasn't there so she spoke to DS Hunter. She knew who he was. He'd been asking all the questions in Cotter's Row. He was the good-looking one with the dark hair and the tan.

'This is Claire Irvine,' she said. 'Kath Howe's sister. I need to talk to you. I'll be at six Cotter's Row tonight at eight o'clock. You've got that, have you? Number six not number two. I don't want Bernie or Marilyn bothered.'

Hunter tried to get her to tell him what it was all about. She could tell he was excited. But she wouldn't. Let him wait.

Downstairs she heard the *Neighbours* theme so she slid off the bed.

'Got a boyfriend at last, have you?' Kim Houghton asked kindly. 'Lovey-dovey phone calls now, is it?'

Claire smiled politely but she did not answer.

Chapter Seventeen

The phone call from Claire Irvine brought the team to life. When Ramsay returned from the Headland he was already fired up. He'd called in at the Coastguard Headquarters in Tynemouth and talked to the man in charge, a confident West Countryman called Morton who seemed glad of the distraction from routine. In the control room the telephone rang continually. Ramsay gathered that members of the public were asking for high-water times to check a safe crossing to Holy Island or to plan a fishing trip to the Farnes. He wished he'd had as much sense when Kath Howe's body was first found.

'I read about the murder,' Morton said. 'Thought you'd have been in touch before.' Rubbing salt into the wound.

'We weren't sure where she was dumped.' Ramsay knew he sounded defensive. 'But the day of the incident, what time was high water?'

'At the Headland?'

Ramsay nodded. Morton consulted a chart.

'Seven twenty-nine in the morning. Just after eight in the evening. Twenty eleven to be precise.'

'Would the cut be full much before that?'

'No. It wasn't a particularly high tide. Say an hour either side.'

Kath Howe had still been alive at eight thirty in the morning. If she'd been tipped into the cut during the day the sea would have been out and she'd have lain there, visible, on the rocks. There had been men drinking in the club all afternoon, kids playing, dog walkers. Even in the rain someone would have seen her. And just before dark Marilyn and her father had been searching. They'd have looked in the cut, worried that she might have fallen. So if she'd been thrown off the jetty it would have been after dark. The eight eleven high tide would have taken her out to sea.

'What about the currents round there? Would she have been washed back to where she went in?'

About that Morton wasn't prepared to commit himself. All the same Ramsay walked back to his car past Tynemouth Priory feeling more elated. At least the case was moving. They'd been asking questions about the wrong time. They'd need fresh statements from all the witnesses, concentrating on their movements during the evening. And more publicity in an attempt to find someone who had seen Kathleen Howe during the afternoon.

Then, when he returned to the station, the team were full of the call from Claire Irvine.

'How did she sound?' Ramsay asked.

Hunter had left the Incident Room as soon as he learned that Ramsay was back in his office. He was hoping to get a bit of credit by being the bearer of good news. Hoping to be in on the action at last.

'Very matter of fact, really. Stubborn. She wasn't willing to give anything away on the phone. You can hear the tape. She'd make a canny witness.'

'If it comes to that.'

'Aye well.' Hunter always tended to optimism. He thought much of his boss's problem was that he was overcautious. Not that Ramsay hadn't had one or two successes lately. Secretly Hunter thought he was a clever bastard. He wouldn't admit as much to the lads, though. He told them he was still waiting for a transfer to the city.

Even Hunter's optimism had begun to strain before the phone call. It was all taking much longer than they'd expected. He'd chased around with the rest of them at first, dragging in the local lunatics and losers for interview. He was still taking responsibility for tracing Kim Houghton's boyfriend, the driver of the red Mazda. He'd even appeared on the television appealing for the man to come forward. He'd been interviewed by the pretty blonde lass who did the local news. He'd always fancied her.

His mam had videoed it and showed it to all her friends.

'Eeh,' they said. 'Your Gordon on the telly. He'd charm the birds out of the trees, that one.'

But Gordon Hunter's charm hadn't been enough to persuade the driver of the red Mazda to come forward. Hunter knew there could be many explanations for this. He had a wife or a permanent girlfriend. He had told his boss he was working at the other end of the country and claimed expenses. He just didn't want the hassle. Or there might be a more sinister reason for his keeping quiet.

Hunter had decided that his next move would be to spend Friday and Saturday night in the clubs in Whitley Bay. The bar staff might recognize the description of the man. If he were a regular, one of Kim's friends might have an address for him.

Of course if Claire Irvine had real information the jaunt might not turn out to be necessary. Hunter considered that possibility with a little regret. He enjoyed clubbing, had already picked out a pretty little DC to be his partner. He wouldn't mind an expenses-paid night out.

Ramsay broke in on his thoughts. 'Give Sal Wedderburn a shout before you fill me in on this phone call. She's spent longer with Claire Irvine than anyone. We could use her opinion.'

Ramsay was grateful for Claire's intervention because he was coming under pressure to use the media more directly. A weeping daughter and a grief-stricken husband might stir the conscience of a friend or relative shielding the killer. So far he had resisted the pressure. He hated the glamorized voyeurism which resulted from filmed emotional outbursts. Anyway, he didn't think it would work. Kath Howe's relatives hadn't shed many tears for her. They might have been shocked by the manner of her death but they would manage very well without her.

Hunter came back to the office with Sal Wedderburn. He let her have the only vacant chair and lounged against the filing cabinet, sulking because Ramsay hadn't thought his opinion sufficient.

'Well?' Ramsay asked. 'How should we play it?'

'I don't think we should go mob-handed,' Sally cut in before Hunter had a chance to open his mouth. 'If she's decided to speak after all this time we wouldn't want to put her off. So I'd say play it casual, understated. As if responding to her call is just part of the general routine.'

'I think,' Ramsay said slowly, 'she's too bright to be taken in by that sort of approach. She didn't phone us just to give information. Not entirely. She phoned because she wants someone to make a fuss of her. That's how I see it.'

'You think she's after the attention? And that's all?'

'Not necessarily. But the attention might be the pay off. She'd need a pay off. She's not a woman who'd give anything away for nothing.'

'How often have you met her?' Hunter was incredulous. He'd known psychiatrists who wouldn't commit themselves to a statement like that after seeing a patient for years.

'Once,' Ramsay said calmly. 'Only once. But that was the impression I got. And her history bears it out, doesn't it? I've spoken to a social worker, Jean Douglas, who supervised Claire's family after her mother died.'

He shuffled through papers on his desk and pulled out a sheet of handwritten notes. He read from them.

'Claire was a late baby. Kathleen was seventeen when she was born. The mother died in a road traffic accident when the girl was two. At about the same time Kathleen left home to marry Bernie. So then there was just Claire and her dad. Social Services monitored the situation but there were never any suspicions that Claire was neglected, no cause for concern at all except for some bed-wetting and nightmares which went on a bit longer than normal. According to everyone she was a very mature little girl, very close to her dad. Not that he spoilt her. If anything she looked after him.'

Sally interrupted. 'But Kath would have *helped*, wouldn't she, sir? It's not as if she and Bernie lived a million miles away. She would have taken some responsibility for bringing up her sister.'

'Apparently not. Mrs Douglas wasn't very complimentary about Kath Howe. When Claire was fifteen the father had a heart attack at work and died. Social Services approached the Howes to discuss Claire's future. It was Bernie who offered her a home. Mrs Douglas definitely had the impression that Kathleen wasn't too keen, but felt that living with relatives was better than foster care with strangers.'

'Did she visit the Howes while Claire was living there?'

'Once. Claire seemed settled, said she was happy. But according to Mrs Douglas she wasn't the sort to complain. She sensed some antagonism between Kath and her sister, and asked Claire about it. Claire said it was nothing and she could look after herself.'

'Antagonism as in anger?' Sal asked. 'As in murder?'

Ramsay smiled. 'Sibling rivalry pushed to extremes? I should have thought that was a little far-fetched.'

'Anyway,' Hunter said. 'Claire can't be the murderer. She was at the Coastguard House all day. Unless you think she stabbed Kath Howe in her half-hour lunch break. With Bernie sitting in the room upstairs.'

'Ah,' Ramsay said. 'I've had a thought about that.' He explained about his visit to the Coastguard headquarters, his theory that Mrs Howe might have died in the evening. Then he returned to his notes, determined to make his point.

'Even if the Howes tried to do their best for Claire, to make her feel at home, it wouldn't have been easy for her. Kath was devoted to her daughter and Bernie seems to have been wrapped up in himself and his magic. I can't imagine either of them giving much time to the girl. That's what I meant when I said she might welcome our attention.'

Hunter wasn't convinced. It sounded very plausible but he'd always been suspicious of social workers.

'So what do you suggest? How should we handle it?'

'I think you and I should go to talk to her. I'm sorry, Sal. I know you'd like to be involved, but so far as we know she hasn't got a boyfriend, has never had one, and I think she'd be flattered by the attention of two men. Even two men like us. I think we might work it best.'

Hunter grinned. He thought that occasionally his boss showed considerable insight. And if that sounded like a sodding social worker's report too, he didn't care.

Chapter Eighteen

Claire had already brought small but significant changes to life at two Cotter's Row.

She'd cleared away some of Kath's things. Not the personal stuff like clothes. Bernie could see to that. But she'd got rid of the monstrous spinning wheel from the front room. At first Bernie has been reluctant to let it go.

'I don't know,' he said. 'Isn't it a bit soon?'

'You don't want to *keep* it?'

'No,' he said uncertainly, then, without any hesitation, 'No, you do what you think best.'

Mrs Coulthard had a friend who was into arts and crafts and she'd given Claire fifty quid for the wheel. Claire hadn't kept the money. It wasn't as if she needed if for herself. She handed it over to Bernie.

'Put it away for Marilyn,' she said. 'For the next time there's a school trip. Kath would have liked that.'

With the wheel out of the way the front room looked really grubby so she'd given it a good clean. She scrubbed the paintwork and shampooed the carpet. There was a nasty stain in front of the grate which she'd never noticed before, but it came up as good as new. She opened the windows for the first time ever, washed the curtains, bought a bunch of daffs on her weekly trip to the supermarket and stuck them in a milk jug on the coffee table.

If Bernie and Marilyn noticed the change they didn't comment.

They did comment on her cooking, though. She cooked a meal every evening. A proper meal. Kathleen always claimed to be too busy to cook. Too disorganized, Claire thought. Too wrapped up in Marilyn and her own improving evening classes. There had never been much except beans on toast or pizza. For a woman who despised modern machines, Kath had taken very easily to the freezer and the microwave. She didn't really think food mattered.

Claire thought food mattered a lot. Now, when Emma Coulthard went shopping to the supermarket on the Otterbridge bypass she asked if she might go too. She filled a trolley with fresh meat and vegetables, cheese and crusty bread. Sometimes she bought treats, taking the money from her wages, not the housekeeping – sticky buns for her and Marilyn and a couple of cans of beer for Bernard. Every evening when she got home she started to prepare the meal. She enjoyed planning for it. She had cooked for her father since she started secondary school. Now she would cook for Marilyn and Bernard.

Tonight the detour to Kim Houghton's house had made her later than usual. She hurried up the poorly lit street eager to begin. It was almost six o'clock. A sliver of light showed where a neighbour's upstairs curtain was pulled back but she took no notice. Let them talk, she thought. I've nothing to hide.

She let herself into the house. Marilyn was in the back room. She had drawn the curtains but she was still wearing her coat.

'Have you only just got here?' Claire kept her voice cheerful. Marilyn had put up with enough interrogation from Kath. 'That's the second time this week you've been late.'

'Choir practice again. I got the five thirty bus. Is there anything I can do?'

Claire shook her head. The kitchen was her territory now. She didn't want Marilyn muscling in. Besides, Marilyn was bright. A couple of years and she'd be away to university if she passed her exams. She should be doing her homework.

Tonight, however, Marilyn didn't take her books straight upstairs. She hovered in the doorway to the kitchen.

'Claire.'

'Yes?' Claire had put on an apron over her working clothes and had already started to peel potatoes. She'd bought some nice slices of lambs' liver the day before. She'd cook them slowly with a rich gravy and lots of onions. Her dad had always liked liver done that way. He'd shown her how to do it.

'I was wondering. . .' Marilyn spoke uncertainly. She was fiddling with the strap of her school bag. 'I was wondering whether we might rent a television. I've been asking round. It wouldn't cost very much.'

'You'd have to ask your dad.'

'But you could put in a word. He'd listen to you.'

Claire smiled. 'I wouldn't mind,' she said. 'Why not?'

'I'll go up then. Do some violin practice before I start my essay.'

Claire splashed vegetable oil into a frying pan and slid in chopped onions from a board. She shook flour on to a plate and picked up the liver slices, turning them with a deft movement to cover both sides with flour, then she rinsed her hands under the tap.

Above the sound of violin scales she heard the front door open. Although Claire could not see the hall from where she was standing in the kitchen, she could imagine what was happening. Bernard would have propped his bike against the outside of the house while he unlocked the door, then he would wheel it in to stand at the foot of the stairs. Kath had wanted him to keep it in the old privy in the back yard but for once in his life he had stood up for himself and refused. He'd said anyone could steal if from there and didn't Kath realize he'd be lost without his bike.

Claire could see his point but if she decided to decorate they might have to make a different arrangement. The rubber end of the handle bar had made a terrible mark on the wallpaper, and quite often there was mud on the carpet.

The front door was slammed shut and Bernard walked through to the kitchen. His cheeks were flushed from exercise and the wind. He beamed at Claire.

'Something smells good.'

In his hand was a plastic lunch box. Claire had taken to making sandwiches for him before he set out to work. He tipped crumbs into the bin, then set it on the draining board.

Claire turned from the cooker to face him.

'I'm going out tonight,' she said. 'Kim Houghton's asked me to babysit.'

'Oh.'

'I thought you and Marilyn would like some time on your own.'

'Yes,' he said uncertainly. 'I see.'

'You should get to know her better. It's important.'

'I ought to practise,' he said quickly. 'I'm doing a party in Otterbridge on Saturday. A Sunday school. They said they'd understand if I wanted to cancel but I couldn't let them down and it doesn't do to get rusty.'

'You *ought* to talk to Marilyn. About her mother. About the future.'

'Oh no, not yet. Now wouldn't be the right time at all.' Panic made him sweat. He wiped his forehead and his upper lip with a handkerchief. 'Of course I will tell her, but later, when things have settled down a bit.'

Claire shrugged and turned back to stir the frying pan. She knew with Bernard it was no good pushing.

'Look,' he said in an attempt to get back into her good books. 'Perhaps Marilyn would like to help me practise. She always used to, when she was little.'

And Claire was pleased to see, on her way upstairs to get tidied up before going to Kim's, that father and daughter were working together on Bernie's magic. She looked in on the scene with satisfaction. Bernie had brought his box of magic tricks into the warm of the back room and Marilyn was sitting on the floor beside his chair sorting through a pack of playing cards. Not really enjoying it, Claire could see, but making the effort. Altogether she thought things were going very well.

It was only as she paused in the hall to put on her coat and glanced into the front room, where all trace of Kathleen had been removed, that she was reminded of a picture in a book she had been given as a child. When she turned to look at herself in the gilt-edged mirror by the door, the thought of the picture remained. It was of a large brown cuckoo with a bright eye and powerful claws tipping a smaller fledgling from a nest. She had been expected to feel sorry for the fledgling, but it had been the cuckoo which had caught her imagination.

Chapter Nineteen

Ramsay and Hunter were outside six Cotter's Row at eight o'clock. Exactly. Ramsay wanted Claire to know that they were taking her seriously. She let them in as soon as they'd rung the bell and Hunter made a joke about her rushing them in before the neighbours could see she was entertaining two strange men. Ramsay wasn't sure how she'd take that. He'd gained the impression of someone prim, old before her time. But although she didn't smile she answered Hunter in the same lighthearted vein.

'They're used to strange men turning up on the pavement outside this house.'

Then she gave a giggle and Ramsay saw that Hunter had already managed to establish a slightly flirtatious rapport.

She was very comfortable in the house. She might have lived there.

'Tea?' she asked. 'Coffee? Kim wouldn't mind, I'm sure.'

'Tea, then,' Ramsay said. 'Thanks.'

She was still wearing her respectable working clothes: a long black cord skirt with opaque black tights underneath and flat shoes; a white cotton shirt done right up to the neck. The effect was severe, that of an Edwardian school mistress or a nun in mufti. Not the type Hunter would usually have gone for at all, but he had slipped into chat-up mode without any apparent effort.

She brought out the tea on a tray, with sugar in a bowl and milk in a jug. The tray had already been laid in the kitchen. Ramsay wondered if she had brought the milk jug from home. It didn't match the cups. It was clear she wanted to make a good impression.

'You not having one, then?' Hunter asked. As she set the tray on the low coffee table he saw she had dark, rather masculine eyebrows. Like two bloody caterpillars, he thought, crawling across her forehead. 'You shouldn't have bothered just for us.'

'That's all right.' She knew there was a can of Coke in the fridge. She would treat herself to that afterwards.

'How can you help us, Claire?' Ramsay asked. 'You *do* think you can help us?'

She hesitated and for a moment he thought he had jumped in too quickly. At last she spoke.

'Certain information has come into my possession.' It was clear she had practised that bit.

'And you think this information might help us find the murderer of your sister?'

'I'm not saying that. I just think you should know.'

'Of course.' He paused. 'You can trust us, you know, not to jump to conclusions.'

'I feel responsible, you see, for my children.' Then, fearing they might have misunderstood. 'I mean the children I look after.'

'You mind the Coulthard bairns, don't you?' Hunter said. 'Three kids under five. I bet they're a handful for a young lassie like you.'

'Young children are only a problem if you don't know what you're doing.' Her response was unexpectedly tart. 'I had two years' training, before they let me loose on kids. Most parents don't have anything, do they?'

The question was flashed at Hunter who seemed uncertain how to answer. He couldn't understand what he had done to upset her.

'What sort of parent was Kath?' Ramsay asked quietly.

'You're not here to talk about that.'

'There's no hurry is there? Gordon and I have all evening. We really would very much value your opinion. As a qualified childcare worker.'

At first Ramsay thought she would refuse to answer. She had her own agenda for the evening's interview. But finally she could not resist.

'If Kath had been my mother I'd have died.' It was said flatly, without any emotion.

'Why?'

'Well, I didn't have it easy but at least my dad wasn't *weird*.'

'What do you mean?'

She ignored Ramsay and turned to Hunter. '*You* can't be too old to remember. When you're a kid you don't want to be different. Not in any way. It's the most important thing. It was bad enough for me. No mother and money tight all the time. If I have kids I won't put them through that. They'll have the same as everyone else. Nike trainers and whatever brand of jeans they want, even if it means me doing without. Dad didn't understand, but at least I didn't have a mother like Kath to show me up. She got it *all* wrong.'

'In what way?' Ramsay asked. She answered him angrily as if he'd interrupted a private conversation between her and Hunter.

'In every way. She wore dreadful clothes. She went into school and made a fuss. She said Marilyn wasn't getting enough homework! She was the only mother to turn up to Sports Day so everyone stared.' She stopped in mid-flow and continued more quietly. 'The worst thing is that she didn't realize. She thought Marilyn appreciated the effort. Perhaps you can't understand. Perhaps it's not the same for boys.'

Ramsay thought it was very much the same for boys. There had been a lad from his village who had gone to the grammar school at the same time as him. His mother had suffered from a mental illness. She had probably been schizophrenic, though at the time she had only been labelled barmy. In primary school the boy had spoken about his mother having to go into St George's, the local psychiatric hospital. Later he learned not to mention it at all.

Once, coming home in the school bus down a narrow road leading to the pit village where Ramsay lived they had come across the woman. It was summer and she had picked a bunch of wild flowers from the hedgerow. She was dancing in the middle of the road, throwing the blooms one by one into the air. The driver had pushed on his horn and muttered darkly about maniacs who should be locked up. The boys whistled and yelled. Eventually the woman, still apparently unaware of the bus, moved to the side of the road.

The boy had said nothing. He had shown no concern for his

mother's safety. His only response has been to send a desperate, pleading glance towards Ramsay, begging him not to betray his secret. Then he had laughed at the woman with the rest of them.

Ramsay, who had never quite been one of the crowd, was tempted for a moment to jeer at the boy and give him away. He was still proud that he hadn't. Now he was trying to come to grips with Marilyn's feelings for her mother.

'I see that it can't have been easy for her,' he said to Claire. 'Kath must have seemed quite different from the other girls' mothers, but they always seemed very close to me. I mean, there were never any rows, were there? Disagreements, perhaps, but no real bust-ups.'

He thought that in all the hours Kath and her daughter had spent walking together they must have developed an understanding. And unlike the schizophrenic's son, Marilyn had cared more about her mother's safety than feeling foolish. She had knocked on the door of a stranger, panic-stricken, when she thought her mother was missing.

'Well,' Claire said. 'Kath was lucky. Marilyn's not the rebellious type.'

'And Bernard?' Hunter asked, allowing himself a little risque grin. 'Was he rebellious?'

'Bernard was devoted to Kath,' Claire said.

'They never had any arguments?'

'He's not the type to row. You'll have seen that for yourself.'

'Deep, then.'

'I've told you. He was devoted.'

They sat for a moment in silence. The sound of next door's television came through the wall.

'Tell me, Claire, what did you do on the Saturday evening after Kath disappeared?'

Ramsay knew he was playing a dangerous game. Claire was itching to pass on her information. Making her wait might make her lose her cool. She might give away more than she intended. Or she might clam up altogether just to spite him.

'We all went to look for her.'

'Together? Separately?'

'Marilyn asked up the street in case any of the neighbours had seen her then she waited in the house. We knew Kath didn't have any keys. Her coat was at home and they were in the pocket. Bernard and I went down the Headland as far as the railway line. By then it was too dark to see, so we went home to see if she'd turned up. Later Bernard went down to the phone box by the club to report her missing.'

'By himself?'

'That's right.'

'Was he away for very long?'

'Just long enough to phone the police.'

'Thank you, Claire. That's very helpful. I'm sorry about the questions, but I wanted to get them out of the way so we could concentrate on what you have to tell us. We're very grateful for your patience, Claire, and now we'd like you to tell us why you phoned us.'

He held his breath, hoping he'd done enough to appease her.

'I wanted to show you this,' Claire said at last. 'I wasn't sure at first but now I think you should see it.'

From her handbag she took a piece of paper. It looked as if it had once been crumpled into a ball, but an attempt had been made to flatten it.

'I suppose I should have showed you earlier. I hoped I wouldn't have to but it's been weeks now and you've still not caught the killer.'

She set the paper on the coffee table. Ramsay let it lie there and read aloud without touching it.

Mr Taverner.

It has come to my notice that you have developed an intimate relationship with someone whom any decent person would consider unsuitable. This is a severe and disgusting betrayal of trust. If this relationship does not cease immediately I will feel obliged to tell the relevant parties.

The letter was written in pencil. There were a number of crossings out. Some words had been scribbled out so fiercely that it was impossible to see what had been written underneath. It was not signed.

'Kath wrote it,' Claire said. 'It's her handwriting.'

'But she didn't send it?'

'Well, she wouldn't have sent this. She always wrote her letters in fountain pen. Not pencil. She said even biro was crude. This was a practice, wasn't it? That's how I came to find it.'

'Where did you find it?'

'There's a bucket by the grate in the back room. We put our waste paper in there, then we use it to light the fire. It was with the newspapers and Marilyn's rough homework.'

'When did you find it?'

'Early on the Saturday morning. The day she died.'

'So it was written on the Friday?'

'Or some time earlier that week. It was right at the bottom of the bucket.'

'Why did you keep it?' Ramsay's voice was bland. He didn't want Claire to think he was accusing her of prying.

'I meant to ask her about it later in the day. I didn't want her making a fool of herself. Or me.'

'You?' Hunter raised his eyebrows, gave that slightly lecherous smile.

'What?' She realized what he was implying, and blushed. 'Don't be daft! I wasn't carrying on with Mr Taverner. But it affected me, didn't it?'

'In what way?'

'It's obvious, isn't it? She was accusing Mr Taverner of having an affair with Mrs Coulthard. Of course that affects me. They'd want to know where she got her information for one thing. The last thing a nanny's supposed to do is tittle-tattle.'

'And did you? Tittle-tattle?'

'I didn't start the gossip,' she said defensively. 'Mr Taverner was there on the day. Kath went up to clean. And then Bernard made it worse.'

'Bernard? What would he know about what was going on at the Coastguard House?'

'He went up there one evening to talk about his magic act. Mrs Coulthard wanted an entertainer for her kiddies' party. You know about that. He found them together then.'

'And he came home and talked about it?'

She nodded.

'What about you? Did you talk about Mr Taverner and Mrs Coulthard to Bernard and Kathleen?'

'They asked what was going on. I said Mr Taverner was around a lot, especially when Mr Coulthard was working late. But I didn't accuse him of anything.'

'And that was enough for Mrs Howe to write a letter like this?' Hunter demanded.

'You didn't know her. Mr Taverner was a teacher, wasn't he? One of Marilyn's teachers. She couldn't have had her darling Marilyn corrupted. Besides, when she got suspicious I expect she kept an eye on the place, looked out for his car. I wouldn't have put it past her. It certainly wouldn't have occurred to her that it wasn't any of her business.' She looked at them, trying to make them understand. 'She was like that. She thought she had a right to interfere.'

'Do you know if she ever sent this letter?'

'Never got the chance to ask her, did I? I came home at lunchtime especially to have a word, to tell her to keep her nose out, but she wasn't there. And I never saw her again.'

'And what's your feeling?' Hunter leant forward so that their heads were almost touching over the coffee table. 'Were they having an affair? You'd know, if anyone would.'

'Well, I never caught them in bed together if that's what you mean.'

'We're not talking about evidence,' Ramsay said patiently. 'As Gordon says, it's your feeling we're interested in.'

'I'd say they were very close. The way they spoke to each other, laughed. As if they shared a joke which no one else could understand. A sort of. . . intimacy.'

'I see,' Ramsay said. 'And do you think Mr Taverner ever received this letter? Tell me, Claire. What's your feeling on that?'

'Put it this way. Since that party he's never been near the house. Not to my knowledge.'

Chapter Twenty

'What do you reckon, then?'

Hunter and Sal Wedderburn sat across the table from him waiting for an answer. Ramsay sipped from his pint. He suspected they had formed an uneasy alliance to push him into action. He had known they were plotting when they both asked, separately, if he fancied a pint after work. It was the day after their meeting with Claire Irvine.

Then Hunter had brought them to this place. An old man's pub sinking into bankruptcy, as the customers who came to huddle over their dominoes died off one by one and the landlady drank away the profits. Not a place Hunter would choose for a social evening but somewhere he knew they would not be overheard.

'Well?' Hunter demanded. Sally, who was brighter than he was, had let him be spokesperson. 'What do we do now? Confront Taverner with the letter?'

'Not until we understand more about it.'

'What else is there to know?'

'The identity of the person referred to.'

'Christ man, we know that already.'

'No,' Ramsay said calmly. 'We know who Claire Irvine *believes* it refers to, but we can't be certain, can we? Mrs Coulthard isn't mentioned by name.'

'So who else could it be?'

Before they could answer, the door swung open and a tiny old lady came in. She scuttled across the stone floor and hoisted herself on to a bar stool with the agility of a child.

'Bottle of Mackeson please, pet,' she said to the landlady who was obviously an old friend.

'Sorry, Kitty hinnie. You won't believe it but the brewery's on strike. They didn't deliver.' No one *did* believe it. The days of brewery strikes were over. The landlady opened the till with a clatter and took out a five-pound note. She waved it towards the youngest of the domino players.

'Nip over to the supermarket, Doug, and fetch Kitty a couple of bottles of Mackeson.'

The man went out and the room returned to silence. Hunter's question still hung in the air. He looked at each of them then answered it himself.

'What about Kim Houghton, the single mam at number six? You saw the inside of her house. She didn't furnish that on Income Support and the whole neighbourhood knows she takes strange men back there. She's classy. I bet she doesn't come cheap. Mark Taverner could be one of her regular callers. Kath Howe might have seen him go in. Like Claire said, she'd probably have recognized his car.'

'Hardly worth killing for, though, is it?' Sal Wedderburn objected.

'What do you mean?' Hunter turned on her. Any understanding between them had disappeared.

'Well, he's free, a widower. She's divorced. Who could object to them spending the night together? Even on a regular basis and even if he slipped her a few quid to buy her fancy curtains. Kath Howe might not have liked it but even if she'd informed the school, who would care?'

Ramsay thought that Taverner would care. He was a fastidious man, a churchgoer, head of religious education at the high school. News that he had paid a prostitute would be more than an embarrassment. The school with its pretensions to traditional values wouldn't like it much either.

'I'm sorry,' Sal Wedderburn was continuing, 'I just don't see it as sufficient motive for murder.'

'But if he was having it off with Emma Coulthard, and Mrs Howe threatened to make the affair public, you think it would?'

Hunter demanded. 'Be a good enough motive for murder, I mean. Just because the woman's married?'

'No,' Ramsay said. 'Not just because Emma's married. But because she's married to Taverner's friend, probably his only friend. If that *is* how it happened.'

Sally, twisting the glass in her fingers, hardly seemed to be listening.

'You don't think. . .' she said, then thought better of it and stopped.

'Yes?'

'Look, this is probably really dumb but it's just occurred to me. The letter doesn't actually say that the person Mark Taverner was having a relationship with was a woman, does it?'

They looked at her.

'Brian Coulthard?' Hunter asked. 'Na! He's not the type.' But she heard, with satisfaction, some uncertainty in his voice.

'Well,' she said. 'It was just an idea.'

'Yes.' Ramsay seemed lost in thought. 'It certainly is an idea.'

'What now, then?' Hunter demanded. 'Where do we go from here?'

'I could have a word with Emma if you like,' Sally offered eagerly, as if she were doing them a favour but kidding neither of them for a minute. Hunter glowered at her.

'I mean she might confide in a woman. If she's been having an affair with Taverner and suspects him of murder she'd be under a terrible strain.'

'And you think she'd talk to you?' Hunter said scathingly. 'She doesn't even know you.'

'Why not? She's hardly going to talk to her husband.'

'It would be a tricky interview,' Ramsay said. 'I don't want either of them to know about the letter. Not at this stage.'

'I don't mind having a go.'

'All right,' he said at last. 'All right.'

'What about me?' Hunter's voice was so loud that the old men looked up from their dominoes.

'Could you talk to Kim Houghton? See if she knows Taverner.'

'I'll speak to her tomorrow.'

'I'm still very keen to trace the driver of the Mazda.'

'I've spoken to every Mazda dealer in the country.'

'We'd best try another tack, then. Weren't we talking about doing a check on the pubs and clubs in Whitley? Do you think you can handle that?'

'Oh aye.' Hunter studied his beer. 'I think I can handle that.'

Sally got to the Coastguard House early. There'd been a heavy frost but now the Headland was in bright sunshine. She parked on the track and pushed open the heavy wooden gates into the garden. It was the first time she'd been inside the walls. She hadn't realized the house was quite so smart. There was new growth on the spindly trees along the border wall, snowdrops and aconites bloomed in the sheltered borders.

Very nice, she thought. Like something out of the home and garden magazine her mother read. She looked forward to see inside the house.

But when she knocked at the door Claire answered.

'Oh,' Claire said. 'It's you.'

'I was hoping to speak to Mrs Coulthard.'

'She's not here. She's gone for a walk, said she needed some fresh air.' Claire sniffed. In the background Sally heard a child's voice. 'She doesn't seem to be able to settle to anything these days.'

'Where did she go?'

'Just out on the Headland. She'll not have gone far. Owen goes to playgroup this morning.'

Sally saw Emma silhouetted against the sun almost at the edge of the cliff. She was carrying the baby in a sling against her stomach and had buttoned her long black coat around the child, so Sally thought for a moment that she was pregnant again, and felt a stab of disgust. Three kids were enough for anyone. She realized almost immediately that, it was impossible for Emma to be so pregnant so soon and when she got closer she saw the baby, its head lolling uncomfortably to one side, fast asleep.

'Mrs Coulthard. Could I have a word?' She didn't introduce herself. Everyone on the Headland knew the team of detectives working on the Kath Howe murder.

'I suppose so. I was just going to walk down to the jetty and back.'

She was still looking out to sea and Sally could study her face without appearing to be staring. She looked grey and tired. There were fine lines around her eyes and her hair could have done with a tint and a perm. Perhaps you're letting yourself go, Sally thought, now your fancy man doesn't visit any more.

'I'll come along with you, then,' she said. 'We can talk as we go.'

They set off over the grass.

'Well?' Emma asked. 'What do you want?' The ferocity of the question surprised Sally. She had planned the interview in advance. It had not been supposed to start like this.

'Actually, I wanted a word about Mr Taverner.'

Emma stopped in her tracks. 'Mark? Why?'

Sally hesitated. She could hardly say, 'Well, I just wondered if you were having an affair with your husband's best friend. Your nanny says you're very chummy. You'll feel a lot better if you tell me all about it.' She saw now that wouldn't work. The problem was that she had expected Emma Coulthard to be quite a different sort of woman. A housewife. Dull and downtrodden. Not sharp and assertive. She tried a different tack.

'Look,' she said. 'In a murder investigation all sorts of details come out. Things which have no possible relevance to the case. Things which people would much rather we didn't know about. In that situation we're always very discreet.'

As Emma looked at her, Sally remembered Ramsay saying that she once held a very high-powered job in industry.

'What exactly are you asking?' Emma demanded.

'If there's anything you'd like to tell me about your relationship with Mr Taverner? Any information which you think you should pass on?'

'I'm sorry,' Emma said. 'I really don't have any idea what you're talking about. Of course I'd help if I could. It's in our interest to have the murderer caught. We live here, after all.' She made a show of looking at her watch. 'I'm afraid I won't have time to finish that walk. I'll have to go straight back. My son starts playgroup at ten and I've promised to give someone a lift. Don't hesitate to get in touch if there's anything I can do to help.'

She swept away down the hill.

Sally Wedderburn was left standing on the cliff. She thought she must look like bloody Meryl Streep in *The French Lieutenant's Woman*, then wondered how she was going to admit to Stephen Ramsay – and to Gordon Hunter – that she'd cocked up.

Chapter Twenty-One

It was Kim Houghton's turn to help at playgroup. There was a rota and once a term you had to do your bit. Some of the mothers moaned about it but Kim didn't mind. The woman who ran the group wasn't much older than her and they always had a laugh.

Besides, she liked kids. In their place. She couldn't have Kirsty messing about with sand and paint at home – there was the carpet to consider – but in the old church hall with its smell of mildew and decay that seemed to cling to the children even after they came home, she could be as mucky as she liked. Kim always made sure Kirsty was dressed in her oldest clothes on playgroup day.

At nine o'clock the phone rang. It was Emma Coulthard playing lady of the manor. She said she was just going for a walk but she'd be back for playgroup if Kim wanted a lift.

'Great,' Kim said. 'But you don't mind going a bit early, do you? I'm on duty.'

She could tell that Emma wasn't too pleased about that, but she thought, sod it.

If Emma hadn't phoned she'd have got a taxi. She couldn't be faffing about on the bus and she was flush at the minute. She was even thinking of putting aside some money towards a holiday with the girls. They were talking about Corfu. She'd always fancied going there. She'd have to sort out something for Kirsty though. She loved Kirsty to bits, wouldn't be without her, but she couldn't have her in Corfu with the girls. It had crossed her mind that Claire might take her for a week. It wasn't as if she was any trouble, and you could tell that Claire would want a child of her own one day the way she fussed over that baby at the Coastguard

House. It would be good practice. Being a nanny was one thing. Looking after a bairn for twenty-four hours a day was quite another.

In the car Kim chatted to Emma about holidays but she hardly seemed to be listening.

Toffee-nosed cow, Kim thought.

The church hall was a barn-like stone building with high arched windows and a stage at one end. The heavy equipment was kept under the stage and it was still being set up when they arrived. Emma stayed to help because the playleader said she didn't want any children left until she could supervise them properly. She stopped in the middle of fixing the heavy wooden slide on to the climbing frame to explain.

'Someone tried to snatch a laddie from a nursery in Otterbridge last week. The police think it was the same person who abducted that kid a month ago. You know, he was at a birthday in McDonald's and he just disappeared. They found him wandering along the seafront at Whitley hours later. We've all been asked to take special care.'

Emma felt the room spin and shut her eyes tight. She couldn't imagine the horror of what the mother had gone through, and still she felt faint.

When she looked again the playleader, red faced and muscular, was staggering across the room with a tray of sand. Emma followed her.

'I could stay and help all morning if you like.' She didn't want to lose sight of either of the boys.

'Don't be daft!' The woman was bringing up three on her own and didn't have much patience for overanxious mums. 'We'll shut the door when everyone's here and you know we never let them go until someone we recognize is here to collect them.'

The room was already starting to get noisy. Boys on trikes played bumper cars, taking advantage of the helpers' lack of attention. Kirsty had found the dressing-up box and click-clacked over the wooden floor in oversized high-heeled shoes. Emma's head throbbed. She wanted to get back to the Coastguard House and Helen.

'All right,' she said. 'If you're sure.'

Still she hung on until the children were sitting in a circle on the carpet and they'd called the register. On her way out she made certain the door was firmly closed behind her.

It was near the end of the session when all the toys had been put away and they were singing 'A Princess Lived in a Big High Tower' that a girl saw the face at the window. The girl was Louise Armstrong who'd flounced off in a sulk because she hadn't been chosen as the princess. They'd told her she didn't have to play if she didn't want to. They'd known she'd come round in the end.

When she screamed the playleader muttered unprofessionally under her breath about spoilt brats. The Armstrongs lived in one of the posh new houses on the edge of the village. She rounded on the girl.

'What's the matter now, Louise?'

Owen Coulthard, the handsome prince, stopped galloping round the circle, and looked.

'There's a man at the window,' Louise said. 'A monster. Or a vampire.'

Louise had older brothers and sisters and, despite her snobby parents, probably watched videos which weren't good for her.

'Don't be silly, Louise. No one can get up there. It's too high.'

Then the head appeared back at the grimy window. They all stared. The man gestured in a way which was vaguely menacing.

'Carry on with the game,' the playleader said grimly. Neither the children nor the adults took any notice. She strode to the door, threw it open and yelled, 'What the hell do you think you're doing?'

He had been forced to climb on to an upturned bin to get to the window. He wobbled for a moment, recovered his poise and jumped down.

'I tried knocking on the door,' he said accusingly. 'No one heard.'

'We wouldn't. We were busy. *If* you knocked we probably wouldn't have heard.'

'I'm looking for Kim Houghton.'

'Now there's a surprise.' She spoke so quietly that only he could hear. More loudly she said, 'She's busy.'

He began to lose his temper. 'So am I, lady. My name's Hunter. I'm a detective. Mrs Houghton will tell you.'

Only then did Kim, laughing so much that she was red in the face and tears were running down her cheeks, come forward to put him out of his misery.

'I suppose you'd better come in,' the playleader said. 'We're nearly finished.'

So then he had to stand inside the hall until the games were over. The children pointed and sniggered at him, encouraged in their taunts by Kim Houghton who called out to him, 'We're doing. "The Farmer's in his Den" now, Sergeant. Do you fancy being the farmer? Or would you rather be the bone?'

She showed no inclination to drop out of her place in the circle to talk to him.

At last the games were over and the parents were let in to collect their children. Emma Coulthard must have recognized him but she gave no sign. Kim called over to her. 'I don't need a lift home thanks, Mrs Coulthard. I've made other arrangements.' Then she gave him a wink so obvious that he knew she'd only done it to embarrass him.

'I've a few more questions,' he said, once the hall was quiet.

'There,' she said, 'and I thought you'd come to ask me out for lunch.'

'We could talk over lunch if you want to.' If Ramsay interviewed witnesses on expenses, he didn't see why he shouldn't, too.

'Na!' she said. 'Look at me. I'm hardly dressed for it. Anyway, I've got Kirsty.'

'Oh.' He felt put out. It wasn't often he was turned down.

'I don't suppose you fancy fish and chips?' she said. 'A walk on the beach?'

'Why not?' Though he'd never been one much for the great outdoors, and the little house in Cotter's Row would have been much more cosy. He hoped that salt water wouldn't ruin his shoes.

They bought fish and chips in Heppleburn and ate them walking along the long sweep of sand which ran north from the Headland. Kirsty ran ahead, jumping from sand hills, poking with a stick among the debris washed up by the tide. She didn't seem to be a child who needed much attention.

Kim ate hungrily. When she finished, she licked the grease from her fingers and sent Kirsty off with the paper to find a bin.

'More questions, you said.'

'Aye.'

'You've still not found the bloke who was with me that night?'

'He's not come forward.'

'Well, I've told you all I can remember. There's nothing more I can do.' She spoke crossly as if she expected contradiction and walked ahead of him.

The beach was almost empty. In the distance an old man was throwing a piece of driftwood for his dog. It was very still, very clear and the power station at the north of the bay seemed close enough to touch. Hunter felt exposed and silly. Apart from his holidays in the sun he hadn't been near a beach since he was a kid. He hurried after her.

'I need to ask about other friends, other blokes you've taken back to the house.'

'What do you mean?'

'Well, you're not telling me he was the first.'

She stopped suddenly. Hunter stopped too and felt the soft sand squelch under his expensive leather soles. She was furious.

'What are you calling me, then? You're as bad as the old grannies in the Row.'

'No,' he said, panicking slightly. 'No You don't understand! What I'm saying is you're an attractive woman. I can't believe the chap in the red car was the first. . .' He paused, tried to find the right word, '. . . admirer you've had since you were divorced.'

She was slightly mollified.

'No, well. People jump to conclusions. Just because I'm friendly, like.'

'I'm sorry. I didn't mean to offend you.'

It occurred to him that he'd learnt a few things through working with Stephen Ramsay, though he'd never let on. Finesse. That was the word. In the past he'd have gone at this witness like a bull at a gate, and got nowhere. Now he'd have her eating out of his hand.

They walked for a few minutes in a companionable silence.

'The thing is,' he said at last, 'you're the only one on the Headland who seems to have anything like a social life. Except the Coulthards, of course, and we're speaking to them too. Whoever killed Mrs Howe knew the place. They knew where it was safe to dump the body, for example. You do see that we have to ask about any visitors you might have had. It's nothing personal.'

'Yeah,' she said. 'I can see that.'

'So if you could give us a list of any people who came to your house. Men or women. Say in the month before Mrs Howe was murdered.'

She looked worried again.

'You wouldn't hassle them, would you? Call at their homes?'

The old Hunter would have asked if she was worried that would be bad for business, but tactfully he kept quiet.

'They're friends, you know,' she said. 'I wouldn't want them to get into any bother.'

'We'll be discreet. I guarantee it. I'll see to it myself.'

'Oh aye,' she said, laughing. 'Discretion's your middle name. I can tell that. Coming to the playgroup and scaring us all out of our wits.'

All the same she sat with him in the shelter of a sand dune while he took out his notebook and she reeled off about a dozen names. She had details of some. She could give their occupations, their addresses. She even knew the names of their children. She didn't seem to resent their other, respectable lives. For others, like the man in the Mazda, she just had first names and brief descriptions.

Mark Taverner's name was not on the list.

'And this is all?' Hunter asked. She had trotted out the names so glibly that he did not believe it was exhaustive.

'Yes!' She was close to being offended again.

'You don't know a chap called Mark? Mark Taverner.'

'Never heard of him.'

'He's a teacher at the high school.'

'Well there you are, then. I never go out with teachers. I can't stand bossy men.'

'Are you doing anything tonight?' he asked casually. If he was likely to bump into her in Whitley he wanted some warning, though if she were there, perhaps she'd be able to point out this Paul to him.

'Na,' she said. 'A quiet night in.'

She stood up and called in Kirsty. Hunter took them home, dropping them at the level crossing so the old ladies in Cotter's Row would have nothing to talk about. For the rest of the day he found dribbles of sand in his clothing: in his trouser turn-ups, in his jacket pockets. Even in the seams of his underpants when he went for a piss.

Chapter Twenty-Two

It reminded Gordon Hunter of being a boy again. Friday night and out on the prowl in Whitley. In those days, though, he'd have had a couple of mates with him for moral support and to take a turn in the fight at the bar.

When it got dark the temperature plummeted. The cars parked in the streets leading away from the seafront glistened with frost and as he breathed in, the cold stung his throat and his nostrils. There was a thin, sharp moon, upended like a smile.

The streets were heaving with people dressed for the dance floor. The lasses wore skimpy little-girl frocks in pastel colours and when they were caught in car headlights you could see their lacy panties and their underwired bras. Though they shivered and hugged themselves that seemed to be more through excitement than a response to the arctic conditions. When he'd been young he'd never felt the cold either. He'd never taken a jacket to Whitley for fear it would get pinched or that he'd get so pissed he'd put it down and forget it. Or one of his mates would throw up all over it in the taxi home.

He walked along the seafront trying to get a feel for the place again. It had been a while since he'd been there and the pubs and clubs seemed to change hands almost monthly. Then their characters altered with the management. Kim Houghton had said she'd met Paul in the Manhattan Skyline. In his youth that had been a place for under-age drinkers, a bar where a thirteen-year-old girl with enough make up and bravado could get a vodka and tonic if the police weren't in and she had an older lad with her. Now it obviously catered for an older market.

It stood on a corner. Once the façade had been painted pink but the salt wind had blasted most of the colour away. A barrel-chested bouncer in a gleaming white shirt, only just held together by straining buttons stood outside the door and a sign said: OVER 21S ONLY. He didn't have to turn anyone away. The high school kids walked straight past. They wouldn't have been seen dead in there. When Hunter pushed through the swing door he could see why.

The music was loud but not ear-shattering and Abba's greatest hits seemed to be on a continual loop. The Manhattan's decor must have been devised originally to go with the name. There were high, tubular steel stools by the bar and a neon cocktail glass, tipped on one side, flashed on one wall. The effect had been spoilt by an attempt to turn the rest of the room into a Mediterranean taverna. A fishing net hung from the ceiling and there was a scattering of rustic tables and chairs. Most of the space was left clear to fit in as many drinkers as possible.

Hunter did not notice the clash in design styles. He slouched at the bar and asked for a bottle of Holsten, then swivelled to take in the other customers, who were lit intermittently by the flashing cocktail glass and strobe lights over the dance floor.

There were a few couples in early middle age trying to recapture their youth and some single men intent on serious drinking standing beside him at the bar. None of them fitted the description of the Mazda driver. The rest of the customers were women. One large party had pulled most of the chairs into a tight circle. An elderly woman seemed to be in charge of bags and coats. The others – aged from sixteen to sixty – got up from time to time to dance. For some this seemed a new experience. They were already very drunk. A works do, Hunter decided. They'd been at the Lambrusco surreptitiously all afternoon, into the bogs to change, then out on the town. Noticing that a tall, dark woman was the butt of all the jokes, he thought it was probably a hen party. When she was too paralytic to stand they'd wrap her in toilet paper and push her up the street in a pram.

He didn't see the hen party as regulars. When Abba reached the end of 'Super Trooper' again, and the dancers collapsed giggling, he wandered across the dance floor and pulled up a chair on the outside of the circle. They giggled some more, but pretended not to see him.

'Ladies,' he said, 'I wonder if you can help me.'

They couldn't help him though they would have liked to. They worked in Otterbridge Town Hall collecting the council tax. They'd hired a mini bus to bring them to Whitley so they could give Maggie a good party before she lost her freedom. It was the first time most of them had been out socially for ages apart from the pictures or the pub. They did have an office trip out just before Christmas but that was always to Newcastle, for a Chinese banquet in Stowell Street. The music started again and Maggie was pulled to her feet. Hunter returned to the bar.

There were three bar staff, all men. They wore white shirts, bow ties and matching waistcoats. They were busy. Not rushed off their feet, that would come later, but too busy to stop work while they talked.

Hunter identified himself. They weren't impressed.

'I'm looking for a chap who was in here Friday night, three weeks ago.' Hunter leant across the bar and shouted so they could all hear him.

'What's he supposed to have done, like?'

'Nothing. But he might be a witness to that murder on the Headland.'

That got their attention.

'He says his name's Paul. He could be a regular. Hanging out on his own looking for company.'

'Aye well. There are plenty of those. But late on a Friday night I could serve my sister and not notice. They shout the order, you pull the pint, you take their money. You look at their hands not their faces.'

'He left the place with Kim Houghton. Do you know her?'

'Kim the blonde?'

Hunter nodded. 'You looked at *her* face then?'

The barman allowed himself a smile. 'We all need a treat once in a while, don't we?'

'Are any of her friends in?'

The man scanned the faces lit by the coloured lights to show willing but he knew they wouldn't be there.

'Na,' he said. 'If they do come in it won't be until later. They have a few drinks somewhere cheaper before they come here.'

'Give me a shout, then, if you see them.'

He bought another bottle of lager and settled on his bar stool to survey the dance floor. Of the hen party only the bride-to-be was worth watching. She had straight black hair and white skin made smooth by make-up. When the light caught her full on the face she had the hint of a moustache but from the back you couldn't fault her.

The two women turned up at eleven, just as Hunter had decided he'd had enough. The music had turned smoochy. Burt Bacharach instead of Abba. The hen party had moved on and the place was filling up with couples. If you pulled a woman in one of the noisier pubs you brought her here to impress her and loosen her up. He couldn't make up his mind whether he should find a club more to his taste to continue his search, or if he should go home. He was hungry and if his mother was still up she'd fix him something – bacon and eggs, a plate of chips. He still lived in the council house where he'd been brought up. He'd never felt the need to move out. It wasn't as if she cramped his style. If he had a lass staying Mam would just bring up two cups of tea to his room in the morning.

The women stood by the bar, sharing a joke with one of the barmen. They might have been a bit tipsy – their faces were flushed and they were enjoying themselves – but they were quite in control. Hunter watched them with appreciation. The one with the perm must be at least as old as him, but they were both fit. Weekly aerobics and an occasional workout at the gym would have seen to that. He didn't see them as joggers. That wouldn't be sociable enough for them. They'd want a chat and a laugh to see them through the pain barrier.

The barman saw him looking and gave him a thumb's up sign. Hunter moved in.

'Can I buy you a drink, girls?'

'We're all right thanks.'

They turned back to their conversation. Both wore wedding rings.

'You're friends of Kim's, aren't you?'

'So?' They were immediately suspicious.

'I just wanted a chat.'

The woman with the perm put an elbow on the bar and leant towards him.

'Why don't you just piss off?'

'No,' he said. 'It's not what you think. My name's Gordon Hunter. I'm a detective with Northumbria Police.' The music swelled: 'Do You Know the Way to San José'. He wasn't even sure they'd heard him. 'Look,' he shouted. 'I don't suppose you fancy a curry?'

They sat in the Taj Mahal, drinking lager. Hunter ordered a vindaloo. They picked at chicken tikka masalas. The blonde with the perm was called Shirley, the younger one was Christine. Their husbands were in business together. Fitted kitchens. That was how they'd met Ray and Kim. Ray had asked them to build a kitchen in a house he was doing up.

Shirley was apologetic. 'Sorry about earlier. Blokes sometimes get the wrong idea, especially when they've seen us with Kim. She's single, isn't she? It's different for her. We're just out for a bit of fun. Friday nights we take it in turns. One week the lads go out for a few beers and a meal. The next they stay in to sit with the kids and it's our turn.' She smiled. 'We're happily married women.'

'Not like Kim.'

'Well, let's put it this way. You'd never have got Kim's Ray to stay in and mind his little girl.'

'Were you in the Manhattan with Kim three weeks ago?'

They thought about it.

'No,' Christine said. 'That would have been the boys' night out.'

'But if you were regulars in the Manhattan you might have met the man we're trying to trace. His first name's Paul. He's in his early thirties, dark, drives a red Mazda.'

They looked at each other. They'd taken to Hunter and they wanted to help.

'There was that guy who was in a while ago, talking about the funeral.' Christine looked to her friend for confirmation. 'Wasn't he called Paul?'

'I believe he was. And Kim certainly took a shine to him.'

'What funeral?' Hunter asked.

'I don't know any details. He was plastered. Said he'd been to a funeral that day. Someone special.'

'When was this?'

'A while ago.' She paused. 'It must have been September. It was the week after we'd come back from Tenerife and we got a special deal because the schools had gone back.'

'And you say Kim was with you then?'

'That's right. She didn't go off with him though. He could hardly stand. She wouldn't have wanted anyone in the house who might be sick on the carpet.'

'Have you met him in the Manhattan since?'

'I have. Once. He seemed really canny. Friendly, you know, asking all about our families, how old the kids were. I had the impression he had some of his own. Kim might have been there that time too.'

'Did he tell you his second name? Give any clue about where he lives or works?'

The women shook their heads. They said he hadn't talked much about himself, hadn't had the chance probably with the three of them carrying on. No one could get a word in when they got together.

Chapter Twenty-Three

While Hunter was preparing for a night in Whitley, Claire Irvine was in Cotter's Row, wondering about driving lessons. It was too late for Bernard to take the plunge. She could see that. He'd never get to grips with driving a car. But someone in the family should be mobile, and she didn't mind having a go. She certainly didn't plan to work for the Coulthards for ever and even if she wanted to, that wouldn't be possible. Soon Owen would start school and Emma might think she could manage the two youngest by herself. Then Claire would be looking for work. Most women wanted a woman who could drive – some even provided a car for running the kiddies around. And if ever she had a child herself it would be nice to be independent.

She thought too that if she could drive Bernard might be able to make more of his magic shows. He hated working in that office. These days it was all market testing and saving money. Although he'd never said, she had the feeling that everyone there made fun of him. He never mentioned any friends.

'If you wanted to go out for a pint after work, you know I wouldn't mind,' she'd said recently.

Kath would never have thought of it, but Dad had gone to the pub with his mates every Friday. They'd played darts, made a night of it.

Bernie had shaken his head. He said he thought some of the chaps went out together but he wouldn't feel right about asking to go along too.

'Besides,' he'd said. 'I like getting home now. It's so cosy.'

Then she'd felt a glow of pleasure and knew she'd done the right thing.

She didn't mention the driving lessons to Bernard. It wouldn't be tactful to make too many changes too soon. People would talk. She'd seen Sally Wedderburn staring at the television the last time she'd come to visit. As if renting a telly was some sort of crime.

She'd forgotten how soothing a night in front of the set could be. They all enjoyed it, though Marilyn wasn't much interested in the programmes themselves. She still disappeared up to her bedroom with her books most nights. She did watch *Top of the Pops* but Claire thought that was just so she could talk about the groups with the other girls at school.

In the evenings Claire and Bernard had developed a routine. She would clear up the meal and wash the dishes, then the two of them would settle in front of the television. At nine o'clock he would make cocoa. They'd call Marilyn down from her room and drink it together. It was, as he'd said, very cosy.

Without a car Bernard had to rely on taxis to get him to the church halls and Scout huts, where he performed for the children. He took bookings for his shows at work and explained over the telephone that he would have to charge travelling expenses on top of his modest fee. Sometimes that put people off. Not people who'd actually seen him perform, though. They thought he was worth every penny.

She could see he was nervous about the Sunday school anniversary party. It was the first show he'd done since Kath's death. He was worried he'd find it hard to concentrate sufficiently to make the tricks work. In magic, concentration was everything.

He'd asked Marilyn if she'd like to go with him, be his assistant.

'We could find you a costume,' he'd said enthusiastically. He would have liked her standing beside him in a sequinned leotard and shimmering tights.

But she'd refused absolutely. She'd told him that she'd arranged to meet a friend in Otterbridge. This was unheard of and Claire thought it was probably an excuse. Perhaps Marilyn was worried that some of the girls would find out. It probably wasn't considered cool to be a magician's assistant.

Claire would have gone with him for support, but she'd already agreed to work for the Coulthards. Emma and Brian had planned a Saturday afternoon out on their own. Another unheard-of occasion.

In the event Bernard needn't have worried about his performance. It was as confident and fluid as ever. Indeed, in the beginning everything seemed to work like clockwork. The taxi turned up on time. He was met outside the church by a pleasant, motherly woman, in a flowery print dress.

'Mr Howe,' she said. 'How kind of you to come.' He could tell she meant it.

The hall had been built very recently. It had a polished-wood floor, a real stage and spotlights. The helpers had set aside a little room for him to get ready for his act. They brought a pot of tea and a plate of home-made cakes. In the hall he heard them shouting to the children to settle down. They were *very* lucky that Uncle Bernie had agreed to visit them. It all made him feel important.

When he stood up to perform there was immediate silence. The faces turned towards him were attentive, scrubbed clean. The girls wore frilly frocks and patent-leather sandals. He would have liked to dress Marilyn in prettier things when she was little but Kath had never cared much what her daughter looked like. The admiration of the children made him feel even better than the fussing women. He knew he would do well.

He chose a boy to help him, picked him out from the front row.

'And what's your name?'

'Alex.' He wasn't the least bit shy.

'And how old are you, Alex?'

'I'm six.'

He wore red braces and a blue tie, a miniature merchant banker. His hair was still damp where his mother had slicked it into place. Throughout the show Alex watched every move Bernard made and gasped as each trick was performed. The audience followed his example and gasped and laughed in all the right places. The adults at the back clapped and shouted compliments.

This time the climax of the performance was not the creation of a birthday cake. Bernard had performed that many times before and was bored by it. Instead he reached into his bowler hat and threw handful after handful of sweets into the audience and then scattered, with a sweep of his arm, a cloud of silver stars which floated down on to the upturned faces like snowflakes.

He gave a deep bow and the room erupted into cheers.

He asked Alex if he'd like to help him pack his magic bag.

'Can I?'

'Of course.'

The two were left on the stage, forgotten, while the children chased round the room after the sweets he'd thrown. The helpers came out of the cloakroom with armfuls of coats.

'I'm going to wait outside for my taxi,' Bernard said. The boy was standing very close to him and he could tell now that the hair was slicked back not with water but a glutinous cream which had a strong and distinctive smell.

'You can come with me if you like.'

Bernard had already been paid. He supposed he should say goodbye to the women but they seemed busy and Alex was pulling him by the hand through a side door.

'Here,' Bernard said. 'Round the back. This is where it'll be.'

There was a short, tree-lined path, which led to the street. It was quite dark. The parents collecting their children must be using another entrance. The boy still held his hand. They were close enough to the building to hear laughter, shouting mothers, but here they were alone. It was starting to get cold again. The boy shivered.

Suddenly a door was flung open and from the oblong of light a tiny woman in a short skirt, leather jacket and high-heeled shoes hurtled towards them. She was followed at a more measured pace by the helper in the floral dress.

The stranger grabbed Alex by the arm and pulled him away from Bernard. For a moment she stood with her arms wrapped around the boy. Her chin was bent towards the child's hair and it occurred to Bernard that at such close quarters the scent of the gel would be overpowering and very unpleasant. She raised her head and said to Bernard. 'What the hell do you think you were doing?'

It was a southern voice, deeper than he had expected, furious. 'I'm sorry?'

'Don't play the innocent with me. If we hadn't come out then you'd have had him away.'

'No,' Bernard said. 'Really. No.'

'You drag him into the dark without telling anyone. . .' She turned away from him in disgust and started on the Sunday school teacher. 'You're supposed to be looking after them. Not letting them wander off with any pervert who wants to abduct them. I should call the police.'

In the end the woman in the flowery dress who was, it seemed, the minister's wife, calmed the situation. She explained who Bernard was and they all agreed to put the incident down to a misunderstanding. The taxi pulled up and Bernard was allowed to climb into it. He tried to say goodbye to Alex but the boy wouldn't look at him. Bernard felt cheated. The day had been so promising and now it was spoiled.

Alex's mother had a short fuse and soon forgot to be angry. When she got the boy home and he told her again what had happened she saw that no harm had been done. She even, felt a bit sorry for the bastard for laying into him. The look on his face!

The minister's wife was not able to treat the event so lightly. She thought about it all evening and then, without discussing it with her husband, who tended to think the best of everyone, she phoned the police station.

'It's probably nothing,' she said. 'If it weren't for all those other incidents I wouldn't bother mentioning it.'

Before her marriage she had worked as a psychiatric social worker. She had met sad adults still troubled by unpleasantness in childhood.

To her discomfort the woman on the other end of the line took her seriously and said an officer would be sent that night to take a statement. Then the following day two detectives, a man and a woman, turned up at the manse and she had to explain again, or at least try to, what it was about Bernard Howe which had made her concerned.

'It wasn't anything he actually *did*,' she told Ramsay and Sal Wedderburn. 'I mean he was very nice. Charming, in fact.'

The house, like the church hall, was new and they sat in a bare living room which still smelled of paint, looking out over an untidy garden. As it was Sunday the minister was busy. She paused. Ramsay looked at Sally, warning her not to speak. In the garden a noisy blackbird was gathering dry grass for a nest. The woman continued.

'We have a number of elderly spinsters who run the Sunday school, and they fussed over him. They had heard, of course, that his wife had died in tragic circumstances. He played up to them. I thought at first he was just being kind. Most men are embarrassed by the attention.'

She paused again. 'I'm not explaining this very well. It wasn't a real, adult conversation. He was behaving like a spoilt eight-year-old. As if all that fussing was due to him. It wasn't normal.'

'I see,' Ramsay said. 'Did he have any difficulty communicating with the children?'

'None at all. They loved him. The little boy who went outside with him wasn't frightened and I'm sure nothing untoward happened.'

'Yet you felt sufficiently concerned, that you contacted us.'

'Yes. There was something about the pair of them, standing there in the shadow hand in hand... Mr Howe didn't seem to realize he was in a position of trust. When we went outside – the mother, of course, was frantic – it was as if he felt no more responsible for the incident than the boy. It was a sort of arrogance. He was the only person who mattered. We were inconsiderate fools to cause a scene.'

Ramsay leant forward.

'Are you saying you think he would be capable of abducting a child?'

She looked back at him, troubled.

'I suppose I am. He'd do it thoughtlessly. Probably not meaning to cause any harm. Just for the company. Not realizing what people might think. The spoilt child again.'

Chapter Twenty-Four

'I knew he was a queer bastard.'

The weather was still cold in the evenings and Hunter stood with his backside against the radiator. It was the Sunday night after the children's party at the church hall. The station was quiet. The three of them were crammed into Ramsay's office.

'So what do we do now?'

'Nothing,' Ramsay said.

'What do you mean?'

'Think about it.'

'What's there to think about? It's obvious, isn't it? Uncle Bernie has a taste for little boys and his wife finds out. So he stabs her. What better motive can there be?'

'Think about it,' Ramsay said again. 'Think about the other abductions. What were the common features?'

'The kids were given sweets. He sat them on his knee and cuddled them but he didn't actually interfere with them. That fits, doesn't it? Isn't that what the vicar's wife said? That Bernie wouldn't have the bottle to *do* anything.'

'You'd admire him more if he had?' Sally Wedderburn spat at him.

'Oh, for Christ's sake, that's not what I said.' He turned his eyes to the ceiling. 'You can't speak in this place without someone twisting your words.'

Moody cow, he thought. Really it took the patience of a saint to work with Sal Wedderburn. They should pay a special allowance for it.

'What was the other common feature?' Ramsay asked.

Hunter looked blank, Sally triumphant.

'He was a driver,' she said. 'Different cars. One red saloon, one blue estate. But each time he drove the kids around and then he dumped them by the side of the road. Bernard Howe doesn't drive.'

'Just because he doesn't usually drive doesn't mean that he *can't.*' Hunter's voice was superior but they could tell he was clutching at straws. 'And using different cars. That would be significant. It might mean that he doesn't own a vehicle but that he has to nick or borrow one specially.'

'I can't quite see Bernard Howe as a car thief,' Ramsay said. 'Can you?'

'So it's a coincidence? Is that what you're saying? The fact that he likes little boys.'

Sally Wedderburn turned on him again.

'Get real. How many calls do you think we've had about the abductions? Hundreds. Probably running by now into thousands. All from people accusing men of liking little boys. It might be a neighbour who watches their kids playing in the street. Or an overfamiliar lollipop man. Or a football referee who puts his hand on a lad's shoulder before sending him off. We've had the lot. At a time like this folk overreact. You can't blame them. Anyone who has regular contact with kids is going to be a target. As you say, it's a coincidence.'

'All the same,' Ramsay said, 'I don't think we can dismiss the allegation altogether.' Working with Hunter and Wedderburn he felt not so much a superior officer as a mediator trying to keep both parties sweet, to find some point of contact. 'Besides anything else it tells us more about Bernard, doesn't it? Informs the picture we already have, at least, of a lonely man with no adult friends, who's chosen a hobby which brings him into contact with youngsters.'

'Like I said,' Hunter interrupted. 'A queer bastard.'

'Perhaps. Anyway I think we should check. Discreetly. If the press gets wind of the fact that Bernard could be involved in the abductions they'll have a field day. There'll be no chance of operating effectively with them baying for his blood. Gordon, find out if he's ever had a licence or owned a car. Sal, have you got the times and the dates the kids were snatched?'

Not so much a mediator, he thought, dishing out the tasks equally so there'd be no cause for complaint. More a bloody nursery nurse.

Sally returned almost immediately with the information. An apparently random list of four dates and times.

'Look at this.' Ramsay was speaking to himself. 'The second was in Newcastle. The second week of January. A Thursday at five thirty. A child was left outside the post office in Eldon Square while his mum dashed in before it closed. Bernard Howe always visits his mother on Thursday. He hasn't missed one, apparently, even since Kath died. He goes straight from work then cycles back to arrive home at about ten. If she can confirm that he's turned up every Thursday since Christmas we can almost certainly dismiss him as a possible abductor. If he wasn't at her house that day.' He looked up at Sally, smiled. 'Well, that will probably mean that Gordon's right and Uncle Bernie has something to hide.'

'Do you want me to check with the mother?'

'No. I'd like to do that. Tomorrow you go and check with the woman who runs the Shining Stars Nursery. She saw someone hanging around on the street the day the kid went missing from there. See if the description matches Bernard.'

'Right.'

On her way out she bumped into Hunter, who was looking despondent. She gave him a wide and patronizing grin.

'No joy, then,' Ramsay said, as Hunter took up his position next to the radiator again.

'Na. Bernard Howe's never had a licence, not even a provisional one and he's never owned a car.'

'We can't rule him out altogether. You know as well as I do that there are ways round the system.'

'Not very likely though, is it?' Hunter knew his boss was just being kind.

'How did you get on in Whitley on Friday night?'

Hunter shrugged. 'It's not been my week.'

'No one had ever met this chap Paul?'

'Oh aye, they'd met him, but they couldn't tell me anything about him. Nothing useful at least. He's still the mystery man. The bar staff at the Manhattan will give me a ring if they think they see him but I don't hold out much hope.'

'You said you didn't get anything useful. Did you get anything at all?'

'Just the fact that he once went to a funeral,' Hunter said flippantly.

'What do you mean?'

'There were two women, friends of Kim's, who think they remember him. The first time they met he was pissed out of his skull. Upset, apparently, because he'd been to a funeral.'

'When was that?'

'Last September. Is it important?'

'Probably not.' But Sheena Taverner was buried in September. Ramsay wondered if that were a coincidence too.

When he left the police station Ramsay drove to the crumbling Edwardian house where Prue lived with her daughter. Prue wasn't expecting him. When she opened the door she was in a striped towelling dressing gown. In the kitchen there was a half-drunk bottle of wine on the table and a pile of plates in the sink.

'Mattie came to supper,' she said. 'I meant to clear up, then I started reading this play. Have you eaten?'

'Not much.' A dubious canteen pie.

'There's some salad. Nice cheese.'

She was distracted. He could tell she was still thinking about the play.

'That'll be great.' He paused. 'I'm sorry to disturb you.'

She shut the book she'd been reading and gave him her full attention.

'Don't be daft. I mean I was half hoping you'd turn up. But I knew you were busy. You will stay?'

He hadn't intended to. 'Of course.'

She poured him some wine, fetched a bowl of leftover salad and a lump of Stilton from the fridge.

'You went to Sheena Taverner's funeral, didn't you?' he asked.

'So that's why you're here!' It was said with resignation, even humour, not resentment. She was determined not to make demands on him. It helped that she was an actress.

'No.' But his acting skills were non-existent.

'What do you want to know?'

'Did you recognize most of the mourners?'

'Hardly any of them. The ones I'd come across through Northern Arts. Other writers who'd done stuff for me in Hallowgate. That was all. I suppose the rest were relatives, friends of Mark's from the high school.'

'Anyone called Paul?'

She shook her head. 'Not that I remember.'

He drank the wine, spread butter thickly on French bread, cut a lump of cheese.

'Were there any rumours about Sheena?'

'What sort of rumours?'

'About a lover.'

She smiled. 'Never.'

'What's so funny?'

'Well, Sheena. If you'd met her you'd understand. Nothing mattered to her but her writing. There wouldn't have been time for another man.'

She poured more wine into her own glass.

'And Mark?' Ramsay asked. 'What about him?'

'Oh, I could understand if he'd had an affair,' Prue said. 'I'm not saying that he *did* have, but I wouldn't have blamed him.'

'You told me once that he doted on her.'

'He did, but he didn't get much from the marriage. He was an admirer. That was his only role. There wasn't any warmth there. If another woman showed him affection I can imagine him falling for it. Head over heels. He'd be desperately guilt-ridden, of course. But it wouldn't surprise me in the least.'

Chapter Twenty-Five

Mrs Patricia Howe lived in a gloomy 1930s villa in a street close to the massive office where Bernard worked. The houses were generally small, squashed-together semis. There were shared drives and makeshift garages in back gardens. It was a street of elderly people and first-time buyers.

Mrs Howe's was the only detached house. It was double-fronted, set back from the road. It had its own garage, rather grand, with a crenellated wall above green wooden doors. The garden had been tidied at some time in the autumn but had received little care since. The paint on the bay window frames had peeled away to the bare wood.

The door was opened by a short muscular woman in a green overall. Her hair was tightly permed, chestnut, a colour which had come, unevenly, from a bottle.

'Mrs Howe?' She was just old enough to be Bernard's mother, though she was not at all what he had been expecting. He could see behind her into a hall lined with dark, stained-wood panels. There was a musty smell of unaired rooms.

'Is she expecting you?' The woman seemed surprised.

'No.'

'She doesn't talk to salesmen.'

'I'm not a salesman.' He was about to explain *who* he was, when she added, 'Or politicians.'

There was a pile of canvassing material on the hall table for a by-election. Prue would be amused that he had been mistaken for a candidate.

'I'm a police officer. A detective.'

'Oh.' She opened the door a little wider. 'I suppose you've got proof.'

'Of course.'

He held out his warrant card. She took it and studied it carefully.

'You didn't mind,' she said. 'You've got to be careful these days.'

'Very sensible.' He could see that she *was* a very sensible woman. 'And you are?'

'Olive. Olive Thomson. Mrs Howe's home help.'

'I need to talk to her, ask her a few questions. Will that be possible?'

'She's not gaga if that's what you mean. Not lost the use of her limbs either. I'm not from Social Services. She pays me to do her housework, has done for years. She thinks it's beneath her dignity to clean the lav.'

'So I could rely on what she told me?'

'Oh aye. She's not one of my easiest ladies but she's got all her marbles.' She looked into a gilt-framed mirror on the wall, fluffed her hair, turned back to him. 'That's probably why she stirs up trouble. Just for the excitement. I don't rise to the bait. I know her too well. If she tries to offend you take no notice.'

'Right,' Ramsay said. 'I'll remember that.'

Olive reached behind her back to untie her apron. 'I was on my way out but I'll show you through first. She likes things done properly. You'll have to speak up. She's deaf and too proud to use a hearing aid.'

Patricia Howe was sitting in a high-backed chair by a French window. She was reading a large-print library book. In the armchair beside her was sprawled an enormous, long-haired tabby cat. It was clear that she had not heard his knock on the door or the conversation with the home help and he stood for a moment watching her read. She was a large woman, with a fleshy chin and wispy white hair pinned back from her face with a tortoiseshell comb. The resemblance to Bernard was obvious. She was heavily made-up and a fine dusting of face powder had fallen on to her grey blouse.

'Mrs Howe, pet, there's someone to see you.'

She turned, saw him then for the first time, then demanded sharply, 'Who is this?' Her voice was hoarse and rasping.

'It's a detective,' Olive said. 'Mr Ramsay. I've checked his card.'

'What do you want?'

Without taking her eyes off Ramsay's face the old woman flapped her hand at Olive to send her away. Olive went.

'I said, what do you want?'

'A few questions. If you wouldn't mind.'

'It's about Kathleen, I suppose. I'm surprised you've not been before.'

'Why's that, Mrs Howe?'

'Well, I knew her, didn't I? As well as anyone. She lived in my house for long enough.' There was a careful emphasis on the word 'my'. 'Oh yes, I knew her.'

'You didn't like her?'

'I didn't kill her if that's what you mean.'

It was supposed to be a joke. She stretched thin lips around uneven, discoloured teeth and cackled. The cackle turned into a violent, racking cough.

'But you didn't like her?'

'No.' The lips clamped shut.

'Why not?' He tried to speak gently but she did not hear.

'What's that?'

'*Why* didn't you like her?'

'She didn't look after him properly. Men need looking after.'

'Did he look after her?' He regretted the question as soon as it was asked, realized that it was Prue speaking.

'Of course he did. He brought in the money that kept her.' For the first time she set aside her library book, let it fall with a crash on to the floor. The cat raised its head, then settled back to sleep. 'Are you married, Mr Ramsay?'

'Divorced.'

'I was always telling Bernard that he should divorce Kathleen. He knew there was a place for him here if he wanted one.'

So, Ramsay thought, if he wanted rid of her he didn't have to kill her. Not on your account. That's what you're trying to tell me.

'They lived here together, you know, when they married.'

'Bernard told me that.'

'Did he?' It seemed to please her. 'They should never have moved.'

'I thought you didn't get on with her.'

She shrugged her shoulders heavily, the gesture of a gracious grande dame.

'Oh, I didn't mind her funny ways.'

'What funny ways?'

She sniffed. 'She had views on everything. Opinions.'

'Shouldn't a woman have opinions?'

'No.'

Except you, he thought. You wouldn't be without them.

'Did you enjoy having a child in the house?' he asked. He couldn't imagine Mrs Howe as doting grandmother, with a pocketful of sweeties, offering to babysit.

'She wasn't any trouble,' Mrs Howe said. 'It's a big house.'

'Was Kathleen a good mother?'

'I suppose she was. I never interfered.'

Ramsay found that hard to believe. He said nothing. Mrs Howe continued.

'I thought Kathleen was too serious. Too pushy. She was determined to turn Marilyn into a blue stocking. She was a pretty little thing. All that white hair. She should have had more fun.'

They sat without speaking. A grandfather clock ticked in the hall. Mrs Howe's stomach rumbled and she belched gently into her handkerchief. The room was heated by large painted radiators and an open fire and was very warm. Ramsay felt drowsy and he wondered if Mrs Howe was falling asleep. Translucent pink lids covered her eyes.

'Bernard and I always had fun,' she said. 'He never met his father, you know. There was only ever Bernard and I.'

Ramsay did not ask if the man was dead or if he had deserted them and Mrs Howe didn't elaborate. Perhaps she had never married.

'We had such good times, the two of us. Such wonderful times. Before he married Kathleen. We went to the cinema every week, then out to supper. We made an event of it. You could then. I wore gloves and a hat. Oh yes we turned a few heads. He was a good-looking man.' She opened her eyes and made a theatrical sweep of the arm towards an upright piano which stood against one wall. 'He played the piano like an angel. And even then he worked magic. He performed for me. He knew how it diverted me.' She sighed. 'We were such very good friends.'

'You must have been disappointed when they moved to Cotter's Row.'

She shrugged. 'One must learn, mustn't one, to let go.' But her eyes were hard and bitter.

'It must be a comfort that he visits so regularly.'

She brightened again. 'Oh yes. Our Thursday evenings are very special times.'

'What do you talk about on his visits?'

'Everything. He has no secrets from me. His work, his plans for the future. . .'

Himself, Ramsay concluded silently. That's why he comes. Not to keep you company. Certainly not to help with practical chores around the house. Not even because you cook cauliflower cheese for his supper. But for the pleasure of talking about himself.

'Did he seem concerned or anxious in the weeks before Kathleen's death?'

'No. If anything he was happier. More the boy he used to be.' She grinned horribly again. 'I thought he'd got himself a mistress. Someone with style. I wouldn't blame him.'

'Did he bring Marilyn to see you?'

'Hardly ever. Once in a blue moon. According to Kathleen I was a subversive influence.'

'When did you last see her?'

'On my birthday. The end of January.'

'That was a Thursday too?'

'Of course. It's always Thursday.'

'There must be weeks when he can't get to see you,' Ramsay said. 'When something turns up at work or at Marilyn's school.'

'No.' She said firmly. 'He's a good boy. He always puts his mother first. The last time he missed a Thursday night was more than a year ago and he only stopped at home then because he had flu.'

'Are you sure of that? He never came on a different day instead?' She turned her whole body so she was facing him.

'What are you saying, Mr Ramsay? That I'm senile?'

And he thought that Bernard's visits were so important to her that she *would* know.

She shut her eyes and waved her hand impatiently to indicate that he should go. On cue the cat raised itself and hissed. Her eyes remained firmly closed as he left the room.

Outside the weather had changed. A sea fret had moved in from the coast. Although it was only midday it was dark enough for the street lights to have come on. The fine drizzle looked like mist but water trickled in drops from bare branches and gutters.

As Ramsay bent to unlock his car, words of Mrs Howe's which he had thought to be entirely malicious seeped back into his consciousness. He stood upright, transfixed. His keys clattered on the pavement.

'Of course,' he said out loud. 'Of course.'

He turned back to the house and saw that Mrs Howe had raised herself. She was standing and staring out at him through the window. The cat, cradled in her arms, bared its fangs.

Chapter Twenty-Six

Sally Wedderburn stood outside the impressive facade of Otterbridge High School. She'd spent all afternoon in the Shining Stars Nursery and the screaming kids had given her a headache. It had been a waste of time as she'd suspected it would be. No one had seen an overweight middle-aged man on the evening Tom Bingham was abducted. Nor a bicycle. Miss Frost's recollection of the man waiting outside in the street was vague. Youngish, slimmish. She wasn't even sure about hair colour. She'd only really seen a silhouette and street lamps gave such a peculiar light.

Sally was at the high school on Ramsay's instruction. She was waiting for Marilyn. The wind carried flecks of ice and she pulled her coat around her as she paced backwards and forwards along the pavement to stop her feet from freezing. She was too nervous to stand still. After making such a hash of her interview with Emma Coulthard she was grateful that Ramsay was giving her a second chance. She was desperate not to screw up again.

An electric bell rang and children began to stream past her, pushing and jostling through the gates. She had to concentrate. It wouldn't do to miss the girl. She had suggested seeing her during school time – that would have been easier – but Ramsay wouldn't allow it. He said it wasn't fair to drag her out of her class. She'd have to explain to her friends what it was about. How could they put her through that?

So Sally stood, watching the children in the identical navy uniforms until the stream turned to a trickle. Still there was no sign of Marilyn Howe. When the staff began to emerge, their arms full of books, she panicked and hurried inside.

The heat of the building dazed her. She was in a wide, wood-lined corridor. Behind a glassed-in reception desk three secretaries were discussing last night's television programmes. A long brass plaque listed the names of old boys who had been killed in the Second World War. Rows of sporting trophies and faded photographs stood in a display case fixed to the wall. She was wondering if Ramsay's instructions on discretion related to secretaries too when a middle-aged woman clattered down a flight of stone stairs behind her.

'Can I help you?' The teacher was on her way out and paused in mid-step, turning back to ask the question.

Before Sally could answer a crescendo of music came from further along the corridor.

'No,' she said. 'Thank you. I'm waiting for a pupil who's in the orchestra.'

'Go through,' the woman said. 'Wait in comfort. You might enjoy it. They're rather good.'

And she was gone. The heavy doors swung together behind her.

The orchestra was rehearsing in a hall which still smelled of the midday meal. There was a stage but the players were sitting in the well of the theatre on moulded-plastic chairs behind a forest of music stands. A sandy-haired flamboyant man in a pink shirt was conducting. Sally was relieved to see Marilyn sitting in the front row, with the other violins. She leant against the back wall of the hall in the shadow. Only then did she recognize Mark Taverner amongst the group. He was playing clarinet, partly hidden by a line of full-grown, acne-covered boys.

When the rehearsal finished Sally stayed where she was. The children seemed in no hurry to leave. They chatted as they put instruments into cases and then they sauntered out. No one noticed her. Marilyn lingered behind to stack the chairs and fold the stands. A couple of girls called polite goodbyes to her, but they didn't stop to help her. Sally thought Marilyn would always, stay behind to clear up. It would give her an excuse for being alone on her walk to the bus stop.

Mark Taverner and the conductor were talking. Suddenly the

conductor looked up at the clock on the wall, shuffled together his music and hurried out. He shouted back to Mark.

'Sorry to leave you to sort things out here. I'm due in Whitley Bay Playhouse in twenty minutes. Auditions for *Cabaret*.'

But Mark made no attempts to help Marilyn with the chairs. As soon as the conductor had disappeared he strode after him, in a hurry, without a word.

Sally emerged from the shadow and walked into the main body of the hall. Marilyn was struggling with the last music stand. Sally nodded towards the door through which Taverner had disappeared.

'What was wrong with him?'

'Mr Taverner? He's a pompous git, that's all. He thinks we should only play serious music. And that he should be conductor.'

Sally was reassured. She'd had the impression that Marilyn was pompous herself, something of a goody-goody. Now it seemed she was like any other teenager, slagging off her teachers.

Marilyn picked up her school bag. 'What are you doing here?'

'I'd like to ask you a few questions. I could give you a lift home. Better than waiting at the bus stop on a night like this.'

'I suppose so.'

'Shall we go for a coffee somewhere? Or do you have to get straight back?'

'They know I had orchestra. They won't be expecting me until six when the late bus gets in. There's time for a coffee if you like.'

The only café still open in Otterbridge was a burger place next to the bus station. It was full of teenagers eating chips and drinking Coke, smoking cigarettes. Marilyn had taken off her school tie and blazer before going in. She'd folded them neatly and left them in the car.

'Won't you be cold?' Sally was wearing two jumpers and a coat.

'I don't care. *No one* wears their blazers in town. What if someone I know comes in?'

They sat in a corner as far away from the smokers as they could get, and drank milky coffee from glass cups. Their conversation was punctuated by the rumble of buses beyond the fogged-up window, the screech of brakes.

'What's this about?' Marilyn asked. Seeing her closely Sally realized that she was wearing make-up. Thin eyeliner, the remains of mascara. A tentative experiment which hadn't quite come off.

'It's rather delicate. That's why I didn't want to come to talk to you at home.'

Marilyn stared at the window, though it was impossible to see anything through the condensation except the distorted yellow glare of bus headlights.

'I think I know what you want to ask.'

'Do you?'

'Go on, though. I'd look a right fool, wouldn't I, if I got it wrong?'

There was no humour in her voice. She sounded terribly weary.

'It's about your father. And Claire.'

Marilyn said nothing, continued to stare.

'Is that what you were expecting?'

Marilyn nodded slowly. 'How did you find out?'

Because Ramsay guessed, Sally thought. He's more of a magician than your father.

She said, 'Things often come up in an investigation. If it weren't for the murder it wouldn't be any of our business.'

'This has nothing to do with the murder,' Marilyn said firmly. 'Absolutely nothing.'

'All the same we do have to ask.'

'They're so stupid,' Marilyn cried. 'They don't realize there's bound to be talk. The two of them living in the same home. They're like kids. Kids playing house. It's so embarrassing.'

'And there is something to talk about?'

'You mean, are they having an affair?' Marilyn demanded. She turned away and blushed.

Sally nodded.

Marilyn cupped her hands around her coffee. Even when she spoke she didn't look up.

'Did Inspector Ramsay tell you that I knocked on his door one evening looking for my mother?'

'Yes. In the autumn, wasn't it?'

'That was the day she found them in bed together. She ran out of the house.'

'It started as long ago as that?'

Marilyn sighed. 'Oh, when I think back I realize it had been going on for ages, years even.'

'Did she talk to you about it?'

'Mummy? Of course not. She'd die.'

'Claire, then?'

'Nobody told me about it. They wouldn't. I'm sixteen but they treat me like a baby. And they were so dumb! It's a small house with thin walls. When I was upstairs in my room working they forgot about me. They assumed I couldn't hear what was going on, what they were saying to each other.'

'They were shouting?' Sally was wondering if the neighbours had heard. If it ever came to court they could do with an independent witness.

'Mummy was a bit hysterical when she found out. I could tell that. I don't suppose it ever occurred to her to think of Claire as a rival. Her little sister, not much older than me. It must have come as a shock. That's why she ran away, forgot all about me coming home from school that day. But no, there wasn't much shouting. Enough for me to work out what was going on but not rows that went on for days and days. Nothing vulgar like that. That's never been our style.'

'How did they work things out?'

Marilyn shrugged. 'I'm not sure.' She gave a little smile. 'I could hardly ask them, could I? I wasn't supposed to know that anything was wrong. I was swotty little Marilyn who only cared about GCSEs and music exams. I wondered at first if Claire would be banished from the house, but things seemed to carry on much as they did before. I presume they both promised to behave in the future.'

'And did they behave?'

'I think they must have done, at least while Mummy was alive. There were no more rows.'

'And after your mother's death?'

'They've tried very hard to be discreet.'

'But not hard enough?'

She paused, looked up and smiled. 'I told you. The walls are very thin.'

'You don't seem very upset. About the relationship between your father and your aunt.'

'I'm not. I mean, I would have been if Mummy were still alive, but now I don't blame them. It's hard to explain. Mummy's dead and nothing's going to bring her back. Why shouldn't they have the chance to be happy?'

Sally chose her words carefully. 'Even if they only achieved that happiness through your mother's death?'

'What are you saying?' Marilyn demanded, though Sally thought she knew very well.

'You told me they couldn't have been involved in the murder. Why are you so sure?'

'They wouldn't have had the nerve. Get real!'

The brash slang which was natural to Sally seemed foreign to her, as if using it were a newly acquired skill. She blushed again. 'I'm sorry, but really it's not possible.'

Sally let it go.

'You must miss your mother.'

Marilyn looked up at her bleakly. 'Yeah, I do. More than I ever would have imagined. She could be a real pain at times but she was always there when I came home from school, asking what I'd been doing, encouraging me. You know.'

Sally nodded.

'Dad does his best but it's not the same.'

'He's too wrapped up in Claire?' Sally spoke lightly, tried to make a joke of it. Marilyn smiled dutifully.

'No. He's too wrapped up in himself. But that's men for you, isn't it? They're all the same.'

Sally wondered who had passed on that particular piece of wisdom.

'What did you do the evening your mother disappeared?' Sally thought she might get extra points for asking.

'Why do you want to know?'

'It's my boss. He thinks it's possible your mother died later than we originally thought.'

Marilyn said nothing. She seemed lost in thought.

'So what did you do that night?' Sally persisted gently.

'Nothing.'

'What do you mean?'

'I stayed in. Dad said it was so someone should be there if Mummy came home. He and Claire went off together. To search, they said.' She smiled wryly. 'An excuse, I suppose. Sick, isn't it?'

A waitress in a red and white checked dress collected their cups. At the counter the lads had finished their chips and were getting rowdy. Marilyn had not even looked in their direction, which was odd, Sally thought. At sixteen raging hormones had given her a radar system which could pick up an adolescent boy at a distance of a hundred yards.

'Got a boyfriend?' she asked.

'No one special.'

'I suppose you're too picky.'

'Yeah,' Marilyn said. 'You could say that.'

Chapter Twenty-Seven

Claire was just leaving work for the evening when the phone went in the Coastguard House. She heard it ringing as she shut the kitchen door behind her but she didn't go back to answer it. She had a meal to cook.

Emma heard the phone but she let it ring. She was bathing Helen in the children's bathroom at the top of the house. A red net filled with plastic toys was strung round the taps and the shower curtain had pictures of the Little Mermaid. A clockwork turtle swam towards Helen, who splashed the water with her feet and chortled. The phone stopped. The answering machine would have clicked on. It would probably be for Brian. Business. Or rugby.

Owen answered the phone before the answering machine was activated. They'd recently bought a cordless receiver – a toy for Brian – and Owen arrived at the bathroom door with it in his hand, proud of himself, expecting congratulations.

'It's Uncle Mark.'

Jesus, she thought. What's he done now?

She lifted Helen out of the bath and wrapped her in a towel. She dried her hands and took the phone. Owen hovered in the doorway.

'Thanks, pet,' she said, trying not to sound too impatient. 'You can go back and play with David now.' She locked the bathroom door behind them then sat on the closed toilet seat with the baby on her knee.

'Yes?' She didn't want to be too encouraging.

'Emma. I've got to see you.'

She took a deep breath. Sometimes Mark reminded her of one of the boys. She had to try hard not to snap at him.

'I'm not sure that would be a good idea.'

'Please,' he said. 'We've got to talk.'

'We're talking now.'

'Come on, Em. You know what I mean.'

'You can't come here.'

There was a silence and she realized she had hurt him, so she added, 'I'm sorry. Not the way things are.'

'No,' he said bitterly. 'I see that.' He paused. 'Could Claire have the kids one evening? When Brian's working?'

Emma gave a little laugh. 'You must be joking. Claire doesn't stay five minutes longer than she needs to these days and overtime's out of the question. She's playing mummies and daddies with Bernard Howe.'

'That's not very kind.' It was the old Mark, disapproving, self-righteous.

'No,' she said. 'Well I don't feel very kind.'

She thought for a moment. She knew he wouldn't give up. 'I suppose I could see you Saturday lunchtime. Brian's working and Claire doesn't mind coming up during the day. Where shall we meet?'

'You could always come here. To the house.'

She thought of the Otterbridge house full of Sheena's books and Sheena's pictures, still smelling somehow of Sheena and always cold. She shuddered.

'No,' she said. 'Not there. A pub. Somewhere halfway between here and Otterbridge so it won't take me too long to get home.'

'The Lamb in Puddywell,' he said. He hadn't had to think about it and it surprised her that Mark, who hardly ever went into pubs could come up with a name so easily. 'Twelve o'clock. I'll see you there.'

Before she could answer he rang off. She pushed the button on the phone and set it on the floor. She wished she'd had the courage to stand up to him. She shouldn't have said that she'd see him.

The bathroom door rattled. The noise startled her and she realized her hands were shaking. Brian shouted.

'What are you doing in there?' He sounded amused, not irritated, which made a nice change.

'Bathing Helen.' What do you think I'm doing? she thought.

'Why the locked door? Teaching her modesty at an early age?'

She smiled despite herself. 'No. Habit I suppose.'

She stood up, holding the shrouded baby against her shoulder and let him in. He kissed her lightly on the lips. He'd been making more effort lately and she was aware of a sudden and surprising surge of affection. They stood together in the steamy room, the baby between them. The smell of talcum powder and the heat made her feel quite faint.

He began to undress. Carefully, as he always did. He hung his jacket on a hook on the door with the children's dressing gowns, threw his shirt into the wicker laundry basket and folded up his trousers. He turned on the taps. He took Helen from Emma, pulled away the towel and held her in the air, so he could press his lips on her stomach to make the farting noise which always sent the boys into hysterics. Then he said, in the gurgly voice he saved for babies, 'You don't mind, do you, Sweetie? You don't mind if Daddy uses your bathroom?' To Emma he said, 'Why don't you stay here? We can talk while you dress her. Before he climbed into the bath he locked the door again. 'Mark hasn't been round lately.' He was lying right back so she couldn't see his face. The words seemed to come from nowhere.

Helen was on the changing mat on the floor and Emma was bending over her, fixing the sticky tapes on the disposable nappy. She kept her eyes on the baby as she answered.

'No. I suppose it's a while.'

'Not since David's birthday,' he persisted. 'Why don't we invite him round for lunch on Sunday?'

'I don't know,' she said. 'I suppose we could.'

He sat up, sending a tidal wave into the toys strung from the taps and continued enthusiastically.

'There's a new place just opened round the corner from the

office. It's brilliant. A real old-fashioned toy shop. I bought some presents for the boys. Kites. Not those dreadful plastic ones that tear as soon as you look at them, but the sort we used to have when I was a kid. Canvas and bamboo. You put them together yourself. If there's any sort of wind on Sunday we could fly them. Mark would enjoy that.'

'Brian!' Emma had to interrupt him. 'Listen. There's something you should know about Mark.'

Brian had been soaping his back. He stopped. 'No,' he said.

She kneeled up. They stared at each other.

'I don't need to know anything about Mark. He's my friend. He's been through a rough time. I want him to be happy. In the same way I want you to be happy.'

He reached out and put an arm covered with bubbles around her shoulder and pulled her towards him. When he kissed her she smelled the baby shampoo he'd used on his hair.

'I don't care what Mark's been up to. You have to understand that, I don't mind. As long as he's happy I don't mind.'

It was as if he expected her, absolutely, to know what he meant.

Because Brian was home early they ate with the boys in the kitchen. Pepperoni pizza from the freezer and baked potatoes in the microwave. Emma prepared a salad, which Brian made into a joke. He put his hands by the side of his head to form ears, pulled his front teeth over his lower lip and said,

'Lettuce. That's rabbit food. Men don't eat *that*.'

The boys made rabbit faces, too, then collapsed into fits of giggles. Even Emma joined in, despite her disapproval. He knew how difficult it was to get them to eat properly. The laughter made her realize how tense they had been in the previous months, and remember that once they had got on very well.

After supper Brian sat her in an armchair in front of the television with a large glass of wine and took the boys up to bed.

'Don't wind them up,' she said. 'Not before bedtime.'

'Of course not.' His voice was solemn but when she looked up he was making the rabbit face at the boys who were waiting in the doorway and as he chased them up the stairs they whooped and screamed with delight.

They'll wake Helen, she thought, not really caring if they did.

She'd finished the wine when he came downstairs.

'Two stories each,' he said with satisfaction. 'And they're fast asleep.' He fetched the bottle from the fridge and poured her another glass.

'Don't you want any?'

'I thought I'd pop out to the club. Just for a quick half.'

A quick three pints, she thought, and why do I have the feeling that he's running away? But she was so grateful for his kindness, so frightened of spoiling the evening, that she let him go without a fuss.

Inside the club it was as cold as always. Brian kept on his overcoat and put on the pair of gloves he found in his pocket, making a show of it, so the regulars all laughed.

He was halfway through his second pint when Kim Houghton turned up with a new man in tow. Brian watched her from his seat by the bar. He'd had his own fantasises about Kim Houghton in the past. He'd imagined what it would be like to knock at the door of the little house in Cotter's Row, to be taken inside . . .

The man was a jerk in a sheepskin jacket and black patent shoes. When he wasn't drooling over Kim he was trying to sell Les a second-hand Cavalier. She'd been in with car dealers before. Perhaps she was trying to work her way through the motor trade. Or perhaps she fancied a little motor herself. The bloke wouldn't have much joy selling to Les, Brian thought with satisfaction. Les had lost his licence the month before through drink-driving. That had given them all a shock, made them watch their step.

Brian wondered what Kim had done with the little girl. Being a single mum didn't seem to cramp her style. He'd seen them together occasionally, the child immaculately dressed, colour co-ordinated, a scaled-down version of her mother. Poor little bastard, he thought. It couldn't be much fun. He'd have to get Em to invite her up to play. Perhaps she'd enjoy flying kites too.

He'd just rescued Les from Kim Houghton's boyfriend by

demanding another pint, when the door opened and two police officers came in. They were in plain clothes but everyone knew what they were. It was the flash young man and the bonny woman with red hair. They stood for a moment, looking around them. All the conversation in the place stopped.

Les rubbed his hands together. He always did that when he was nervous.

'Yes, folks,' he said. 'What can I get you?' Pretending he didn't recognize them, that they were just ordinary punters, though the day they found the body they'd been practically camping out in the place.

Brian could tell that the man was tempted. He was gasping for a drink. But the woman said, 'Nothing, thanks. We'd just like a quick word with Mrs Houghton.'

They took Kim to a table in the corner so that not even the boyfriend could hear what they were saying, then the three of them walked out. The car dealer looked foolishly after them, finished his drink and followed. There was the sound of a car engine. He must have started his company car and driven away.

'What was all that about then?' Brian said. 'Do you think she's been arrested?'

Les gave a gappy grin. 'Na!' he said. 'No handcuffs.' He gave a lecherous wink.

Brian felt himself becoming flushed, though handcuffs had never featured in his fantasies about Kim Houghton. He'd imagined a wardrobe full of dressing-up clothes. A school uniform. Black stockings. Tarty red underwear. But nothing really kinky.

He decided he'd go. Emma would appreciate it if he wasn't too late back. Besides, Les wouldn't want to risk a lock-in for after-hours drinking with the police on the Headland.

It was even colder outside than in the club and he walked quickly past the jetty and into Cotter's Row. There were still lights on in Kim Houghton's house but he was surprised to see that the car the detectives drove was not parked there. It was pulled up right against the pavement outside the Howes' place. And from inside came the sound of raised voices.

Chapter Twenty-Eight

'How did you know?' Sally had demanded. 'How did you know that Bernard and Claire were having an affair?'

'It was something Bernard's mother said. I suppose we should have realized before. Considered it at least.' He saw it as a failure of his, this refusal to consider the obvious. It was another sort of arrogance.

'It really changes things, doesn't it? I mean if they were working together we've got motive and opportunity.'

'I suppose we have.'

Although this too was obvious he resisted the enthusiasm. He wasn't ready yet to make an arrest. She was like a hypomanic kid on the eve of her own birthday party. She couldn't keep still. She bounced around the office on the balls of her feet and came to rest at last with her bum on the window sill.

'When you first suggested it I couldn't believe it,' she said. 'I mean he's old enough to be her father. What a creep!'

I suppose he *is* old enough to be Claire's father, Ramsay thought. Prue's friends who were into self-enlightenment and therapy would make a lot of that. It was plausible enough. They'd say that Claire, who had recently lost her father, was looking for a substitute. If the couple ever came to trial there would be a probation officer's report before sentence and he could predict almost word for word what would be said about Claire's bereavement. But he thought something quite different was going on in the relationship. It wasn't a father Claire was looking for but a child. Someone to take care of. And Bernard Howe had never grown up.

'Surely we've got enough to bring them in for questioning,' Sally said. She was as macho as Hunter when the mood took her. *She'd* persuaded the girl to talk. Now she wanted a bit of glory and a result.

'Probably.' Ramsay spoke calmly.

'We'll go for it, then, shall we?'

'No,' Ramsay replied. 'Not yet. We'll talk to them at home. Separately if we can. That shouldn't be a problem. They're not sophisticated enough to put up any resistance.'

'But why not here? Formal questions. In the Interview Room with the tape running. They'll be blaming each other within minutes.'

'Because the press will get to know.' He was annoyed by her callousness, disappointed in her. He'd supposed that because she was a woman she'd look at things differently. And didn't that make him every bit as much of a bigot as Hunter? He tried to contain his irritation.

'You know as well as I do that if we say a witness is helping the police with their inquiries the world assumes he's guilty. There's the girl to think of. And what if they're innocent? It's easy enough for us. We just move on to another case. But they'll have to put together some sort of life and that's not easy when the neighbours are whispering murder.'

Sally turned away without saying anything. Sometimes she thought Hunter was right. Despite his reputation Ramsay was getting old and soft. He was perceptive enough but he didn't have the guts to see a thing through.

'Where's Gordon?' Ramsay asked.

'In the canteen.' Sulking, she thought. Because I got the girl to tell me about Bernard and Claire.

'I want him in on this too.'

She was going to ask why but managed to bite her tongue just in time.

When they got to Cotter's Row only Marilyn was in. They heard her clatter down the stairs to come to the door. She'd changed from her uniform into washed-out jeans and a sweater. When she turned to let them in Ramsay saw the label on the jeans pocket. It wasn't one that any of her friends would have recognized. Her mum had probably bought them for £5.99 from a stall on Blyth market. Prue's daughter wouldn't have been seen dead in them.

'Claire's baby-sitting for Kim Houghton,' Marilyn said. 'Dad's gone with her.' Then, speaking directly to Sally, 'I suppose they wanted a bit of privacy.'

'When do you expect them back?'

She shrugged.

'Not till late. They said not to wait up.'

'Bring them back here now, Gordon.' Ramsay spoke quietly but they could tell he wasn't going to be pissed about. 'Find out where Kim Houghton is and get her home. If necessary Sally can baby-sit until she gets back.'

As soon as he'd spoken he knew Sally wouldn't like it. She hadn't joined the force to be a childminder.

'That *is* all right, Sally?' With hardly a trace of sarcasm.

'Of course,' she said huffily. She started away from the door then turned back hopefully. 'Unless Marilyn wants to do it. It might be less awkward for her to be out of the house.'

'No.' For some reason he couldn't even quite explain to himself why he wanted Marilyn there. Perhaps to remind Bernard and Claire of their responsibility. Or to represent Kath Howe. Because no one else had liked her very much and that wasn't a good enough reason to let a killer get away.

It took half an hour to fetch Kim Houghton from the club. Sally decided that as Kim was just down the road she wouldn't be needed as sitter. Ramsay could wait that long. In number two Ramsay waited downstairs alone. Marilyn offered him tea. When he declined she went back upstairs to her room. To someone without experience of teenagers that might have seemed strange or rude, but Prue's daughter ignored all adult visitors to the house as a matter of course. A matter even of honour.

He was glad of the silence and the opportunity for thought. He went into the living room intending to rearrange the furniture to his liking before the interview and he was struck by the change in the place. When he had looked in on his first visit to the house it had been cluttered, uninviting, dirty. It still looked as if it was never used, but much of the junk had been taken away and it was spotless. There was a smell of furniture polish. He thought the carpet had been cleaned. He supposed Claire had been spring cleaning. Her way of making a fresh start? Or something more sinister?

Hunter came in.

'They're on their way. Kim and her fancy man were just down at the club.'

'This house was searched, wasn't it?' They had been looking for letters, an address book, some indication that Mrs Howe knew her murderer.

'Yeah. The day after the body was found. You suggested it and Mr Howe gave his permission.'

'But properly searched?'

'Well, we didn't pull up the floorboards. I mean the chap had just lost his wife. Be sensitive, you said.'

Because there had been no real suspicion then that Mrs Howe had been killed in the house. And if anything had been hidden after the murder it would be long gone now. Still, Ramsay thought, it wouldn't hurt to get a team in.

He and Hunter interviewed Bernard first. They took him into the front room.

'By man, it's like an ice box in here.' Hunter shivered to make his point. Bernard switched on an electric fire, but it seemed to have little effect on the temperature.

Ramsay, remembering what Marilyn had told Sally about thin walls, had suggested that the women might like to watch television while they waited. The noise from the back room was distracting but at least the interview would not be overheard.

Bernard was red faced, blustering, defensive. There were three easy chairs in the room, all covered with the nylon stretch covers which are advertised in mail-order catalogues. Ramsay motioned him to sit down.

'I don't know what this is all about,' Bernard said. 'Really, it's not on.'

'Come on, man.' Hunter was chummy. He perched on the arm of Bernard's chair. 'You can't expect to keep things quiet when you sneak off for a night together. What do you think Kim made of the two of you turning up on her doorstep? She'll not have thought you were there to play Scrabble.'

Bernard blushed a deeper crimson, said nothing.

'Or didn't you turn up together? Is that how you worked it? Claire went first, then you trotted on down when the coast was clear?'

There was no answer. Hunter's voice hardened.

'Is that how you worked it?'

'Yes.' It was a scarcely audible mumble.

'Well, all this secrecy has really landed you in the shit.' Hunter was all smiles again. 'You do see, Bernard, that the only way to get out of it is to answer all our questions? If you lie to us again we'll think you've got something else to hide. Beside your little affair, I mean.' He got up from the arm of the chair, looked down on his victim. 'You do see that, Bernard, don't you?'

'Yes.' Despite the cold he had begun to sweat. 'But we didn't really lie.' He was panicking and the words came out as a babble. 'Not about anything important. Not about Kath's murder. If you'd asked us we'd have told you.'

'What would you have told us?'

'Well, that Claire and I had become . . .' He paused. '. . . friendly.'

Hunter walked away in apparent disgust. He stood with his back to the fire, his arms folded, watching.

'Tell me,' Ramsay said gently. 'When did you and Claire start to become "friendly"?'

Bernard looked at him suspiciously. He, too, had changed from his work clothes. He was wearing olive green cords, worn thin at the knees and a Marks & Spencer's patterned sweater in lilac and pink. A Christmas present, Ramsay supposed, from his mother. Claire would have had more taste and Kath would have considered it an extravagance.

'What do you mean?'

'Was it soon after Claire came to stay with you?'

'She wasn't under age!' The panic had returned. 'She was seventeen.'

'Didn't it occur to you that you might be abusing a position of trust?' Ramsay asked.

Of course it didn't, he thought. That's what the Minister's wife said when you wandered off into the night with the little boy. Like the spoilt child you are you did just what you felt like. You didn't consider the consequences at all.

'Abuse never came into it,' Bernard said. 'You ask Claire. We were happy together. That didn't seem wrong.'

'I don't suppose that's how Kath saw it.'

'No,' Bernard muttered. 'Kath didn't understand. Not at first, anyway.'

'How did she find out?'

'It was September. Claire hadn't started working for the Coulthards. She'd finished at the college but she couldn't find a job so she was home a lot. My office works flexitime. If I do enough overtime I can have the occasional half-day off. We knew Kath was going to be out that afternoon. She was doing a course at the Open Door Learning Centre. Word processing. She thought she'd be able to help Marilyn with her school work. It was every Wednesday. But the tutor was ill so she came back early.'

'She didn't come home because she suspected you were being unfaithful?'

Bernard winced at the word, shook his head. 'No, she didn't suspect anything. That might have been easier. It was the shock. That's what floored her.' He stared past Hunter. 'You should have seen her face.'

'What happened?'

'She ran out into the street. It was getting dark. I heard a screech of brakes. Some fool driving too quickly up Cotter's Row. I thought she'd killed herself. But she was only frightened.'

'You went after her?'

'Of course. I was worried. We both were.'

'Were you?' Ramsay's voice remained polite but faintly sceptical.

'Yes! We didn't want to hurt her. That's the last thing we would have wanted. That's why we'd kept our friendship secret.'

'Not because you were afraid Kath would want it to stop? That she'd cause a scene?'

'Not exactly.' He paused. 'When we'd made sure she hadn't been run over we thought it would be better to give her some time alone. That was what she wanted. I was booked to do a magic show. I took Claire with me. I thought by the time I got back Kath would have calmed down.'

And none of you considered Marilyn, Ramsay thought, coming home and finding no one here.

'Had she calmed down?'

'In a way. It was horrible. She cried. I'd never seen her cry before. She wasn't angry. She blamed herself. When we got in Marilyn was in bed and Kath was sitting in her chair in the kitchen with tears running down her cheeks. I'd have done anything to make her stop.'

'So you and Claire promised to break off your relationship?'

'No!' He seemed astounded by the notion. 'We couldn't do that. We love each other.'

'I don't quite understand, then, what happened.'

'When we'd had time to think about it we realized that nothing need happen. That things could go on just as before.'

That's not how Marilyn tells it, Ramsay thought. She told Sal that Claire and Bernard stopped being 'friendly' when her mother found out. Was she deluding herself? Or is Bernard lying again?

Bernard was continuing. 'Kath didn't want to leave. We were quite happy for her to stay. If we were discreet there shouldn't be any upset or disruption.'

Hunter couldn't contain himself. 'And she was ready to go along with that? To share your bed at night knowing you were screwing her little sister on your afternoons off.'

Bernard seemed horrified. He looked to Ramsay for support. No one had ever spoken to him like that before. Ramsay said nothing.

'We worked things out in a civilized way,' he said, very much on his dignity.

'Wasn't your wife jealous?' Hunter demanded. When he went

out with a lass he expected undivided attention. Any flirting or funny business and she'd be out on her ear.

There was a brief silence.

'If she was, she was too proud to show it,' Bernard said. 'She was a little withdrawn for a while, but things soon settled back to normal. Kath was frightened of being on her own. That's why she agreed to the arrangement.' Deliberately ignoring Hunter he sat up straight and turned to Ramsay. 'And that, Inspector Ramsay, is why I had no need to murder her.'

Chapter Twenty-Nine

Claire sat very straight with her hands in her lap and her ankles crossed. Her dark hair was pulled away from her face. She wore no make-up. She hadn't been given the opportunity to talk to Bernard about his interview but she didn't seem curious. She waited for the questions like an earnest schoolgirl before an oral language exam.

Hunter had been sent into the back room to watch television with Bernard. It was Sally's turn to sit in on the conversation. But it was Ramsay's show. He was the examiner.

'Let me take you back to the day your sister was killed,' he said.

She said nothing. If there was any reaction it was a faint amusement.

'You came home for lunch?'

'Yes.'

'And to see Mr Howe?'

She raised her thick, dark eyebrows. 'You know about Bernard and me,' she said. 'I suppose Marilyn told you. I thought she'd guessed more than she was letting on but Bernard couldn't see it. It's probably for the best. There was no need to drag us away from Kim's, though. We'd have told you if you'd asked.'

'That's why you came home that lunchtime? You knew Marilyn would be out?'

She nodded.

'You must have thought Mrs Howe would be out too. That was part of the deal, I presume, that you'd wait until you had the house to yourselves before . . .'

'Making love?' she finished impassively. 'Yes. There was no formal

181

arrangement. No rules. But it wouldn't have been kind, would it, to do that while Kath was in the house?'

'Was it kind to have an affair with her husband?'

She didn't answer but he didn't think that the question had disturbed her. He left it and moved on.

'What made you think Kath would be away from home that lunchtime?'

'I thought she'd planned to go into Otterbridge with Marilyn on the bus.'

'She told you that?'

For the first time Claire seemed unsure of herself. 'I don't remember. I suppose she must have done. Otherwise I'd have stayed at the Coastguard House for lunch.'

They stared at each other, then Ramsay asked again, more slowly.

'Well, was it kind to have an affair with your sister's husband?'

She put one elbow on her knees and leant forward, eager to make him understand.

'Kath was a strange woman, Inspector. She didn't feel emotion. I don't think she was upset even when our mother died. . .'

'You were too young to remember that, surely?'

'I remember that I was upset. And that Kath was never around to comfort me. There were no cuddles at bedtime. I don't think she ever read me a story. As soon as she could she left to marry Bernard.' She paused. 'I don't blame her. I don't think she was capable of emotion.'

'She cried when she found out about you and Bernard.'

'Yes,' Claire agreed. 'But that was because her pride was hurt. She never loved Bernard. Not truly. Not like me.'

The self-justification, Ramsay thought, of mistresses everywhere.

'Did she love Marilyn?' he asked. 'I presume she cuddled Marilyn and read her bedtime stories?'

'Oh yes,' her voice remained light and cool but somewhere under the amusement he thought he detected a note of jealousy. 'Kath surprised them all when the baby was born. For the first time in her life there was something she cared for. She wasn't much good at the practical side. So clumsy apparently that they thought she might drop the baby. But there was plenty of affection. Perhaps too much.' She stared up into Ramsay's face. 'It's not the same, though, as love between adults.'

'Is that really what you and Bernard have?'

'What do you mean?'

'When the relationship started you were seventeen. Only just an adult.'

'Age has never mattered to us.' She paused. 'Bernie didn't corrupt me if that's what you're saying.'

'No. I'm sure he didn't.'

From the room next door came a swelling soprano singing the backing to a deodorant advertisement.

'What I don't understand,' Ramsay said, 'is why Kath didn't ask you to leave. You claim there was no great bond between you. And it's not as if you would have been homeless. You were just about to start work for the Coulthards. It's normal, isn't it, for nannies to live in? They would have had the space to put you up.'

He paused, then continued as if the idea had just come to him. 'Or perhaps she *did* ask you to leave, but not then. She waited until she was sure you were settled at the Coastguard House, and you had somewhere suitable to go. She would take her responsibility for you very seriously. I have the impression of a very principled woman. Is that why she didn't throw you out immediately? I wonder if that's what provoked her death. She couldn't go along with the pretence any longer. She wanted you out.'

'Kath never asked me to leave,' Claire said grandly. 'She knew that if I went, Bernard would come too.'

'I wonder if you really believe that.' Ramsay was apologetic. 'It seems to me that Bernard is a man who likes his comfort. His routine. Kath might not have been a brilliant homemaker but she shopped and cooked and washed for him. She let him play with his magic tricks and his ventriloquist's doll. She really didn't make any demands. If he'd left the family he would still have been financially responsible for Marilyn and for Kath. There'd be your wages of course, but there wouldn't have been much money for a decent home of your own. I'm not sure if Bernard would have enjoyed slumming it in a flat or a bedsit. Even with you. It's not what he's used to and he's not a man, I'd say, who likes change.'

Claire said nothing and Ramsay went on. 'But let's assume that you're right. Let's assume that Kath wouldn't have thrown you out because she couldn't risk his leaving too. That would make sense. Above all she wanted to make a stable home for Marilyn. Bernard would be a part of that. That alone would explain why she was prepared to tolerate the position . . .'

'Quite,' Claire said.

'But I can envisage certain circumstances which she would never be prepared to tolerate.'

He looked at her as if expecting a response.

'I don't understand.'

'I don't think, for example, she would put up with your living here if you were pregnant. You're not pregnant, are you?'

'No!'

'Because if you were, Kath would find it impossible to pretend to herself that Bernard was just being kind to you, as substitute father. She would have to admit that the relationship was – how did you put it – a love between adults. And a new baby would be competition for Marilyn. It really wouldn't work, would it?'

'I'm not pregnant!' The words came out as a scream.

'No,' Ramsay said. He was quiet and sympathetic. More like a doctor than a policeman, thought Sally, who was watching spellbound, all thought of the earlier criticism of her boss forgotten. 'No, you're not pregnant. But you'd like to be, Claire, wouldn't you?'

Sally thought the girl was going to scream at him again, but she nodded silently. Sally wanted to go up to her and put her arm around her and tell her not to let Bernard bug her, because all men were bastards. Except Ramsay, who was a bloody genius. But Ramsay was going on, ignoring Claire's obvious distress.

'I've seen you with the Coulthard children,' he said. 'But I suppose it's not the same if they're not your own.'

'Bernard always said he didn't want any more children.' She gave a little smile. 'He said it was the mess and the clutter he hated.

184

Nappies in buckets. Spilled food all over the floor. But that was because Kath wasn't very good at it. It doesn't have to be like that.' She looked down at her feet. 'And that was probably an excuse. He knew Kath wouldn't like it. He was afraid of her.'

'Did you think you'd talk him into it? There's plenty of time, after all. You're very young.'

'I wasn't sure.' She looked up bleakly. 'He can be stubborn when he wants to be. And *he's* not so young.'

'But you thought that with Kath out of the way there'd be more chance he'd change his mind?'

She nodded enthusiastically and they realized again that she was hardly more than a child herself. 'I thought he'd see how well I'm running the house. How cosy and cheerful everything is. And he'd see that if I can manage to hold everything together when I'm working, a baby wouldn't need to get in the way.'

'He didn't see it like that though, did he, Claire? Bernard wants you all to himself. He doesn't understand how important it is to you to have children. How can he?'

'I tried to make him understand!' she cried. 'I arranged for us to be on our own this evening so we could discuss it, but he wouldn't listen.'

'What a terrible waste!' Ramsay said. 'After you'd made the plans. Bernard will never know what you went through, what courage it must have taken. You knew Kath didn't go to Otterbridge. You said you needed to talk to her about Bernard and arranged to meet her at the jetty at lunchtime. No one could see you in all the sleet and the rain but still it must have taken some nerve. To stab her, push her into the water. Throw the knife after her then walk back to the house as if nothing had happened. Poor Claire. You killed your sister and it was all for nothing.'

But while he was speaking he knew it couldn't have happened that way. Because at lunchtime the tide was out and he couldn't believe a body could lie, unnoticed, on the shore all afternoon.

She looked at him, open-mouthed.

'Or did it happen later?' he asked. 'You slipped out of the

Coastguard House while the party was in full swing and killed her then.'

'No,' she said in a whisper. 'I didn't kill Kath. How could you think that? I lost my father and my mother. She was the only relation I had left.'

He regarded her gently, with pity.

'Then it was Bernard,' he said. 'Bernard killed her. For you. And that's why you didn't tell us about your affair.'

'No,' she said again, more firmly. She had quite regained her composure. 'Neither of us killed her. And there's no way that you'll be able to prove that we did.'

Without asking his permission she stood up and walked out. The exam was over.

Ramsay had come in his own car, which he had parked in the alley at the back of the houses to avoid the impression of a police raid. Bernard showed him out through the kitchen door into the yard. The others had left already. Ramsay switched on his torch to light his way through the debris. There was an old tin bath with a pile of clothes pegs lying in the bottom, a wheelie bin and a ceramic tub which looked as if it had been newly planted with seedlings. Perhaps Claire was trying to extend her civilizing influence to the yard as well as the house.

As the torch beam flashed past the shed which had once been the outside lavatory, he saw that the door was closed with a heavy padlock. What did Bernard own that was of sufficient value to be locked away? His bike, but that was still propped against the wall in the corridor inside. He thought again that he had grounds for a thorough search of the house and the yard, but imagined the effect on the family of a team ripping the place apart and put off the decision again.

A splintered wooden gate led from the yard to the alley beyond. Ramsay stood there for a moment and looked through the uncurtained window into the house. Bernard and Claire stood in the kitchen facing each other. She put her hands on his shoulders. He pulled her awkwardly towards him so her head rested on the pink and lilac sweater. He stroked her hair.

Ramsay was moved by this sentimental gesture, then thought his sergeant would think him a sentimental fool. Although Bernard Howe's domestic situation obviously fascinated Hunter, he would sneer at it. How could anyone take that relationship seriously? Ramsay imagined that the information was already being passed on to the other members of the team. 'He had a bloody harem I tell you, the paunchy fat bastard. Two women and one of them young enough to be his daughter.' He'd try to keep the envy from his voice but he'd probably not manage it.

He felt a voyeur, that by standing there, looking in, he was sharing Hunter's salacious interest in the family. He unhooked the latch and moved into the alley. From his car he could see up the Headland to the Coastguard House, lit by a security light, gleaming white through the greyness and the drizzle. A beacon, he thought. Metaphorically at least. What most of the families in Cotter's Row aspired to. A BMW in the garage. A machine to wash dishes. A nanny to mind the children. Comfort and security. Wasn't that why so many people played the lottery every week?

He had climbed into the car and begun the slow drive down the narrow alley when it came to him that the situations between the Coulthards at the top of the hill and the Howes at the bottom might be very similar. Bernard had managed his compliant ménage à trois without disturbance or conscience. Why should Emma Coulthard not be doing the same thing? He had assumed that if she were sleeping with Mark Taverner she would want to keep the fact secret from her husband. But the two men were friends. Friends who shared everything. Perhaps they were sharing Emma too.

Chapter Thirty

It was Friday night. At the club Les had hired a stripper and for once the place was full. There were cars parked all along the jetty. When Emma left the house to fetch a bucket of logs she could hear the music, a thumping insistent bass.

Kim Houghton could hear the music even inside the house. It taunted her. A night at the club wasn't her idea of a thrilling evening, but it was better than staying in on her own. She'd asked Claire if she'd like to babysit but Claire had refused. Which was pretty snotty of her, considering the fiasco which had happened during the week. Kim had almost said to her, 'Hey lady, I think you owe me an evening. At the very least. How do you think I felt being dragged out of the club by two police officers? In front of all those people?'

But Kim hadn't said that. You could never tell how Claire would react and if she'd decided to take offence, Kim could have lost a regular sitter. And a cheap one.

She was tempted to wait until Kirsty was asleep and go out anyway. Kirsty hardly ever woke up once you put her to bed and even if she did she was a sensible kid. She wouldn't do anything silly or make a fuss. The club was only just down the road, so she could pop back every hour or two to check everything was OK. Once she got there she was bound to meet someone she knew. Some bloke who'd buy her a few drinks for the pleasure of her company.

Then she thought she'd better not risk it in case the cops were still lurking on the Headland.

There wasn't any police presence on the Headland that night. Ramsay had sent the team home.

'We could all do with some time away from the case,' he'd said. 'Put it in perspective. Come back with some fresh ideas.'

Hunter thought it wasn't perspective they needed but proof. Evidence. He was quite clear in his own mind that Bernie Howe and Claire Irvine had worked together to kill Kath Howe, had plotted it in advance. He understood Ramsay's caution. Blow your nose at the wrong time and the CPS would refuse to take a case, but that didn't mean the pair weren't guilty.

He left his car at home and walked to his local. His mam was still out with the girls from her work. Fridays they stopped for a pizza and a few glasses of Spanish wine on their way home. She'd be back later to cook his supper.

The lads were in the back bar where they always sat. When he'd joined the police he'd lost most of his mates from school and the regulars at the Hastings Arms were the nearest he had now. They were watching Sky Sport on a giant television – Newcastle United had a vital Cup match on the following day and the talk was all about that. Hunter wasn't sorry they didn't ask about the case. There wasn't much to boast about, after all. There were six of them crowded round a small table and they each bought a round of drinks.

He left the pub well before closing time and walked home, staggering a bit on the step up to the front door. His mother had his meal ready for him and he ate it from a tray in front of the television. There was no pudding, though. He thought she could have run to a pudding, especially as he hadn't been home for his tea for weeks.

She had taken the tray away and he was lying back in the chair, watching the television through half-closed eyes when his mobile phone rang.

'Yes?' Automatically, still looking at the scantily dressed women who hosted the new Channel 4 chat show.

'It's Steve. From the Manhattan Skyline.' He heard music, shouting, laughter and he had to strain to catch the words.

'Yes?'

'That man you were after. Paul. He's in again.'

Before Hunter could answer the phone went dead. He didn't stop to think. Certainly not that he was probably way over the limit and shouldn't be driving. He grabbed his jacket and shouted through to his mother in the kitchen, 'I'm off out, Mam. Work.'

She came into the hall, drying her hands on a tea towel he'd brought her back from Limassol.

'All right, pet.'

'I'll be late back so don't wait up.'

'I won't, then. Mind you take care now.' But she said it easily. She knew Gordon had always been able to look after himself.

He arrived at Whitley Bay without realizing quite how he'd got there, only knowing from the time on his watch that he'd driven too fast.

The seafront was full of people and noise. A line of teenage girls staggered in a conga across the road in front of his car, cocking their legs like a row of incontinent puppies, moving to some rhythm he couldn't hear. A plump boy was throwing up in the gutter.

Outside a hotel, which had once been a respectable place for families to stay, a fight was going on. A cheering crowd had gathered, blocking the way of a bouncer who had ripped off his bow tie, wanting some of the action too. People streamed across the road in front of Hunter's car to get a better view of the fight. He leant on his horn but they took no notice. Eventually he turned the wheel and pulled the car on to the wide pavement of the Promenade, clipping his wing mirror on one of the ornamental wrought-iron lamp-posts.

He pushed his way into the Manhattan Skyline. Customers were waiting four deep at the bar and he almost produced a riot by elbowing through them until he was facing the man in the patterned waistcoat who'd been working the week before.

'Is he still here, then?'

The man, concentrating on pulling a glass of beer, seemed not to hear. Hunter thumped his fist on the bar.

'You phoned about the bloke I was looking for. You said he'd come in.'

The barman set the glass down carefully.

'Aye. He did.'

'Well, where is he now then?'

'I don't know, do I?'

'What do you mean?'

'He came in, had just one drink, then he went.' He was still listening to the customers' shouted orders and stood, balletically poised, reaching a glass to the optic with one hand, taking the cap off a bottle of cider with the other.

'For Christ's sake!' Hunter thumped the bar again, almost weeping with frustration.

'What did you expect me to do? I could hardly lock him in the bog, could I? If you wanted me to make a citizen's arrest you should have said on the phone. I didn't need to ring you.'

'Is there somewhere quieter we can talk?'

'Are you joking? If I stop now I'll get the sack.'

'If you don't stop now I'll close this place down. Tell that to your boss.'

There was an exchange with a middle-aged man who sat on a stool at the end of the bar. Steve beckoned Hunter to follow him. They walked down a dusty corridor past the toilets and into a bare, windowless room with a formica table, a sink and a couple of kitchen chairs. On the floor there was a pile of women's magazines – Hello! and Homes and Gardens – a kettle, some grubby mugs and a catering tin of instant coffee.

'I've got five minutes,' Steve said. 'And that comes out of my break.'

'Get that kettle on. You've got as long as it takes.' Hunter sat on one of the chairs and put his elbows on the table. He had a headache. 'Where did Paul go when he left here?'

'I've not got a clue. I'm not a mind-reader.'

'Well, tell me exactly what happened.'

The kettle boiled. Steve made the coffee, tipped in damp lumps of powdered milk. He stirred it but there were still dandruff-sized specks of white floating in the greasy liquid. Hunter drank it, not caring.

'He came in just before I rang you. I didn't recognize him at first.'

'When would that be? Three quarters of an hour ago?'

'Something like that. It wasn't so busy, anyway. Before the big rush.'

'Was he on his own?'

'Aye. But he didn't want to be. He was looking for Kim Houghton. That's when I realized it was him. He asked if she'd been in.'

'Had she?'

'No. I've not seen her for a while now. I told him that.'

'Why did he come here looking for her?' Hunter was speaking almost to himself. 'He knows where she lives. Why didn't he go to her home? Unless he thought we'd be on the Headland, looking out for him.'

'You're the detective. But I don't think he was capable of what you'd call rational thought.'

'What do you mean?'

'I'd say he'd had a few. Only one pint in here, but if you ask me he'd been drinking before he arrived. He wasn't roaring drunk. But a bit on the emotional side. It takes some people that way.'

'Why? What did he say?'

'"You don't understand. You don't know what it feels like to be lonely."' Steve put on a fair imitation of a maudlin drunk. 'Something like that. He got even more sorry for himself when I told him Kim wasn't about.'

'But he didn't tell you where he was going next?'

The barman shook his head. 'If he'd been an ordinary customer I'd have been glad to get shot of him. I thought he'd start crying in his beer. I can't stand the ones who turn suicidal.'

'Nor me.'

They shared a moment's silence in contemplation of people who wasted the effect of good beer. Steve seemed to have forgotten his boss's instructions to be back in five minutes. He lifted his empty mug to offer Hunter another coffee but Hunter was overtaken again by a sense of urgency and shook his head.

'Have you got a description of him?'

'Nothing different from what I told you last time.'

'What was he wearing?'

'Black jeans, white shirt, newish black leather jacket.'

'Right. I'll see you, then.' He fought his way through the crowd and into the street.

He checked Idols, Forty Second Street and The Big Apple. Occasionally he glimpsed a leather-coated back, dark hair. But when he got a closer view the man was too fat or too young. He only accosted one suspect and *he* turned out to be a Scot with a Glaswegian accent and a wife called Gillian who'd been hiding in the ladies. Then he went outside and looked in the side streets and the car parks for a red Mazda, thinking he must look dead dodgy. If some woodentop saw him he'd be pulled in on suspicion of nicking cars. Eventually he gave up.

It occurred to him that he should get someone round to the Headland in case Paul turned up there looking for Kim, and even that he should go himself to warn her. She might invite him in. In the end he didn't do anything. He was supposed to be off duty. He was tired and he was, he realized now, still pissed. All he wanted was to get home without bother and go to bed.

When his mam heard his key in the lock she got up to make him cocoa. He took it to bed with him and swore out loud because she'd forgotten to turn on his electric blanket.

Kim Houghton started on the vodka as soon as she'd put Kirsty to bed. It was a present from a security alarm salesman who travelled abroad a lot with his work. She didn't usually like drinking alone but tonight she was so fed up that she thought she deserved a treat. She wouldn't be able to sleep anyway. The music from the club would keep her awake. And the thought of all those people having a good time.

Kim watched the late film on the television and then went upstairs. She was standing at the window, about to draw the curtains when she saw a car she didn't recognize parked on the other side of the street, outside Bella Charlton's house. Bella's nephew and his family must have come to visit her at last. It annoyed Kim to imagine the old witch still up, having a party, while she was on her way to bed. Alone.

Chapter Thirty-One

Emma woke with a start to the sound of Brian's alarm. She'd taken a pill the night before and hadn't even heard Brian come in. Probably just as well, she thought, looking at him. He scarcely stirred when the alarm went off and the smell of beer and stale cigarette smoke still clung to the clothes he'd folded up on the chair.

She got up to make tea and found that the boys were already out of their rooms. They were sitting on the kitchen floor surrounded by string and brown paper. They'd unearthed the kites which Brian had bought and hoped to keep for a surprise until the following day. Owen was looking at the picture on the box.

'Can we fly them?'

'Not today. You'll have to make them first and Dad's going to work.'

'He's not gone to work yet?'

'No. He's still in bed.'

When she took a cup of tea to Brian, with the usual couple of paracetamol, they were sitting on the bed. Owen was fixing together lengths of bamboo cane and Brian was propped on one elbow, bleary-eyed, supervising the construction.

'*Dad* says we can fly them.' Owen was triumphant. He'd already got the hang of playing one off against the other.

'Did you?' she asked.

Brian shrugged. She could tell he was disappointed but he hadn't been able to refuse.

'Do you have to go to work?' At weekends he didn't make appointments. It was just a matter of catching up. She held her breath, wondering what she'd do about Mark if he decided to stay.

He hesitated.

'Yeah, I do. Something important. You know.'

She went downstairs without answering.

After days of gloomy drizzle it was perfect weather for kite flying. The sun was shining and there was a blustery wind. Emma put out a line of washing and the sheets flapped and swooped, so bright in the morning sunshine that they hurt her eyes.

Brian came down. He was wearing jeans and an open-necked shirt and she wondered if he'd changed his mind and decided to stay. It seemed, though, that the pull of business was too great in the end. She watched him drive off with mixed feelings. As the time to meet Mark got nearer she realized she would have been glad of an excuse not to go.

She told the boys firmly that they would have to wait until after lunch to play outside. Claire would be looking after them then. It would be something for them to do. She thought it would be good for Claire too, to wrap up warm and get some fresh air. Constructive play was important and recently the nanny seemed to have lost her enthusiasm for the job. It was almost as if she resented the time she spent with the children.

Emma was already planning how to give Claire the sack. She knew now wouldn't be a good time. It would be insensitive, to say the least, so close to Kath's death. But for all sorts of reasons she'd made up her mind that the girl would have to leave.

Claire was predictably grumpy when Emma told her about the plans for flying kites.

'What about Helen?' she asked.

'It's not cold outside. She'll be fine in her pushchair.'

'I'm not sure I can cope with them all. You know what David's like if he gets in a strop.'

'Nonsense!' Emma, who was already irritated by the demands being placed on her by Mark, felt like giving the girl a shake.

'Where are you off to, then?' Claire demanded. She watched Emma button her smart coat and take her car keys from the hook on the kitchen wall.

'I'm meeting a friend for lunch,' Emma said snootily, implying, Not that it's any business of yours, anyway.

'You won't be back late, then?'

'No,' Emma said. 'I won't be back late.'

But then, just as she was on her way through the door, the misgivings which had been troubling her all morning made her reconsider. Why did she have to meet Mark? When they were together he was too persuasive. She could say all she wanted on the phone. Ignoring Claire's curiosity, she turned back into the house.

She took the phone into, her bedroom and pushed the buttons impatiently. The line was engaged. She waited for a couple of minutes and tried again. This time she got through. It rang three times then switched on to his answering machine. She didn't bother leaving a message. He'd be on his way to the pub. She called goodbye to the children and went out to her car. Whatever Mark had done she couldn't leave him sitting there, waiting for her.

She drove slowly down Cotter's Row. At the weekends there were lots of parked cars. Some of them were pulled on to the narrow pavement but still there was only just enough room to get through. As she approached the club she saw Marilyn Howe walking back up the Headland towards her home. She was striding purposefully as she always had done when she walked with her mother, her eyes fixed ahead of her.

Emma arrived at the pub in Puddywell exactly on time. She had expected Mark to be there already. He should have been if he had set off from Otterbridge when she had phoned and he had seemed so insistent when he had arranged the meeting that she had not contemplated that he might be late. But his car was not parked in the road outside and there was no sign of him in either of the bars.

She bought a bottle of mineral water and took it to a table with a view of the road. Sunlight filtered through the dusty window and showed up the grime on the floor. She had dressed carefully for the meeting. Smart clothes always gave her confidence. Now she wished she had worn something more suitable, less conspicuous.

The pub was almost empty and the barmaid, a large, jolly girl who seemed scarcely old enough to serve, was inclined to chat.

'Are you waiting for someone?'

Emma pretended she had not heard and the girl disappeared into a room at the back to make a toasted sandwich for a big man in overalls and wellingtons.

The door opened and Emma turned, her recriminations already prepared, expecting apologies and excuses. But Mark did not come in. She watched a young couple in black leather, crash helmets under their arms, go to the bar and order drinks. They switched on the juke box and the room was filled with the same repetitive electronic music which had been coming from the club the night before.

Emma stood up and went to the phone. The barmaid had returned to her post and watched her with sympathy. Emma dropped her purse, scattering change all over the floor, retrieved ten pence and dialled. The phone rang. The answering machine switched on. She spoke as much for the watching barmaid as in the hope that Mark would respond.

'If you're there, Mark, please pickup the phone.'

The barmaid who had seen her speak, but had been unable to hear the words over the music, smiled.

'A mix up over times, was it?' she asked, as Emma returned her glass to the bar.

'That's right,' Emma said.

'Men! What are they like?'

She sat in her car deciding she would give him ten more minutes. When the time was over she considered driving to his house. Despite everything, she felt concerned for him, responsible even. Then she thought that with three kids, not to mention Brian, she did enough of the mothering thing. She didn't need Mark as well. She switched on the engine and drove back to the Headland and her children, thinking that perhaps she'd had a lucky escape.

The level crossing was down. The train moved so slowly that Marilyn Howe on full power would have been able to overtake it. At last the lights stopped flashing and she pulled away. In Cotter's

Row an old man was washing his car and she had to sound her horn to make him move his bucket from the middle of the road. He seemed oblivious to everything except the shine of the chrome on his Escort.

She had expected Claire and the children still to be inside. Claire was stubborn and Emma wouldn't have put it past her to find an excuse not to fly the kites. But as she approached the Coastguard House she saw Owen racing across the grass. The kite was in the air behind him, its tails twisting crazily in the wind. She stopped the car and got out to watch.

'Having a good time?' she shouted.

He noticed her for the first time, lost his concentration and stumbled. The kite plummeted to the ground. 'Brill,' he said. She pulled him to his feet.

'Where's Claire?'

'She took Helen into the house. She needed changing.'

'Is David with her?'

'I suppose so.'

He began to wind the string clumsily round his fist.

'We'd better go into find them.' She didn't really like Owen being beyond the safety of the Coastguard House wall. 'Did Claire play with you?'

'Yeah. She's not as fit as you, though. She got all red and hot and she only had one go.'

'Perhaps she needs more exercise.' Emma felt a superior amusement. She did step aerobics twice a week in Otterbridge Church Hall. 'Hop in and I'll drive you the last little way.'

Claire was in the kitchen. She was still flushed and slightly out of breath. She was fastening Helen's dungarees.

'You're back early,' she said, more peeved than grateful for Emma's arrival.

'I said I wouldn't be late.'

Claire looked at Owen. 'Where's David?'

'I don't know.'

'I asked you to keep an eye on him while I changed Helen.'

Owen was unconcerned. 'I know, but he came up with you. For a wee.'

'Get Owen some juice,' Emma said to Claire. 'I'll see to him.'

They had built a downstairs bathroom next to the utility room so the boys could come in from the garden without carrying mud to the rest of the house.

'David,' Emma called. 'What are you doing?'

There was no lock on the door and she pushed it open. The plastic step which David used to reach the toilet was in its place but there was no sign of the boy.

She told herself to stay calm. She shouldn't overreact. She went back to the kitchen, then shouted his name up the stairs. There was no reply.

'When did you last see him?' she demanded of Claire.

'About ten minutes ago. Helen was grizzling. I could tell she needed changing. I asked the boys to come in with me but they wouldn't. I warned you I wouldn't be able to cope with them all outside.'

Emma knelt down. She tried to keep her voice steady as she spoke to her son.

'Are you sure David came into the house?'

'Not really.'

'What do you mean?'

'I was flying the kite. I was the only one who could really make it work. It went really high. All the string was unwound. I thought David might like to hold it. He could, if I helped him. But when I turned round he wasn't there so I thought he must have gone in with Claire.'

Emma stood up and took the baby from Claire. She held Helen tight, trying to control her temper. She didn't want a scene in front of Owen.

'Go and look for him outside,' she said tightly. 'There's an old man washing his car in Cotter's Row. He might have seen something. I'll search in here.'

For a moment Claire didn't respond. She went to the fridge and poured Owen a glass of juice. She handed it to him.

'I expect he's in the house somewhere, hiding,' she said. 'I was in the bathroom, changing the baby. I wouldn't have heard.'

'All the same. I'd like you to look outside. Now.' She couldn't believe that Claire was being so obstructive. 'Please.'

'All right. I'm going.' Claire stamped out sulkily.

Emma began her search of the house. There was no immediate sign that David had returned there. His coat had not been thrown on the floor. He had not been rooting through the kitchen cupboards for crisps or chocolate. She moved methodically from room to room, praying for an explosion of sound, an upturned chair, a cry of boo. Owen followed her. They walked in silence. Emma opened cupboard doors and looked under beds. When she was convinced David wasn't in the house she returned to the kitchen. She sat Owen on her lap.

'Can you remember anything which might help?' she asked, trying to keep her voice normal, unflurried.

He shook his head and began to cry.

Until now Emma had been able to believe that this was one of the regular scares she inflicted on herself. If she lost sight of Owen for a moment in a supermarket or he was the last to come out of playgroup she convinced herself that some harm had come to him. It had become an automatic anxiety, a superstitious way of warding off danger. Now she knew that the danger was real. When Claire appeared back at the kitchen door Emma looked up at her without hope.

'You didn't see him?'

'No,' Claire said. 'No one's seen him.'

'I'll phone the police, then.' It was a relief to have something to do. She dialled 999. Later she phoned Brian at the office but there was no reply.

Chapter Thirty-Two

The police set up a roadblock just beyond the level crossing. Brian Coulthard saw it on his way home but nobody stopped him. The two officers standing in the sun weren't interested in cars coming on to the Headland, only those on their way off.

Ramsay sent Sally Wedderburn to wait with Emma Coulthard at the Coastguard House. At first she'd objected.

'I've had nothing to do with the child abductions since I joined the murder team.'

'Don't you think this is connected with the murder?' he asked, as if he were surprised she'd not worked it out for herself. She hadn't liked to ask what he meant.

Still she'd been reluctant to go. She and Emma Coulthard hadn't exactly hit it off when they first met and this support role wasn't really her thing. She wasn't much good at comforting conversation and endless cups of tea, letting the kids play with her radio and climb all over her lap. All the same she supposed it was an opportunity of a sort.

When she got there Emma Coulthard hardly seemed to recognize her. The woman was sitting on a stool in the kitchen. She was very upright and her face had a hard, sculpted look caused by all the muscles tensing through an effort of will. Sally realized she was afraid that if she relaxed for a minute she'd break down. She had the other children to think of. Sally admired that.

'Is there any news?' Her voice was controlled too.

Sally shook her head. 'Not yet. They've put a road block down by the level crossing. They're stopping all the cars.'

'It's too late. He'd been gone twenty minutes when I phoned you.'

'Not necessarily. There's been a convoy of trains to the power station this afternoon. The crossing's been down for a lot of that time. Besides, it's not certain yet that David's been abducted, is it? You said he was the sort to run away. We've a team searching the shore. There are plenty of places he could be playing. And the roadblock's there as much to ask for witnesses as anything else. People visiting the Headland might have seen him.'

'Yes.' The logic of the reply seemed to reassure her. 'Yes, I see.'

'Where's your nanny? We'll need to talk to her.'

'I sent her home. I know it's not really her fault but I was afraid I'd have a go at her. Say something I might regret later. We need someone to blame, don't we, at a time like this? Besides ourselves, of course.'

Then she did seem about to break down, but the door opened and Brian Coulthard came in. He ran across the floor towards his wife. His black shoes were very shiny and Sally thought he moved like one of the ballroom dancers who take part in Latin American competitions on the television late at night. He took Emma up in his arms, and held her while she sobbed out the story.

Sally mumbled something about having to call the office and wandered through to the living room where a small body sat forlornly on the floor. She let him press the buttons on her radio and talk for a moment to Inspector Ramsay, who was waiting for news at the police station.

Hunter stopped at the roadblock on his way through to the Headland. It didn't hurt to give the lads a bit of support, and whenever he saw his mates in uniform doing a routine task like that it made him feel good he still wasn't one of them.

A blue estate was coming down the road from the direction of the club and he pulled his car into the verge and got out to watch a PC flag it down.

The driver was dark, unshaven. He looked like Hunter felt after twelve pints of lager and a couple of hours' kip on a strange sofa.

'Could you give us your name please, sir?'

'Hooper. Paul Hooper.'

'Any identification to confirm that, sir?'

He pulled out a wallet and handed over a credit card.

'Are you the registered keeper of this vehicle?'

'No. It belongs to the company I work for. Otterbridge Motors.'

'That's the one with the big showroom at the retail park off the bypass.'

'Aye.'

Later Hunter was to have nightmares about that scene. He ran it over and over in his head. Because he almost stood aside and let the man drive away. He watched the PC look in the boot and ask his questions about a small lad wandering the Headland on his own and he almost failed to make the connection. But not quite. At the last moment he stepped forward, almost shoving the constable out of the way as he stuck his head through the driver's window.

'Mr Hooper,' he said. 'What was your business on the Headland?'

Then, when there was no immediate reply.

'Been to visit Kim Houghton again, have you?'

'I don't know what you mean.'

He wouldn't be a bad-looking chap, Hunter thought, if he had a shower and a shave. He knew how to dress. The leather jacket was folded up on the seat next to him.

'Kim Houghton's got a friend named Paul. A guy just like you. And he was on the Headland the night before a woman was murdered. We've been asking him to come forward, but he never did. Strange that, isn't it? In a case when an innocent woman's been killed you'd think he'd be only too pleased to help the police. And now a little boy's gone missing too. So tell me, Mr Paul Hooper, what is it exactly that you've got to hide?'

The man leant forward so his head touched the steering wheel. Then, to Hunter's disgust, he began to cry.

They wasted no time in interviewing Hooper. The boy was still missing. Ramsay was aware throughout of the clock on the wall, the minutes ticking away.

'Where is he, Paul? Where's David?' The question, like a refrain, punctuating the other questions.

At first it was impossible to work out what was going on. It wasn't that he was unco-operative. He seemed only too eager to answer their questions. Except the important one, which he seemed not to hear.

'Where is he? Where's David?'

He said he wanted to explain. He needed help. So did Marie, though she'd never admit it. That's why he'd spent the night on the Headland. Because he wanted to think. At first Ramsay left the questions to Hunter, who found it hard to get a word in.

'I didn't mean them any harm,' Hooper said. He leant right across the table. It seemed he was going to grab Hunter by the shoulder to make him understand. 'You do believe me about that, don't you? I wouldn't have hurt them for the world.'

'Who are we talking about here?' Hunter demanded. 'Mrs Howe or the little laddie? And what, exactly, did you do with the little laddie, Paul?'

'I put him back!' Hooper sat back. He was surprised, indignant. 'I put them all back. You know I did. I bought them sweets, played with them, and then I put them back. On a busy street with lots of people so I knew they'd be safe.'

'Who did you put back, Paul?'

'You know! Stop playing games!' He hit the table with the palm of his hand. Mad as a snake, Hunter thought. He hated interviewing loonies. You never knew where you were with them. Hooper continued, counting on his fingers as he listed the names.

'The first was William Samms. The second was called Toby. I never knew his other name. That was in Newcastle outside the post office in Eldon Square. The third was Ricky Elton. I took him from the McDonald's on the estate where I work. The fourth was Tom Bingham. He came to me. I was looking through the nursery window and he came running out. He thought I was his dad. I pretended I was. It was our secret. Four boys. I never took a girl.

I thought a girl might get upset more easily and cry. I would have liked to take a girl but I couldn't risk it. Not unless it was someone who'd met me before.' He paused, then blurted out guiltily, 'Kim Houghton's got a girl. Kirsty. As pretty as a picture.'

'And that's why you went back to the Headland, wasn't it, Paul? Not to see Kim, but to see Kirsty. That's why you were looking for Kim in Whitley last night. Because Kirsty wouldn't have got frightened and upset, would she, Paul? You wouldn't have been a stranger to Kirsty.'

It was Ramsay, speaking for the first time. Hooper was startled, as if he'd forgotten the inspector was there, but he nodded fiercely in agreement.

'So why didn't you do it?' Ramsay asked. 'Why didn't you just knock at the door and ask if you could take Kirsty out? Kim wouldn't have minded.'

Hooper mumbled something.

'Or wouldn't that have been as much fun? Not as much fun as snatching a child when no one was looking. Is that why you took David instead? Where is he, Paul? His mum wants him back.'

Hooper looked up.

'Who's David?' he asked.

'Why did you do it, Paul?'

'Marie and I have been trying for a baby for ages,' he said conversationally, as if he were talking to a mate in a pub, not answering a question. 'We went for all the tests. We put our name down for treatment but we couldn't afford to go private and there's such a queue. It's more common than you think, you know, infertility.

'Then while we were still on the waiting list Marie fell pregnant. We couldn't believe it. She had a little boy. Jordan. As round as a barrel and bouncing with health. That's what everyone said. He died. Cot death last autumn. No one knows why. He'd be three if he'd lived . . . So it was back to the beginning of the queue, wasn't it? And money in the NHS tighter and the waiting list even longer. We put down our names to adopt. Or foster. But they wouldn't have us. They said we were too emotional after the baby died Unstable.'

He broke off abruptly, began chewing his fingernails.

'Where's David?' Hunter said. 'David Coulthard. The little boy you took from the Headland this afternoon.'

'I didn't take anyone from the Headland,' he repeated automatically. Then, in a more animated voice, he went on. 'It was like you said. I went to Whitley last night, looking for Kim. I'd been really low. I thought I could have a few beers, go back to Kim's house, play with Kirsty in the morning. I told Marie I was working away.'

'Didn't you realize we'd been looking for you?' Hunter demanded. 'If you'd met up with Kim she'd have phoned us straight away.'

'No,' he said. 'I didn't think.' And they realized that was probably true. He was too wrapped up in himself, in his own need for comfort. 'Kim wasn't there. So I drove out to the Headland. I looked in the club because I thought she might be in there, having a drink with her friends. Then I waited outside the house. Kim wouldn't have recognized the car. We take different ones from the garage. It depends what's been sold. I didn't knock at the door. There might have been a babysitter. I wouldn't have known what to say.'

'What did you hang around there for?' Hunter asked.

'I thought Kirsty might be on her own,' he confessed. 'Kim leaves her sometimes. She doesn't deserve a kid, does she? But Kim was there. I saw her draw the bedroom curtains. I suppose I could have gone in but by then I couldn't face her. All that chat. Having to be nice. You don't have to do that with kids. So I drove down to the jetty and went to sleep in the car.'

'Until two o'clock in the afternoon?' Hunter asked, as if he didn't believe a word of it.

'Yeah. I mean I wasn't asleep all that time. I went for a walk along the cliffs. To clear my head. Like I said, thinking. I knew it couldn't go on. If you hadn't picked me up at that roadblock I'd have given myself in anyway.' He looked up at Hunter. 'How did you know I was there?'

'We didn't.' Hunter was quickly losing patience. 'We were looking for David Coulthard, the little boy you abducted from the Headland. Now stop pissing about and tell us what you've done with him.'

'I've already told you. I didn't take a little boy. I would have liked to spend some time with Kirsty, but I didn't see her either.'

Ramsay slipped silently from the room. Paul Hooper was biting his thumbnail again and looked very much like a little boy himself.

Chapter Thirty-Three

In Cotter's Row Ramsay waited for Sal Wedderburn to join him before knocking at the door. He saw her walking briskly down the track, her hands in her jacket pockets. He knew she would be glad to have escaped the Coastguard House.

'How are the Coulthards bearing up?'

She shrugged. 'It gets harder, the longer it is without news.'

'You left someone with them?'

'Grace Newton.'

Ramsay nodded. Grace was soft and plump, famous for her laziness. She was irritating to work with but she'd be unflappable, reassuring.

'Do you know where Emma Coulthard went this lunch time?' Sally said. 'To meet Mark Taverner. She came right out with it in front of her husband. She said she'd explain to him later. He didn't seem bothered. As if it hadn't come as any surprise that they were meeting.'

'How long did she spend with Mark?'

'She didn't. Apparently he arranged to meet her in a pub and he never turned up. That's how she was back on the Headland earlier than she'd expected.'

'Has he phoned the Coulthards since, with any explanation?'

'Not so far as I know.'

Sally was impatient to knock on the Howes' door and get on with the interview, but he stood on the pavement for a moment and considered what this could mean. Wild explanations occurred to him, a bizarre conspiracy theory in which Mark had phoned

Emma to keep her off the Headland while her child was taken. Ramsay was distracted by the coincidence.

'I suppose his car might have broken down,' he muttered. 'Something like that.'

'Are we going in then?' Sally demanded.

'We'll talk to Mr Taverner later. When we've finished here.'

Marilyn opened the door. She was wearing the same jeans, the same jumper.

'Is there any news?' she asked. 'Claire told me what happened. You read about these things, don't you? But you never dream they'll happen here.'

Ramsay had the impression she was repeating a phrase she'd heard. Perhaps the neighbours had said the same thing about her mother's death.

'Where is Claire?'

'In the backroom.' She lowered her voice. 'She's ever so upset.'

'Is your dad in?'

'No. He's working this afternoon. A private party. The taxi came a while ago. He needed a taxi to carry all the stuff he's got. He's trying a new act: ventriloquism and magic combined. So he had to take Charlie.'

'Charlie?'

'The ventriloquist's dummy.'

Ramsay wondered what the men on the roadblock would make of that, then thought, with a constriction of the stomach, that they might not even stop the taxi. They were looking for a private car. They might just wave it through.

'Where's your dad working?'

'I don't know. Newcastle, I think. Somewhere smart. Jesmond. Gosforth.'

'Does he keep an appointment diary?'

'Yeah, but he'll have it with him. Why?'

'We'll need to talk to him. He might have seen something.'

'Are you joking? He was in his room, practising. You could have the Blyth Town Band marching in the street outside and he'd not notice.'

'Can we go through, then, and talk to Claire?'

'Sure.'

Although the fire wasn't lit, Claire was sitting in her usual chair by the side of the grate. She was still wearing her outdoor shoes and her coat. There was a newspaper on her knee but Ramsay could tell she wasn't reading it.

'I suppose Mrs Coulthard told you it was my fault,' she said, still staring at the paper.

'I haven't spoken to Mrs Coulthard.' Ramsay took the other seat, Bernie's seat, beside her.

'I told her I wouldn't be able to manage the three of them outside. She knows David's a tinker. He hasn't got any sense of danger. He's always running off and he'd follow anyone.'

'I think she probably blames herself more than you.'

'Yeah, well. It's my living, isn't it? I might never work again if people get to hear about this.'

'You haven't asked if there's any news of David.'

'I'm not daft. You'd have told me if you'd found him.' She turned for the first time to face him. 'You haven't found him?'

He shook his head. She stared back at the newspaper. 'That's it, then. Someone's had him away. You'd have found him if he was still on the Headland.'

'Not necessarily.'

'What do you want?'

'Do you mind if Sally looks round? We're searching all the houses is Cotter's Row, in case he just wandered in through an open door. Is that the sort of thing he might do?'

'He might,' she conceded. She wiped a hand across her forehead. Her cheeks were flushed but still it didn't occur to her to take her coat off. She paused for a moment. Ramsay nodded to Sally, who left the room.

'A nanny's not supposed to have favourites,' Claire went on. 'But he was the one I liked best though he wasn't easy. He was always into mischief. Like I said, a real tinker.'

'Tell me what happened today.'

'I only agreed to go in as a favour. I don't usually work weekends.'

'Did Mrs Coulthard tell you why she needed you to work?'

'A lunch appointment, she said. She was all tarted up.'

'Was it usual for her to go out on a Saturday?'

'No, if she's going to meet her friends it's usually during the week. Weekends most people spend with their families, don't they?'

'I suppose they do.' Unless they're policemen, he thought. 'When did she ask you? Was it a last-minute arrangement?'

'Not really. She fixed it up a couple of days ago.' She wiped her forehead again. 'So I got there and the kids were already wound up. Their dad had bought them kites and they wanted to go out to fly them.'

'Did you go out straight away?'

'No. I gave them dinner first. To be honest, I thought if we waited a bit the weather might change. Not even Mrs Coulthard could expect me to take them out in the rain.'

'But it didn't rain.'

'No.' Claire turned in her chair so she was facing him again. 'So I thought I'd better get it over with. I put on their coats and I took them out. I had Helen in the pushchair and the boys carried the kites. David wanted to help though the kite was bigger than him. They played nicely enough for half an hour then I realized Helen needed changing, so I said "That's it, boys. Time to go in now. You can play again with your dad tomorrow."

'But they weren't having any of that, were they? David threw a tantrum. He's that sort of age. If I'd had him on his own I'd have picked him up and carried him into the house. I don't stand any nonsense. But I had Helen in the pushchair screaming and Owen with a face like thunder. He looks just like his mother when he's in a mood and he's stubborn as a mule. So I said, "OK. You can stay for a bit longer, but you'll have to keep an eye on David." And I took Helen back to the house. Of course, Mrs Coulthard picked that minute to turn up.'

'Did you see anyone else out in the Headland?'

She shrugged. 'A couple of dog walkers. It was sunny. That sort of day.'

'But no one you recognized?'

'An old lady with a Jack Russell who lives at the end of the Row. The Laidler kids. They're allowed to run wild.' The gang who'd found Mrs Howe's body, Ramsay thought.

'Was there anyone who took a special interest in the children?'

'Not that I noticed. I had my hands full.'

'Yes,' he said. 'Of course.'

There was a moment of silence.

'Did you see a man on his own? Thirtyish. Unshaven.'

'Oh him. Yes. But that was earlier, when I was on my way up to the Coulthards'. He was walking down the cliffs to the jetty.'

'You didn't see him when you were out with the children?'

She shook her head. 'You don't think I'd have left them if there'd been someone like that hanging around?'

Sally Wedderburn came back into the room.

'Well?' Claire asked.

'Nothing.'

'Do you know where Bernie's working this afternoon?' Ramsay asked.

'A private party in Gosforth. A doctor's kid. Bernie went there last year too. That's why he had to work out a different routine. You can't do the same act twice.'

'Where exactly in Gosforth?'

'I don't know the address. It's one of those big houses that look out over the Town Moor. I'd have fancied going if Mrs Coulthard hadn't asked me to work. Like I said, I only agreed to do her a favour.'

'Would you mind if we looked out the back?' Ramsay asked. 'A team's searching all the yards in the street but it'll save you being disturbed later if we do it now.'

'Do what you like,' Claire said, but she didn't move.

'I'll open the back door for you,' Marilyn said. She had been in the room all the time, sat up to the table listening.

They trooped through the kitchen after her. Claire stayed where she was. Even with just the three of them the yard seemed crowded. They had to duck to avoid the washing on the line. A row of large vests and elephantine underpants billowed gently.

God, Sally thought, it was enough to put you off marriage for life. Her boyfriend was slim and fit but perhaps Bernie Howe had once been like that.

Ramsay stood in front of the shed. It was red brick, like the house. There was one small window, which was so covered in coal dust and cobwebs that it was impossible to see in. He tried to pull the padlock open but it was locked.

'Where's the key?'

'In the kitchen,' Marilyn said. 'But there's nothing inside. Claire bought the padlock. She's trying to persuade Dad to keep his bike in there but he never remembers.'

'All the same,' Ramsay said. 'I think we'll check.'

'OK.'

He watched her return to the kitchen and take a key from a shelf just inside the back door. Like the padlock it was shiny and solid.

The key turned smoothly but the paving stones in the yard were so uneven that at first he could only pull the door open a fraction.

'There's a knack,' Marilyn said. 'You have to lift it.' She stepped forward. 'I'll do it if you like.'

'No,' Ramsay replied quickly. 'That's all right.'

Because even with the door open just a few inches, the late afternoon sun slanting over the back wall into the yard lit up a patch of the concrete floor. The floor wasn't dusty, which is what he would have expected, but there was a dark stain as if oil had been spilled there. Ramsay hoped that it was oil.

Chapter Thirty-Four

Ramsay hesitated. He heard gull cries, the distant sound of a train. Inside the house Claire must have switched on the television because there was a short blast of music followed by excited speech. From the shed, silence. He turned back to Marilyn.

'I'll tell you what you could do,' he said. 'Put the kettle on. I'd love a cup of tea.'

'All right.'

She returned to the house. Ramsay shut the kitchen door firmly behind her and gave the shed his full attention. He gripped the door close to the hook through which the padlock had been fastened and lifted it, pulling it towards him at the same time. Sunlight flooded in. Now the stain on the floor, rusty coloured, looked more like blood than oil. The corners were still in shadow.

The shed was split into two compartments. One, presumably, had housed the privy. In the other coal was stored. The spaces were separated by a chest-high brick wall and looked like animal stalls. There were no tools – Bernard Howe obviously had no interest in DIY – except a small trowel which had been newly purchased, Ramsay thought, to plant up the tub in the yard. A defunct vacuum cleaner lay on its side. In one corner was a pile of threadbare clothes destined for a charity shop. A plastic sack with AGE CONCERN written on it had been folded over the partition wall. And on top of the pile of clothes lay a small child. His head was thrown back uncomfortably. His arms, palms upwards, were outstretched.

The boy was alive but sleeping. His face was dirty and stained with tears. He opened his eyes and began to whimper.

Sally crouched beside him, making reassuring noises, but she seemed afraid to touch him and it was Ramsay in the end who picked him up. He was still half asleep and he didn't struggle. He'd wet his pants and Ramsay felt the damp seep through David's quilted trousers and on to his shirt. He was holding the boy so close that he could feel his heart beating.

'Give Grace a call,' he said. 'Tell her to put the Coulthards out of their misery. But tell her not to give any details. Just that he's alive and well. She can come and fetch him. I don't want the Coulthard's turning up on the doorstep. We'll have discretion all round. I want no lynch mobs here.'

'How did Claire hope to get away with it?' Sally demanded. 'She didn't even stop us coming out here to look.'

'I don't think there was any intention of getting away with it. It was a gesture.'

If it was Claire, he thought, still unsettled by the coincidence of Mark Taverner's failure to keep his appointment with Emma. Remembering the padlock key lying on a shelf close to the kitchen door which was always kept open. So obvious. Brass like the padlock and shiny. Hunter would tell him that he was making things too complicated and that for once in his life he should accept that the obvious answer was probably the true one.

'I know she was daft about babies. But did she really think she could keep him here, like some sort of doll?'

Sally had worked herself into a rage. Just because she didn't fancy motherhood herself didn't mean she couldn't get upset when kids were ill treated. The thought of the kid locked in the dark shed, scared out of his wits, made her want to vomit.

The kitchen door had a glass panel and through it Ramsay could see that the room was empty. The kettle had switched itself off but there was no sign of Marilyn. He supposed she'd wandered through to chat to Claire and had her attention caught by something on the television. Unless she'd been watching from the kitchen, had seen them retrieve the little boy and had gone to warn Claire.

'Go in,' he said sharply to Sally. 'Don't tell them anything. Just make sure neither of them do a runner.'

Then he stood in the yard, still holding the silent three-year-old, waiting for Grace to arrive to take him away. He hoped the high walls would protect him from the prying eyes of neighbours. He supposed, considering it for the first time, that Prue would think herself too old to have another child.

Grace turned up in the back alley, driving Emma's car with the baby seat in the back. David allowed himself to be strapped in without any fuss.

'You'll arrange for medical checks,' Ramsay said.

'The GP's a friend of the family. He's already on his way.' She leant back against the car. 'What do I tell the family?'

'Nothing. Say you don't know how he came to be found.'

'That's true enough, isn't it?'

'I'm sorry. I don't know much myself yet. Tell them I'll be up later this evening. I'll talk to them then.'

She drove away. After the disruption of the search in the Row, Ramsay had expected the car to draw attention. A nosy neighbour in an upstairs window seeing the child would be enough to start a crowd. But the street was unnaturally quiet. Then he realized there was a Cup game. A five o'clock start to suit the television. The first time Newcastle had reached the semi-finals for years. They'd all be in their front rooms, draped in their black and white scarves.

In the back room the women were sitting in silence. Marilyn was reading a book. *Lord of the Flies.*

'I'm sorry about the tea,' she said. 'I started reading when the kettle was boiling. And I got engrossed. I'm doing if for my GCSE wider reading course.'

Absent-minded, he thought. Like her father.

'When do you expect Bernard home?' he asked.

'Marilyn looked up from her book to the clock which stood on the mantelpiece. 'Any time now.'

Claire stirred. 'Have you finished? Are you going to leave us in peace? I've a meal to cook.'

'I thought you'd like to know,' Ramsay said. 'David Coulthard's been found.'

'Is he all right?'

'Apparently.'

'Oh, brilliant.' But her attention was held by the television. 'I thought I'd go down in the records as the nanny from hell.'

She didn't ask where he'd been discovered. 'I suppose he did wander away, get hidden somewhere?'

'Something like that,' Ramsay said. Then: 'I wonder if you'd both mind going to the station with Sally to make a statement. For our records. To clear the matter up. I'll be along later.'

'Now?' Claire said. 'Bernie'll be in any minute wanting his tea.'

'If you wouldn't mind. We'll drop you back later.'

He could see that Sally was working up a head of steam, imagined her exploding with, 'What sort of games do you think you're playing, lady? I suppose you want us to believe that the kid shut *himself* in your shed.'

'If I could just have a word, Constable, please.'

Shocked by the formality she followed him into the hall. There he said, 'Take her through her statement again. Don't give anything away. Hang on to her until I get back. And while you're there get someone to trace the taxi driver who dropped Bernie Howe in Gosforth. I want the exact time he was picked up. And find out where Mark Taverner's hiding.

'What about the girl?'

'Take a statement from her too. I don't want her here on her own when her dad gets back.'

When they had all gone and he had the place to himself he went to the kitchen, switched the kettle back on and made himself a mug of instant coffee. Newcastle must just have scored because through the wall he heard a concerto of yells and cheers. He took his mug into the back yard and knelt to look at the stain on the shed floor. He was quite certain it was blood. But it was not, as he had feared, the child's blood. David had not received even a scratch. Ramsay knew the rules. If he suspected that this was a scene of crime he should seal it off, call in the experts, make every effort to reduce contamination of the forensic evidence.

But if this was the scene of the crime he believed, it had happened weeks ago and contamination would have already occurred. And he was curious.

He started with the shed. In the compartment half filled with coal there was a tin bucket and a shovel. He moved the coal from one corner to another until he was satisfied that nothing had been hidden beneath it. He rummaged through the pile of discarded clothes. There was nothing but a short piece of bamboo which had fallen from the kite David had been flying. He must have held on to it while he was carried away.

Ramsay remembered what Emma had said: 'His speech is very poor for his age. They say there's nothing really wrong. Boys are often slow developers. But he gets frustrated when he can't communicate.'

It seemed unlikely then that David would be able to tell them who had abducted him. They would have to work that out for themselves.

Ramsay returned to the yard. His back ached. The shed wasn't quite high enough for him to stand upright. He noticed that since his last visit the plants in the ceramic tub had come into flower. There were early polyanths, yellow and deep scarlet.

On impulse he took the bamboo cane and poked it into the loosely packed compost and soil in the tub, prodding carefully through the roots, trying not to disturb the flowers. Then, when he was sure something was hidden there, he fetched the trowel from the shed and lifted out each polyanthus separately and set it on the yard. He took a pair of disposable gloves from his pocket and pulled them on, then fished in the tub with his hands. Despite his care, loose soil spilled on to the paving stones.

He reached into the tub like a child in a lucky dip and pulled out a kitchen knife. An ordinary bread knife with a plastic handle and a serrated blade. The knife that had killed Kathleen Howe. He replanted the polyanthus and went back to the house to await the arrival of Bernard.

Chapter Thirty-Five

When Ramsay got back to the police station he saw Marilyn sitting in the waiting room. She was reading a magazine which must have been left by another visitor. It was full of glossy pictures of filmstars, articles on fashion and shopping and 'How to Keep Your Man'. She seemed engrossed. She looked very tired. Her face was the same colour as her white hair.

'They've finished with me,' she said.

'I'll get someone to take you to your gran's,' he said. 'Your dad's there.'

'What about Claire?' She didn't ask what Bernie was doing at his mother's. Ramsay didn't explain. Bernie could tell her what was happening in Cotter's Row, about the scene of crime officer in the back yard, the constable at the front door fending off the neighbours and the press.

'Don't worry about Claire. I'll bring her over later.'

'How's the little boy?'

'He's fine.' He had spoken briefly to Grace. She'd told him that the Coulthards weren't demanding explanations at this stage. They were just relieved that the ordeal of waiting was over. He knew he would have to visit the Coastguard House – he was starting to suspect how much Emma Coulthard had deceived him – but he could allow them time with their son before he intruded.

In the Interview Room he found Claire with Sally Wedderburn and Newell, another member of his team. He gave his name for the tape and sent Newell away, then sat impassively and let Sally get on with her questions.

'Why did you do it, Claire?' Sally asked wearily. It wasn't the first time the question had been asked.

'Why did I do what?' Claire wasn't intimidated by the surroundings or the questions. She certainly wasn't intimidated by Sally Wedderburn. In her stolid, solitary way she almost seemed to be enjoying herself, to be enjoying at least Sally's discomfort because the interview wasn't progressing as she'd hoped.

'Why did you bring David Coulthard down the hill and lock him in your shed?'

'I didn't.'

'So how did he get there?'

'You tell me. You're the police officer.'

Ramsay could sense that Sally was on the verge of losing her temper but he didn't intervene. She'd come across more irritating suspects than Claire Irvine in her career and he wouldn't always be there to bail her out. She took a deep breath.

'You're not suggesting that a three-year-old locked himself in your shed?'

'Why not? He could have. As a sort of game. Hide and seek. I've told you he was that sort of kid.'

'And locked the padlock from outside?'

'Well, someone else could have done that, couldn't they? Not realizing he was there.'

'What sort of someone else are we talking about here, Claire? You don't exactly get a stream of visitors through your back yard, do you? Or have I missed something?'

'It could have been Marilyn. Or Bernie.'

It could have been Bernie, Ramsay thought. His taxi didn't collect him until after David Coulthard went missing. He said, 'We've talked to Marilyn and Bernie. Neither of them touched the padlock this afternoon.'

'Well, it wasn't me. What would be the point?'

And that had been troubling Stephen Ramsay all afternoon. He couldn't work out what was the point of the abduction. And where it fitted in with Kath Howe's murder. If it did.

'Perhaps you didn't mean any harm,' Sally said. 'Perhaps you just wanted to teach David a lesson, a bit of discipline, while Mrs Coulthard was out of the way and couldn't interfere. Because he's a naughty boy, isn't he? Not just lively, but naughty. And Mrs Coulthard won't have it, will she? She talks about his frustration but that's just an excuse. She doesn't have to cope with his tantrums day after day.'

Ramsay sat forward, impressed. This was more the sort of performance he'd been expecting from Sally. She continued, 'Perhaps this afternoon was the final straw. He was excited, let out on the Headland, suddenly with enough space to run around. I bet he went wild. So you thought you'd have to put your foot down. You'd see it as your duty almost, part of your job to teach him some respect. You told him if he didn't behave you'd shut him up in the dark. But he didn't behave, did he? So you had to carry out your threat. You'll have been told that at college. Don't make threats you're not prepared to carry out. You didn't mean to leave him there though, did you? Not all afternoon. Just while you took Helen up to the Coastguard House to change her nappy. You knew he'd be safe in there.'

Claire sat very still. She stared ahead of her and said, nothing. Encouraged, Sally went on, 'Then Mrs Coulthard spoiled it by coming home early. You couldn't tell her you'd locked David in a coal hole as a punishment. She wouldn't have been very impressed by that. My impression is that she doesn't have time for old-fashioned discipline. I don't suppose she even lets you smack them. So on the spur of the moment you made up a story about him disappearing. After all these child abductions she believed it. And worried herself sick all afternoon.'

Claire began to clap her hands, very slowly.

'Very good,' she said. 'Oh yes, very good. I almost believed it myself.'

'Do you admit that's what happened?'

'Of course not.' Claire was dismissive. 'I love kids. I've been properly trained. I wouldn't treat any child like that. Besides, Miss Clever Clogs, when Mrs Coulthard got in she sent me out down the Headland to look for David. If it happened like you said, why didn't I just let him out of the shed and pretend I'd found him wandering? He couldn't tell her any different. He can't talk. Anyway, what were the other kids doing while all this was going on?' She paused, then shot a knowing look at Sally. 'Your dad lock you in the coal shed when you'd been bad, did he? That'd explain a lot.'

Suddenly and shockingly Sally blushed.

'Could we go back to the padlock, Claire,' Ramsay said gently, as if he were musing to himself. 'You do admit that you bought that?'

'Yeah. I didn't like Bernie's bike in the hall. It left mud on the carpet. So we thought we might persuade him to leave it outside if we had somewhere secure.'

'But this afternoon his bike wasn't in the shed.'

'No. He must have forgotten when he got in last night.'

'You didn't remind him?'

'Na! He'd had enough nagging from Kath.' She must have thought that sounded callous because she added limply, 'You know what I mean.'

'But when I came to talk to you a couple of nights ago his bike was in the hall then too.'

'So? It's going to take him a while to get used to it.'

'There's a stain on the shed floor,' Ramsay said. She didn't answer. 'At first I thought it was oil from Bernie's bike, but now it seems Bernie doesn't keep his bike there very often. For some reason he seems to have taken a real dislike to the shed.' He paused, but still she didn't speak. 'So I took a closer look at the stain and it looks much more to me like blood. We think it might be Kath's blood. We'll be able to tell. There are tests now. You know what that means, don't you, Claire?'

'I'm sure you're going to tell me.' But despite the flip response she watched him anxiously, frowning so the thick eyebrows met.

'We think that's where Kath was killed. Or if she wasn't killed there she was put there soon after she died. Are you surprised about that?'

'Of course I'm surprised. If it's true.'

'Then later, when the tide was high, she was moved to the jetty and thrown into the water. That's what we think must have happened. I'd say it would take more than one person to do that. Or someone who had a car. Have you any idea who that might have been, Claire? How do you think the body was moved to the jetty?'

'How the hell would I know?' She glared at him.

'But you must have noticed the stain in the shed?'

'Of course not. It's got a mucky floor. What's one more stain? Anyway, I don't go in there very often.'

'But you must go in every day. To fetch coal.'

'Na!' she said. 'That's one of Bernie's jobs. When he remembers.'

She gave a little cry and put her hand to her mouth in a gesture of dismay.

'You've been trying to make a nice home for Bernie and Marilyn, haven't you? Since you took over the running of it. You want everywhere to look nice. Is that why you planted the tub of flowers in the yard? That was you, Claire, wasn't it? Kath would never have thought of it.'

But before she could answer there was a knock on the door and Hunter came in.

'Could I have a word, sir?'

He kept his voice even but Ramsay could tell he was excited.

'Why don't we take a break now, Claire?' Ramsay said. 'I'm sure you could do with a break. Sal, you make certain that Claire gets a cup of tea.'

In the corridor Hunter couldn't keep still. He paced backwards and forwards, talking all the time.

'I've been taking the statement from Hooper,' he said. 'The child abductor. I know we've cleared him of the Coulthard abduction but I started the interview. . .'

And you wanted to be sure the arrest was down to you, Ramsay thought.

'. . . so I decided I'd take him over that Saturday when Kath Howe was murdered. All along we thought he might be a possible witness.'

'Did he see anything on the Headland?'

'Not exactly. When he left Kim Houghton's house he went to the phone box by the club to call his wife. To check she was all right, he said, but it was to establish his story about him working away for the weekend, to say he was on his way home. He chatted for a few minutes then he left the Headland. Guess what he did next?'

Ramsay had begun to guess what Paul Hooper had done next but he was a kind man and he didn't want to spoil Hunter's story. At the end he even pretended to be surprised.

'Has anyone tried to contact Mark Taverner this afternoon?' he asked.

'Aye. Like you said. But all we get is the answering machine.'

'He'll be at home. Fetch him in. I want to talk to him before I go.'

'And where will you be off to then, sir?'

Ramsay smiled, pretending again. Letting Hunter believe he was relishing the job. 'Where do you think?'

Chapter Thirty-Six

He took Sally Wedderburn with him to Newcastle. In the car he explained to her what it was all about, but since Claire's dig about her own childhood she seemed to have lost interest in the case. She wasn't even shocked.

Ferndale Avenue was full of parked cars and they had to stop in the next street and pull up on to the pavement. As they walked to the house they had glimpses through an occasional uncurtained window of family groups gathered round Saturday evening television. At Mrs Howe's the curtains were drawn. There was a curtain at the front door too and they waited for Bernard's mother to draw it back before she let them in. She seemed too excited to be surprised to see them.

'Come in, come in,' she said, sounding almost jolly. She was wearing a maroon velveteen dress – a best frock put on for the occasion – and held the cat to her shoulder so it looked like a fur stole. It stared at them with watery eyes. Its fishy breath wafted to them across the doorstep.

'Come in,' Mrs Howe said again with a touch of impatience. 'We're having a little recital. Bernard has often told me how musical Marilyn is but I hadn't realized until now the extent of her talents.' They stepped into the hall and they did hear rather plodding piano music coming from the living room. 'If we're lucky we might persuade Bernard to do some magic for us later.'

She released the cat, leaving it stranded on her shoulder, and clapped her hands in appreciation and as a childish gesture of delight at the piano piece which had just stopped. Ramsay realized she had achieved just what she had always wanted. Her son was back home with her. For a while at least. Through an open door Ramsay saw a Victorian dining table laden with the remnants of a high tea.

The living room was as hot as it had been on his previous visit, but Bernard was sitting with his chair pulled up close to the fire. He was wearing carpet slippers. When he had returned to Cotter's Row after performing his magic tricks to the children of Gosforth Ramsay had explained that he and Marilyn might be more comfortable if they moved elsewhere for a while. It seemed odd that he had chosen to bring carpet slippers with him, then Ramsay realized that these slippers had been bought by Mrs Howe and kept at the house in Ferndale Avenue for Thursday evenings. And in readiness for the time when Bernard, as he surely would, recognized his mistake and returned home.

As they entered the room Marilyn turned on the piano stool to face them. Bernard looked up from the fire but he did not stand up to greet them. Ramsay thought he was full of food, as lazy as the cat now settled on Mrs Howe's knee.

Sally sat on an upright chair in a corner. Her face was lit from below by an ugly table lamp with a porcelain base. It made the skin under her eyes look dark, like bruises.

'I wonder if I might have a few words,' Ramsay said.

'Where's Claire?' Bernard asked. 'Is she all right?' But really he seemed not too bothered. He was asking because it was expected of him.

'Oh yes. She's been very helpful.' For the moment Ramsay had forgotten about Claire. What would happen to her now? 'I expect you're wondering what's going on at Cotter's Row. You'd like me to explain what all our people are doing there.'

'Routine, you said.' Bernard shifted. On the arm of his chair there was a glass bowl containing chocolates in brightly coloured cellophane wrappers. He reached out and took one, unwrapped it carefully and dropped it into his mouth. 'Because that child was found in our shed.'

'There's a bit more to it than that.'

'Oh.' He shook his hands out in front of him and began to

stretch and flex his fingers. Ramsay supposed it was an exercise to keep his hands supple for the tricks of illusion. He found the movement and Bernard's contemplation of the dancing fingers so irritating that he wanted to scream at the man to sit still. Instead he continued calmly.

'We found blood on the floor of your shed.'

'But I thought the boy was fine. That there was no harm done.'

'He was imprisoned for two hours. A terrifying experience for a child that age.'

Because he was looking out for it he saw Sally Wedderburn in her corner tense then force herself to relax.

'But an accident surely. That's what I was given to understand.'

'No,' Ramsay said. 'No accident.'

The hands fluttered to rest in his lap. 'And the blood?'

'I'm surprised you didn't notice that. You must have been in there every day for coal.'

'Yes. And it was clear enough when you pointed it out. But we didn't notice it None of us did. We had other things, I suppose, on our minds.'

'There will be tests but we believe the blood is your wife's.'

'You think that Kathleen was killed in our shed?' He didn't seem shocked by the thought. Rather, he seemed to think it mildly amusing. Here, in his mother's warm living room he obviously thought himself above suspicion, quite safe.

'Perhaps. Or left there until it was convenient to dispose of the body.'

Bernard seemed to consider the matter. His head was tilted to one side so the long strands of his hair almost reached his shoulder.

'Dispose of the body *how*, Inspector?' he asked at last.

'We believe that it was loaded into the boot of a car, parked in the alley behind your house, and driven to the jetty. Again, there are tests which will prove the matter.'

A smile appeared on Bernard's round, white face.

'It's clear then that you can't suspect one of us, Inspector. The shed must have been used without our knowledge. We don't own a car. We don't drive.'

'Of course,' Ramsay continued, as if Bernard had not spoken, 'it's possible that the murderer had help to move the body.'

There was a moment of silence. The cat sneezed then began to pad rhythmically, catching the velveteen material of Mrs Howe's frock in its claws. She continued to stroke it. Ramsay thought that her deafness had probably excluded her from the conversation. They had been speaking rather quietly. She gave the impression of listening but had no idea what they had been talking about. Certainly now she seemed unaware that they had stopped and when Ramsay spoke directly to her, clearly and loudly, she answered without hesitation, assuming perhaps that it followed naturally from what had gone before.

'Do you drive, Mrs Howe?'

'I do. I learned as a girl in the war. In the Land Army.'

It was hard to imagine her dressed in overalls driving a truck.

'And you own a car?'

'Certainly. A Standard Ten. I gave Bernard lessons in it. I could tell almost from the beginning that he would never make a driver. His co-ordination was satisfactory but his concentration let him down. He would have been a menace on the road.'

'Do you still drive, Mrs Howe?'

'Of course. Why should I not? I'm old but I'm not senile, Inspector.' She gave a complacent smile. It seemed not to occur to her to ask why the questions were being asked.

'Regularly?'

'I give Olive a lift to the supermarket once a week so she can stock up on groceries for me. In the old days I'd enjoy a spin in the countryside but alas not any more. I'm too anxious at the prospect of breaking down.' She shook her head, grieving for her jaunts into the hills. 'It would be different if Bernard would come with me occasionally but he claims he's too busy.'

'Mother!' Bernard interrupted. Then to Ramsay: 'What are you saying, Inspector? That my mother is implicated in some way in this crime? That's ridiculous.'

'No!' The cry was involuntary and came out as a shrill scream. Marilyn even stamped her foot to demand their attention, so hard that her body was thrust backwards and Ramsay thought the piano stool would tip over. With her frizzy hair and her petulant face she looked like an adolescent version of Violet Elizabeth Bott.

'You came here to talk to me,' she said. 'You came here to find out why I killed Mummy.'

Chapter Thirty-Seven

Ramsay had not meant, with his questions to Mrs Howe, to provoke Marilyn to confession. He was not sure now why he had brought up the subject of her car. Out of malice, perhaps. Spite. Because the case had dragged on for weeks longer than it should have done. Because Bernard, lounging in front of the fire, was annoying him. To put Marilyn at her ease. He had not expected the outburst.

He turned to the girl. 'We have a great deal to talk about,' he said.

'Yes.' She had twisted strands of her white hair into a thin, stiff thread. She put the end into her mouth.

'But not here. In the police station. Then we can get someone to help you and make sure we don't catch you out with awkward questions. We have to do it properly. For your sake and Mr Taverner's.'

She looked up.

'You know about that?'

'We know most of it. We still need your help.'

'Here,' she said. 'Now.'

'I'm sorry. I don't think that's a good idea.'

'Why not? There are two of you. My dad's here and my nan. If you take me to the police station I won't speak at all.'

So Marilyn told her story there, still perched on the piano stool, to the audience of adults gathered in the semicircle around her.

'When did your relationship with Mr Taverner begin, Marilyn?' Ramsay asked.

She seemed gratified by the description, pleased that he was taking it seriously.

'Last autumn. Just before his wife died. I went to his classroom after school to ask about some homework. He was sitting at his desk with his head in his hands. I thought he was ill. Then I saw he was crying. I talked to him but he didn't even realize I was there, so I put my arm round his shoulder. I didn't think about it. I mean I'd fancied him for ages but it wasn't like that. I was just sorry because he was so upset.' She paused. 'He turned around and he held on to me. As if I really mattered to him. It was the most wonderful moment of my life. Whatever happens now I've still got that.'

Ramsay was too kind to tell her that at that moment, in the classroom, Mark Taverner had been so desperate that he would have clung to anyone.

'I held him until he'd finished crying. By that time I'd missed the bus. I told him Mummy would panic if I was late so he offered me a lift. On the way home he stopped the car.'

'Where?'

'In the lay-by near that empty farm house on the edge of the dene. He talked. About his wife and how difficult it was at home. I was the only person he had to talk to. Everyone else was sorry for her. They didn't think about him.'

Nonsense, Ramsay thought. There was Brian. But Brian was all action. Perhaps he was so busy shouting at consultants and being indignant on Sheena's behalf that he didn't have the time to listen.

'He started to cry again. I held on to him and he kissed me.'

'And then you made love?'

She nodded. 'He didn't force me,' she said defiantly. He wondered what she had made of the groped encounter in the car. He imagined it passionless, selfish. A moment of violence and madness. Hardly the stuff of teenage fantasy.

'Was that the only time?'

She nodded again, reluctantly. 'It didn't mean he didn't care. His wife died soon after. He couldn't see me then, could he? I understood that. I was prepared to wait.'

She paused. Ramsay looked at Bernard Howe. He had his back to the fire now, he had turned his chair to face his daughter when she began to speak. He made a small ineffectual movement towards her – whether of support or condemnation Ramsay could not tell – then, the effort proved too much for him, he sank back into his seat and closed his eyes.

Marilyn continued. 'I tried to talk to Mark, Mr Taverner. He said he was sorry and that it should never have happened. I'd caught him at a vulnerable time but that was no excuse. I said he didn't need an excuse.' She caught her breath. 'By then I was sixteen. It was legal. He said that didn't matter. Because he was a teacher and I was a pupil it was wrong.' She was becoming agitated. 'He didn't mind spending time with Mrs Coulthard, though. She's married, isn't she? That's wrong too.'

'He wasn't having an affair with Mrs Coulthard,' Ramsay said gently. 'She was a friend, someone to talk to.'

'But he could have talked to me!' It came out as a cry. He was reminded of David Coulthard in the middle of a temper tantrum. She gave a little sob. 'Did he tell Mrs Coulthard about me?'

'I think he probably did. He felt very guilty about the way he treated you.'

'It wasn't fair. He thought I was a baby. Not that you could blame him. Look at me. No decent clothes. No make-up. Do you know what Mummy called him? The baby-snatcher.'

'Why did you tell your mother about him?'

'I was angry.' He could already see that she was subject to rages. Usually they were hidden by politeness and good manners. Occasionally they would be uncontrollable.

'Why?'

'Dad had gone up to the Coastguard House to discuss doing magic at the party. He saw them there together. He said when he got here she was half-naked. Are you *sure* they weren't having an affair?'

'Quite sure.' Because he had already discussed this with Mark Taverner. Mark was sitting still in the Interview Room at Otterbridge police station. When they'd brought him in he hadn't stopped talking. Ramsay supposed that someone with his background would be into confession.

'Couldn't you tell anyone else about this?' he'd asked.

'I told Emma about Marilyn, and the letter I got from Mrs Howe. She promised not to tell Brian. She didn't want to. She thought it would upset him to know I'd done something like that.' Mark had lowered his voice, forcing himself to come out with the words. Confession again. 'That I'd seduced a schoolgirl . . . Then after Kath Howe died she wouldn't see me.'

'Did she suspect you of killing Mrs Howe?'

'I don't know.' He was shocked by the thought. 'Perhaps she did.'

'Why couldn't you talk to Brian Coulthard? I had the impression you were very close.'

'I tried. Several times. It was as if he didn't want to know.'

He believed you were having an affair with his wife, Ramsay thought but did not say, and he wanted you to be happy so he didn't stand in the way.

Mark had looked up from the varnished table which was scratched with graffiti like one of the old desks at school.

'I think Marilyn's been following me. When she threatened the kids I believed her.'

In Mrs Howe's overheated room in Ferndale Avenue Marilyn waited impatiently for more questions.

'What did you tell your mother?' Ramsay asked. 'Everything?'

'Don't be silly. Of course not.'

Of course not. Because if Kath Howe had known what had gone on in the teacher's car she'd have rushed up to the school immediately, accusing him of rape, demanding his prosecution and immediate dismissal. And because kids never told their parents everything.

'What exactly did you tell her?'

'That Mr Taverner fancied me. That he'd given me a lift home and kissed me. That as soon as I left school we'd live together.'

The fantasy.

Marilyn continued. 'I didn't mean to tell her. I was angry and it all came out.'

'So she wrote to him, threatening to tell the authorities.'

'I couldn't understand why she made so much fuss. There was

the same age gap as between Claire and Dad and she put up with that.'

There was a silence broken by Mrs Howe's snoring. Her head had tilted back and her mouth was open. The cat jumped from her knee to be closer to the fire but she didn't wake.

'I think we should go to the police station now,' Ramsay said. It wasn't only that he wanted a watertight case. It was because he wanted her to plead guilty. He couldn't bear the idea of her going through a trial.

'No!' she screamed. She flung her arm in front of her like a Nazi salute. Warning him to keep his distance, threatening to push him away if he should try to move her. A gesture again of the furious child. 'I want to tell you how I did it.'

And in the end it was easier to sit back and listen. In the stuffy room he'd run out of energy. If she had a tantrum he didn't want to have to drag her away.

'I didn't plan it,' she said more calmly.

'No.'

'But she was driving me crazy. It was bad enough before. Never letting me out of her sight. Always wanting to know what I'd been up to. After I told her about Mr Taverner it was a hundred times worse. She'd sent him the letter. You'd have thought that would be enough for her.'

'But it wasn't.'

'That Saturday morning she wanted to come to school with me. She said she'd sit in the back of the hall. Check that nothing was going on. Can you imagine what the others would think? What *he* would think? I just couldn't allow it to happen.'

'So you didn't walk together to the bus stop?'

'No.'

Her eyes were bright and feverish.

'What did happen, Marilyn?'

'We had a row.'

'In the house at Cotter's Row?'

She nodded. 'Claire had gone to work. Dad was upstairs. I don't suppose he noticed.'

They both looked at Bernard. His eyes were open but he was staring into space. Perhaps he was dreaming of a perfect illusion. Doves, silk scarves, a vanishing woman.

'I told Mummy she couldn't come with me. I'd be a laughing stock. She said in that case *I* wasn't to go either. I could resign from the choir. She said it was a shame but perhaps it was better all round. She wasn't unsympathetic to Mr Taverner. He'd been through a terrible time. It was probably better not to put temptation in his way. Then she took off her coat and sat down at that dreadful spinning wheel. She pumped at the pedal with her foot and round it went, making the whining noise. Clack, clack, clack. Horrible. Like a bird. So I couldn't argue with her.'

She paused.

'I could see then that it would always be the same. She'd never let me alone, even when I was grown up. She'd always be at my shoulder, telling me what to do. Clack, clack, clack. I'd be different and lonely and frumpy. Always a Bill.'

'So you killed her.'

'I fetched the knife from the kitchen and stuck it into her back. I pushed it right in up to the handle. There wasn't as much mess as you'd think.'

'Did she cry out?'

'Not really. A little gasp. I don't think she realized what was happening. When she was quite still I pulled her into the shed. I didn't want to look at her.'

'Weren't you worried that someone would go in there to fetch coal?'

'No. Claire was at work.' She nodded towards her father. 'And he was practising for a performance. It wouldn't have occurred to him. I banked up the fire and left a bucket of coal by the hearth.' She stretched and gave a clever little girl smile. 'Actually it all happened very quickly. When I looked at the clock I saw I still had time to get to choir.'

'But you missed the bus.'

'Yes. There was a train coming. A man in a red car had been

forced to stop too. He saw I was upset and offered me a lift into town.'

Paul Hooper. If he'd come forward immediately they'd have cleared up the case weeks ago. But he'd had his own reasons to be frightened of the police.

'And after choir you persuaded Mr Taverner to bring you home. You told him what you'd done.'

'I told him I'd done it for him. That was true in a way. Mummy wasn't a threat to his career dead, was she? We waited until after the party. Bernard and Claire were searching for her in the dene. Though I don't suppose they were looking too hard. We loaded the body into the boot of the car and threw it off the jetty.' She looked up at him. 'No one cares much that she's gone, you know.'

'I think you care,' he said. She flinched as if he had slapped her but said nothing. 'At least I hope you do.' Still she ignored him.

'Why did you take the child, Marilyn? Surely there was no need for that.'

'Mr Taverner went all weedy on me. He said he was going to the police. Of course he had to discuss it with Emma Coulthard first.'

She said the name in a sneering, high-pitched la-di-da voice.

'I phoned him from the club this morning. I told him he'd better watch out or I'd hurt those kids. I told him he mustn't see her.'

'Did you mean it?'

'Of course I meant it. Then I saw the little boy. Claire had gone back to the Coastguard House. I told him it was a game. "Let's hide from Claire," I said. It was easy as pie.'

'You must have realized there'd be a search and we'd find him.'

She shrugged. She'd been jealous of Emma Coulthard, rejected by Mark. She'd snatched David to get her own back. There'd been no logic to it.

'You'll have to come with me now.'

She pulled her fingers through the wiry hair in an attempt to make herself presentable.

'I know.' She nodded again towards her father. 'He doesn't have to come, does he?'

'Not unless you want him to.'

Bernard Howe did stir sufficiently to come to the door to see them off. He put his hand for a moment on his daughter's shoulder.

'I'm sorry,' he said. 'About Kath. I should have done something about her.'

She pulled away and stood for a moment on the step, waiting for Ramsay and Sal Wedderburn to join her. Then she strode off down the street, her back straight, her arms swinging at her side.

CPSIA information can be obtained at www.ICGtesting.com
Printed in the USA
LVOW07s1601050215

425854LV00006B/626/P